# The Next Step

Book Two of The Last Stop Series

# The Next Step

Book Two of The Last Stop Series

Michael H. Burnam

LODESTONE BOOKS

Winchester, UK
Washington, USA

First published by Lodestone Books, 2017
Lodestone Books is an imprint of John Hunt Publishing Ltd., Laurel House, Station Approach, Alresford, Hants, SO24 9JH, UK
office1@jhpbooks.net
www.johnhuntpublishing.com

For distributor details and how to order please visit the 'Ordering' section on our website.



ISBN: 978 1 78535 575 2
978 1 78535 576 9 (ebook)
Library of Congress Control Number: 2016945050



A CIP catalogue record for this book is available from the British Library.

Design: Stuart Davies

Printed and bound by CPI Group (UK) Ltd, Croydon, CR0 4YY, UK

Dedication and Acknowledgements

My sincere thanks to my team:
My loving wife, Jessica. Half the fun of writing is discussing story ideas with her.
The real life models for the characters Al and Bet, my grandchildren Helena and Jonah.
A very sad goodbye to Suzanne Phillips, intellectual property lawyer and close friend who left us in 2015. Suzanne knew how to pick up my writing spirits when they were becalmed. See Dick's words to David on page 210.
Last, to our cat Micetro. Read the book and you'll understand why.

Michael Burnam, MD

# Prologue

The crowd chanted *"Mick—ey! Mick—ey!"* so loudly the floorboards shook.

Ernie peered around the curtain and withdrew out of sight. "Better get out there, Mick, before they tear the place down."

*"Mick—ey! Mick—ey!"*

Mickey closed his eyes, trying to lose himself to the rhythm of the sounds.

The chanting grew louder, faster. *"Mick—ey! Mick—ey!"* People stamped their feet and the auditorium trembled with anticipation.

Ernie tossed the Sphere from hand to hand like a juggler. The glowing device the size of a grapefruit contained advanced alien technology—the prize the Europans gave Earth when Mickey passed the Test.

The producer tapped Mickey on the shoulder and shouted over the din, "Remember what happened in Chicago." The Sphere encounter in Chicago had coincided with Oktoberfest. Several inebriated people in the audience had rushed the stage.

Mickey signaled to one of the stagehands and mouthed the words, "Show Time." The curtain rose and the audience jumped to their feet, clapping and screaming. The sound in the auditorium became deafening.

Ernie remained behind the curtain while Mickey walked slowly to the center of the stage. A hush fell over the crowd. At first Mickey stared back without smiling. Then he thrust both arms into the air like Rocky Balboa—pandemonium!

When it seemed the building would shake apart, Ernie walked out and joined Mickey. Mickey wore his usual sport coat and tailored pants. Ernie always dressed from head to toe in silver, the color of the space-faring residents of Jupiter's moon Europa, although he was born in Chicago. As soon as he appeared holding the Sphere, the auditorium became silent with all eyes riveted on the alien device.

Ernie's silver garment reflected back the glare from the stage lights highlighting beads of sweat on his forehead. Sphere encounters made him nervous. Nobody knew why the Europans selected him, a former Marine Ranger and boat mechanic from Twin Lakes Resort in the California High Sierra Mountains, as the keeper of the Sphere, not even Ernie. Nobody cared either, except Mickey. Mickey had become obsessed with the Test, Ernie, the Sphere…everything Europan. The more he thought about the Europans' Test and the Sphere, the less it all made sense! Vickie could see his growing funk and more than once had encouraged him to let go of the past, often with her characteristic colorful language. "Stop being effing jealous about David going to Europa instead of you! You wouldn't have left Earth anyway. You won't even leave home! Besides, hasn't the Sphere already cured psoriasis and provided the formula for cold fusion? Who knows what it's going to do next? Why can't you be happy? Stop being a jerk."

As Mickey and Ernie bowed one last time signaling that the evening's main event was about to commence, the audience got to their feet again clapping and whistling. At the back of the auditorium a group of Sphere Cult members raised signs and yelled the loudest while waving around miniature Sphere Cult key rings with lights inside. After several minutes of it, Mickey raised his hands for quiet and the audience took their seats.

Vickie sat front row center bracketed by her mother Marie, who preened for the cameras, and Melanie Dilman who rose from broadcasting obscurity to Pulitzer Prize-winning journalist by breaking the story of alien contact.

Melanie thrust her microphone under Vickie's chin. "We're here with one of the original Europans."

"I'm from Burbank, California," Vickie interrupted.

Melanie's smile could curdle milk. "Always modest, how

sweet... What are they going to do tonight, *dear*?"

"I don't—" Vickie began.

Melanie faced the microphone and talked over Vickie. "They fixed the ozone layer last week and wiped out malaria the week before." She batted her eyelashes. "What will it be this time, *dear*?"

"What?" Vickie pretended to have trouble hearing Melanie over the buzzing of the crowd. Thanks to her Europan-enhanced senses, Vickie could hear a gnat sizzling on a light bulb at the back of the auditorium.

"I *said*, what miracle are they pulling out of the Sphere tonight, *dear*?" Melanie shouted.

Vickie cupped her hand over Melanie's ear and shouted back. "You've seen this show before, haven't you?"

Melanie gestured the cut sign to her sound technician, then smiled unctuously at Vickie. "In broadcasting it's called a lead-in, *dear*." She repositioned the microphone under Vickie's chin deliberately bumping it. "Remind our audience what's on tonight's agenda. A few words should be enough...maybe finish by blowing a kiss to Mickey?"

Vickie sighed. "Everybody knows what's going to happen."

Melanie made the cut sign again and continued smiling...at least her teeth did. "Just a hint, *dear?*"

Vickie knew that Melanie had the temperament of a pit bull. She leaned towards the microphone. "The people on stage ask for something, and if it's okay with the Sphere, the answer pops out—just like the friggin' Wizard of Oz. How's that?"

Melanie made the cut sign again. "Erase that part," she snarled at her soundman.

Vickie's mother tugged on her sleeve and Vickie turned away from Melanie. "All the networks are here. Why don't you announce it tonight?"

"Announce what?"

"Your engagement."

"We're not engaged."

Marie *smiled* at the cameras and spoke out of the side of her mouth. "You can tell *me*, I'm your mother."

"When he asks me, I'll let you know." Vickie faced forward.

Mickey scanned the young faces in the audience eagerly waiting for the Sphere encounter to begin. He hoped they still had normal lives ahead of them, lives filled with both bruises and triumphs, the way life should be. Too late for me, he thought, forcing himself to keep smiling.

Unlike Mickey, the rest of humanity saw the alien hard drive in Ernie's hand as a gift ushering in a golden age on planet Earth, and why not? The Europans claimed to have achieved the pinnacle of evolution. Besides being immortal, they'd traveled everywhere in the galaxy worth visiting and knew everything worth knowing. But when Mickey and his friends were brought to Europa after Mickey passed their test, only two of the aliens were still functioning. They were too dumb to realize that even immortal know-it-alls need some kind of purpose to keep going.

After enhancing the teens' bodies with technology that extended their lifespans and increased their capabilities, the Europans explained the purpose of their test and why they tried it out on Mickey. Mickey realized now that, lost in the wonder of riding in a flying saucer and meeting aliens, he would have believed in the tooth fairy.

The Europans explained how they'd planned to save themselves by reintroducing a dash of chaos to their world and then spending a few milliseconds of every day undoing it. Fortunately for them, the galaxy is filled with sentient organic races, one more unpredictable and crazy than the next. The Europans were convinced that a colony of such beings was sure to make a mess of things. Cleaning up the mess would provide something for them to do besides calculating the value for pi, which they'd already done.

Mickey heard the crowd murmuring with anticipation, but

couldn't stop thinking about the Europans. True, their wondrous city in a bubble under Europa's ice offered infinite possibilities, but that was precisely the problem! The organic races brought there so far couldn't deal with it. Invariably one crazy individual schemed to control everything, which meant eliminating everyone else. The arrogant aliens weren't smart enough to realize that they needed an organic race with the trait of benevolence, a species that knew how to share.

They searched the galaxy for such a race for several millennia, testing organic species from multiple worlds without success. More and more Europans inactivated, until there were only two still computing. For the Europans, planet Earth was the last stop. Because Mickey passed the Europan's test by demonstrating benevolence, the Europans gave humanity the Sphere, supposedly as a reward. Actually, Ernie maintained sole custody of the Sphere and only he could touch it without painful consequences. Everyone on Earth, including Vickie, considered the Sphere a 'gift from the gods.' Mickey kept reminding her that the Trojan Horse was a gift too.

He glanced at the Sphere. The damn thing came with a catch. Earth's history books referred to it as the Choice (usually as a footnote in small print). To gain access to the advanced knowledge inside, a male and female from the group of Mickey and his friends, Mickey, his best friend David, Pam, and Vickie, needed to agree to become Europa's version of Adam and Eve. Mickey knew he'd been the logical choice, and so did everyone else. Besides that, by then he and Vickie were becoming an item. But with time running out before the Europans' deal expired, along with the last functioning Europan, Mickey realized he couldn't leave home. If David and Pam hadn't gone instead, the Sphere would still be on Europa in a city full of inactive alien computers with legs.

*Everybody expects me to pretend things are great and we'll all live happily ever after,* Mickey thought. What a joke. He wouldn't admit it publically, but if he had another chance to take the Europans' test, he'd deliberately flunk it. He had one purpose now, to figure out what the Europans were really up to before it was too late. Only he could see the Sphere for what it really was, a ticking time bomb that would destroy the world if nobody shut it down.

Ernie raised his hands for quiet, his right hand holding up the glowing Sphere. At the sight of it, the pandemonium in the auditorium stopped. Even the Cult members returned to their seats. As expected a few people fainted, the ones standing too long straining to see from the cheap seats.

Ernie beckoned off stage with his free hand and a procession of olive-complected men appeared from behind the curtain. The leader, a Johnny Depp look-alike, stopped a few paces from Ernie and bowed.

"Where are you folks from?" Ernie asked.

Behind him, Mickey's eyes scanned the audience until he found Vickie. Marie waved to him making sure the networks spotted her, especially Melanie Dilman. Marie's lips mouthed, "That's my daughter's fiancé." Mickey ignored her and stayed focused on Vickie.

The leader approached the microphone and cleared his throat. "Your honor—" he began.

"Just Ernie." Ernie hated formality almost as much as he hated crowds.

"Of course." The leader bowed again. "Oh great and *Just Ernie…*"

Ernie shook his head. "Let's get right to it. What do you want to ask the Sphere?" Everyone was waiting for this moment and the leader of the people on stage had one chance to phrase his question correctly. To receive any useful information from the Sphere, he had to ask for something with humanitarian value, not a container of gold bars to pay for the accidental death of the pool maintenance guy making eyes at his wife. If the group's leader failed, his people would walk away empty-handed and he'd have to face an angry crowd outside.

"A moment please." The leader huddled with his entourage in animated discussion.

Ernie faced the audience. "Everybody knows how this works. If we ask the Sphere the right question"—he held up the Sphere causing a chorus of gasps—"this little guy gives us the answer." He looked at the leader. "Are you ready?"

The leader glanced at his associates one last time, then straightened his posture and cleared his throat. "Oh great and powerful alien temple of knowledge—"

"Just spit it out," Ernie interrupted.

The leader cleared his throat again, this time louder. "Our children die from intestinal diseases caused by polluted water. Please tell us how to provide clean water for our people."

Ernie waved to someone offstage and a large screen descended from the ceiling. The anticipation in the auditorium reached a level "10" on the Richter scale. Ernie held the Sphere high and a beam of light shot from it filling the screen with symbols, equations, and images. Two scientists in the group on stage edged closer and studied the screen. After conferring, one of them turned to the leader and nodded. Smiling with gratitude, the leader shook hands with Ernie and the auditorium thundered with applause. Mickey smiled but kept looking straight ahead. Only Vickie knew how he really felt.

The Sphere's main antagonist was in the audience that night, General Moreland Westlock, head of America's not-so-secret-anymore Defense Intelligence Agency. The general earned his notoriety when he blew his covert agency's cover by botching the capture of the flying saucer while being videoed by Melanie Dilman and broadcasted live to the entire world. Judging by the scowl that never left his face, he hadn't forgotten.

Mickey stood outside the auditorium, waving goodbye to the last of the audience filing out. A few people remained, including several Cult members and some folks standing in line waiting for autographs. Being shy, Ernie always left this part to Mickey and had slipped out the back door the moment the curtain went down.

When the Sphere arrived on Earth and people learned how to ask it the right questions, the world began changing. Not everybody liked it. Governments and special interest groups who preferred the good old days of war, famine, pestilence, and disease, kept trying to steal the Sphere to put a stop to it. No one could pull it off as only Ernie could touch the Sphere. Besides that, he, Mickey and Vickie had Europan nannites circulating in their blood, microscopic machines constantly repairing and strengthening their bodies giving them extended lifespans and unusual powers. The Sphere Network, as Ernie called it, linked them together, including Pam and David, day and night. Pam and David lived four hundred million miles away, but Mickey and Vickie could communicate with them whenever they wanted using their palm discs linked to Ernie's special television.

Mickey signed autographs until the last person in line edged forward, a teenaged boy. Mickey took the boy's paper and pen. "What's your name?" he asked.

"Harvey."

Mickey scribbled a message, the same one every time, and signed it. "What grade are you in, Harvey?"

"I don't go to school anymore," Harvey replied.

Mickey handed Harvey back the paper and pen. "How old are you?"

"Thirteen."

Mickey studied Harvey's face. "You must be smart if you've already graduated."

"Don't need to go to school. Everything I need to know is in the Sphere."

Mickey's dark thoughts began flooding back. "What do you want to be when you grow up?"

Harvey looked confused.

"What kind of job do you want?" Mickey persisted.

"Why do I need a job?"

Mickey's heart sank. "Don't you want to do something with your life?"

Harvey puffed out his chest. "I'm joining the Cult."

# Book I

# Chapter One

Mickey lay awake all night staring at the ceiling. When morning light seeped through the window shades, he eased out of bed, grabbed his clothes, and dressed in the bathroom. After making sure Vickie still slept, he tiptoed to the front door, slipped on his shoes, and activated a touchpad mounted on the wall that summoned an automated car already waiting for him at the curb with its door open and a woman's face smiling from the vid screen.

"Good morning," she said. "The ambient temperature is twenty-two degrees Celsius, wind four kilometers per hour from the southwest with no chance of rain today. Where would you like to go?"

Mickey slumped into the seat. "Five years into the past."

With a soft whoosh, the door closed. "I am unfamiliar with that address. Additional information is required to process your request."

"Never mind," Mickey muttered. "Take me to 16888 Catalina Street, Burbank."

The car started in motion heading for the main line to join a train traveling west. "Estimated time of arrival eight minutes. Would you like to listen to music en route?"

"The Fifth Dimension," Mickey replied sullenly.

"The universe has only four dimensions. Please restate your request."

"Fuck off."

"I am not programmed to respond to that request." A list of psychiatric facilities within a five-kilometer radius appeared on the vid screen. "Enjoy the ride."

Five minutes later, the car detached from the three hundred mile an hour train and resumed autonomous motion. It stopped three minutes later in front of David's old house on Catalina

Street.

Mickey walked to the perimeter of the house's force field and stopped. He had been ten years old the day he moved in across the street, shy and painfully introverted. David had ridden up on his bike. "Hi," he'd said, peering inside the back of the moving van. "My name's David, but you can call me Davie. I live across the street." He'd spied Mickey's bike in the van. "Wanna go bike riding some time?"

The two boys had spent almost every day together after that, riding their bikes, lying on Mickey's bed jawing about life, and five years later hopping a ride on a flying saucer to the moon and then to Europa with Vickie and Pam. Mickey felt the embers of anger always smoldering inside him burst into flame. Thanks to the Europans and their Test, he'd never be able to go bike riding with Davie again. They'd taken his old life away and given him a new one, whether he liked it or not. He wasn't sure how much longer he could take it.

After a backwards glance at his old house, Mickey held up his palm, his silver disc implanted by the Europans flashed twice, and the force field extended around him allowing him inside.

As he started up the familiar walk the front door opened. For a moment Mickey half-expected to see David, but Ernie stood in the doorway instead sporting his signature smile. "Hey, Mick! Wasn't expecting you. Come on in."

Mickey rushed past Ernie into the house without exchanging greetings.

Ernie had occupied the house after David's parents divorced. He didn't change anything, except to bring along his favorite recliner chair and special television, the one he, Mickey, and Vickie used to stay in communication with Pam and David on Europa.

Mickey walked to the living room and picked up a framed photograph from the mantle. The photograph taken six years earlier showed he and David at the resort they visited every summer until David left for Europa. In the photograph, Mickey was holding up a rainbow trout with a grin on his face while David grimaced. Mickey stared at the photo fighting back tears.

Sensing his discomfort, Ernie dropped into his favorite chair and pointed at the couch. "What's on your mind?"

Mickey remained standing. "I have a few questions for the Sphere."

Ernie picked the Sphere off the coffee table. "Fire away."

"Start with this one. Why is what's happening on Earth now any different than what happened on Europa?"

Ernie frowned. "Not sure what you mean."

"The Europans almost became extinct when they ran out of things to do, right?"

Ernie nodded. "Everybody knows that."

"The same thing's happening to us."

"No it isn't," Ernie scoffed.

"Yes it is! Ask the Sphere what the human race is supposed to do next." Mickey's voice went up an octave.

"What're you talking about, Mick?"

Mickey paced around the room. "Ask it what humanity's supposed to do for our next big achievement. Build our own flying saucers and explore the solar system? Why bother? We can see a travelogue of the entire galaxy from the comfort of our easy chairs. How about finding a cure for cancer, or discovering the formula for cold fusion? Don't need to. That stuff's already posted on the internet." He stopped pacing. "And ask the Sphere what the human race is supposed to do with itself besides becoming fat and useless."

"You know you can't ask the Sphere that kind of stuff, Mick. You have to ask a straightforward question, like how to make strawberry pancakes." Ernie forced a smile.

"Then ask it why the Europans picked Davie instead of me."

"We both know the answer to that one," Ernie replied. "You wouldn't have gone."

"I never had the chance!" Mickey shouted.

"Of course you did."

"Remember the aura when Davie and Pam held hands?" Mickey challenged. "It started as soon as we got back from Europa, *before* the Europans told us about the Choice. How come nothing happens when Vickie and I hold hands?"

"I don't know, but what difference does it make?"

"It means the Choice was rigged. The Europans had already chosen Davie and Pam, and I want to know why."

# Chapter Two

## Jupiter's Moon Europa

The aquaski sped through Europa's ocean just beneath the thirty-kilometer-thick shell of ice. As the submersible the size of a two-man jetski banked back and forth, the Europan designated R141 nicknamed Romeo wrapped two silver appendages around the aquaski's saddle to hold on. The aquaski's pilot Al, short for Alpha, grinned and poured on the power. His twin sister Bet, short for Beta, radioed for him to slow down. The more cautious of Pam and David's twins, Bet was born one full minute before Al. She liked to refer to herself as the "big sister" which really ticked off her brother. The closer Bet's aquaski moved to the forest of ice stalactites, the more she reduced speed.

Al noticed his sister slowing down and increased power. "Why are you slowing down?" he sent to Bet on an open communication channel.

"Perhaps your sister's action is wise," Romeo said to Al on the aquaski's intercom.

"You chickening out?" Al asked.

Romeo pondered his response for two milliseconds, which qualified as serious consideration for an Europan. "Why would I choose to leave this location with a domesticated Earth bird?"

Despite the razor-sharp stalactites looming ahead, Al increased speed yet another notch. "It's an expression that means you're scared," he replied.

The colored lights on Romeo's face flashed with a riot of color. Al saw the colorful display reflected in his bubble helmet and tried not to laugh.

"Fear is an emotion. I have none," Romeo said.

Al chuckled. "Then explain why you're holding on so tight the ski's frame is bending?"

"My apologies, Master Al. I was performing normal maintenance by testing the frame's tensile strength."

Bet saw her brother pulling farther ahead. Frowning, she increased speed.

"Mistress Bet," said Juliet, the nickname for the Europan designated J232 riding behind her, "I believe it would be prudent to slow down." Although Juliet looked identical to Romeo, it acted differently, not only its pattern of speech but its mannerisms—if sentient robots had mannerisms. At times it seemed almost feminine. Bet had observed it with flowers draped over its head when the Europan believed it was alone. She had begun referring to Juliet as "she".

"Okay, I quit!" Bet sent to her brother. Her aquaski coasted to a stop.

"A wise decision," Juliet said.

Bet heard Al's voice, this time not via her helmet radio. The twins could speak telepathically. Nobody knew about their telepathic ability, not even their parents. Al stopped his aquaski within a meter of a giant stalactite. *"I knew you would,"* he sent. He reversed direction and used the aquaski's thrusters to maneuver next to Bet. Romeo relaxed his grip.

"You're driving like a crazy person," Bet said to her brother on an open channel.

"It's boring skiing in circles in the same area day after day," he replied.

"I prefer boring to getting killed."

"There's nothing to see around here but water," Al complained. "Why can't we go someplace different for a change?"

"For your safety."

"I'm tired of being safe." Al turned his aquaski back towards the forest of stalactites.

Romeo sent to Juliet on a private channel, "The twins are about to engage in their favorite activity."

"What activity is that?" sent back Juliet.

"The best word in the Earth database is mischief," Romeo replied.

Al accelerated between two of the stalactites. "Come on," he shouted.

"We're not supposed to go in there!" Bet reversed thrust bringing her aquaski to an abrupt stop. "I'm your big sister and I order you to come back, *now*!"

"You're not my big sister, but you're a wuss," Al radioed back.

"That does it," Bet muttered. She started after her brother.

Al weaved his aquaski around the frozen pillars of Europa's ocean for several minutes and stopped. Bet's aquaski coasted to a stop next to his. "Why are we stopping here?" she asked.

"This place looks interesting," Al replied. They had stopped in a column of water free of stalactites large enough to accommodate a Europan flying disc. The column continued above through the surface ice and below to the bedrock of the ocean floor.

"I find it necessary to point out, Mistress, that it would be unwise for you to remain in this location," said Juliet. Geysers of water heated by Europa's core occasionally shoot to the surface melting the ice. Being caught in such a geyser on an aquaski could prove dangerous, possibly fatal to beings made from flesh and blood.

"Let's go down and have a look." Al pointed the nose of his ski downward and began to descend into open water.

Bet craned her head over the side of her aquaski following Al's path. "We're not allowed to go down to the ocean floor," she radioed. Al's aquaski had already shrunk to a small dot of light.

"Your sister is correct," Romeo said.

"Just a little farther," Al replied.

"This whole area's off limits." Bet switched to telepathy. *"Mom's going to kill us if she finds out."*

"Stop being such a wimp and get down here," Al radioed

back. "I see something."

"No," Bet said.

"Dude, come down here!"

"This better be good."

Juliet sent to Romeo on a private channel. "I have heard the children use the term Dude before. Can you explain what it means?"

"The children communicate using a very complex linguistic algorithm," Romeo replied. "I am still analyzing it, but I have observed that within its structure a number divided by zero has a discrete value. It's called Dude."

"The quotient of any number divided by zero must be zero," said Juliet.

"Precisely."

Juliet vocalized the sound a hinge makes when it needs oil. *"Grreech."*

*"What was that?"* Al sent to Bet.

*"She's pretending to clear her throat."* Bet sent back.

*"Europans don't have throats."*

*"Don't say anything. She gets defensive if you ask her about it."*

*"Why do you keep referring to Juliet as she?"*

Bet started downward. "The water's getting warmer," she said on an open channel.

"Because we are descending over an active volcano," Juliet replied.

Bet radioed Al. "Are you crazy?"

"Stop worrying. I don't detect any seismic activity." Al coasted to a stop in the heated water of the volcano's caldera.

"It is unwise to stop here, Master Al," cautioned Romeo. "Seismic events can be unpredictable."

"What's that?" Al's aquaski shot past the caldera's rim and down to the ocean floor. Bet stopped her descent well above.

"Your brother's actions are most unwise," Juliet said.

"Come on! You gotta see this," Al sent. "There's something

weird on the ocean floor."

Before Juliet could protest, Bet pinpointed her brother's location and engaged her forward thruster.

The two aquaskis hovered side by side with their spotlights aimed at a pyramidal mound of rock jutting from the ocean floor.

"You brought me down here to see that?" Bet asked.

"Does that rock pile look right to you?"

"I don't spend a lot of time staring at piles of rocks, baby brother. Let's go home."

"Romeo, is that a natural structure?" Al asked.

"The probability of a lava protrusion assuming that precise shape and proportions is estimated at zero point one percent," Romeo replied.

"See, I told you," Al said.

"Great." Bet turned her aquaski around. "Can we go home now?"

"Wait a minute." Al stared at the rock pyramid. "Romeo, check the database. How long has it been here?"

"The database shows only flat ocean bottom at this location for the last one hundred thousand years," Romeo replied, "but seismic activity can alter the local topography at any time."

"Which is why your mother warned you not to aquaski here," Juliet added.

Al nosed his aquaski closer. The rock pyramid loomed over him measuring twenty times as tall as the ski. "I see an opening like a door," he said, "that shouldn't be here. Let's see what's inside."

"Master Al..." Romeo cautioned. Al's aquaski disappeared inside.

"Get's weirder by the minute," Al radioed to Bet. "Come take a look."

"I'll give you three minutes, then we go home. You got that?" Bet engaged her forward thruster entering a chamber inside the pyramid. The lights of Al's aquaski ascended above her and disappeared.

Al radioed to his sister. "Get up here. I see something."

Bet accelerated after him until her aquaski popped out of the water inside a hollow space. Al's aquaski rested several meters away beached on a ledge of rock. The aquaski's spotlight illuminated a rock wall carved with lines of symbols. The wall appeared to be tinted blue.

Bet beached her aquaski next to Al's and dismounted onto the ledge. She shined her helmet light around the chamber. "What is this place?"

"Haven't seen writing like that before," Al said. "Romeo, analyze those symbols."

Romeo dismounted and approached the blue wall. He projected a beam of light illuminating the symbols.

"Figure anything out?" Al asked.

Romeo didn't reply.

"Romeo?"

Juliet dismounted her aquaski and moved beside Romeo. She shined her light on his face. "Respond," Juliet said. Romeo remained silent and motionless, his face showing a static field of blue with a black square in the center of it.

"Is he malfunctioning?" Bet asked.

"No malfunctions have been recorded in these forms since they were created," Juliet replied.

"Great. Fix whatever's wrong with him and let's get out of here."

"And make a recording of those symbols," Al added.

Juliet moved closer to the wall of symbols. When she played her light across them, she too became immobile with the same pattern on her face.

"Juliet?" Bet said. When Juliet didn't answer, Bet turned to her brother. "What's going on?"

Al shook his head. "Not a clue. But it must have something to do with this place, and those symbols. I'll make a scan so we can decipher them later."

"Do it fast," said Bet. "If we're late, mom's going to kill us."

Al looked around the chamber. "Remember mom's story about King Tut's tomb? Maybe this place is cursed."

"Mom told us about the Tooth Fairy too," Bet replied. "What do we do about Romeo and Juliet?"

"How may I assist you?" Romeo asked.

A moment later, Juliet became active too.

"I register a reboot of my neural nexus," Romeo said.

"As do I," Juliet added. She switched to a private channel with Romeo. "Why did this occur?"

"I have no explanation," Romeo sent back.

"We're going home, *now,*" Bet said.

Al frowned. "Bet's right. You two go straight to the skis and *don't* look at those symbols,"

"Why?" Juliet asked.

"We'll explain later," Bet replied. "Just do it."

# Chapter Three

The house had the appearance of a twentieth-century Earth home with a peaked shingled roof and an old-fashioned veranda. David sat on the steps gazing up at a black canopy dappled with twinkling stars. Pam eased down beside him holding two glasses of lemonade.

David pointed at the stars. "There's Virgo and that's Sagittarius." He sighed. "Except the sky isn't real. None of this is."

Pam handed him a glass. "This is. Picked the lemons myself this morning. One hundred percent four-dimensional fruit swimming in Europa's finest desalinated water."

David smiled at his wife. "Four dimensional lemons. I remember the first time you called them that."

"Calmed your nerves, didn't it?" Pam took a sip. "Maybe the sky's a projection..."

"And the house is constructed from force fields," David added.

"But it's home." Pam laughed. "Sure makes remodeling easy."

David found Pam especially beautiful when she laughed. Her dazzling smile could light up any room, even a fake one. Seeing her smile was usually enough to brighten his mood, but not today.

"Our lemon trees are real," Pam said. "And we'll have apricots and oranges before you know it."

"What about the pterodactyls perched in the lemon tree's branches? Those beasts are freaking weird."

"Those so-called beasts are magnificent, and they don't eat the lemons."

"What do they eat?" David asked.

"Rodents."

"There aren't any rodents on Europa," David said.

Pam looked away. "There weren't."

"You resurrected prehistoric rodents?"

"Modern rats work fine." Pam tried to sound nonchalant.

"I can't believe you did that!"

"The pterodactyls have to eat, Honey. We can't feed them lasagna."

David held up his hand, stopping her from telling him anything else he didn't want to know. They sipped their lemonades.

"Where are the kids?" Pam asked.

"Out on their aquaskis, as usual," David replied.

"They're late," said Pam, frowning. "If it's possible to get into mischief, those two will find a way."

"Romeo and Juliet are with them. Nothing can happen."

"In case you haven't noticed, our two favorite Europans are acting a little strange these days."

David chuckled. "You mean when Juliet goes into the garden and picks daffodils?"

"And Romeo follows after her with his lights flashing." Pam stood. "Here come the kids. I told you. They look guilty." She put her hands on her hips and adopted a stern expression.

"Hi, Mom," said Bet, trying to sound nonchalant.

Al tried not to make eye contact.

"I'm waiting," said Pam.

The twins looked at each other.

"Where are Romeo and Juliet?" David asked.

"With the aquaskis," Bet replied.

"Think I'll have a talk with them."

"They're having some issues," Al added.

"Such as?"

"They're, um, broken."

"Not likely," David scoffed. "Nothing breaks down around here, especially Europans." He started towards the marina.

"Inside," said Pam, pointing towards the house. "Clean up.

Then it's homework time."

"Mom!" Al exclaimed. "My favorite show from Rigel III is on now."

"Record it. Quantum mechanics, not reality vids tonight, Mister."

Bet edged towards the front door.

"Not so fast, Missie. Don't you have homework to do?"

"I don't think so," Bet said innocently.

"What about chores?"

"Don't have any of those either."

"The Menagerie?" Pam prompted.

Bet cringed. "What about it?"

"The duckbill dinosaur pen needs mucking. Grab a shovel."

"Have you seen how much *excrement* those things put out!"

"Take a big shovel, honey. You'll finish sooner."

They stored the aquaskis on elevated platforms adjacent to the City's main force field; an area David called the marina. When he arrived, Romeo was underneath one of the skis performing maintenance.

"The twins said you guys had some problems out there today," David said.

"Both Aquaskis are operating within specified parameters," Romeo replied.

"Not the skis, you and Juliet."

"An unscheduled software reboot occurred, but all neural functions remain optimal

David was about to ask how it happened when everything was perfect on Europa and never broke down, but instead pointed at a pink glob stuck on the underside of one of the skis. "What's that?"

Romeo extended a tentacle and pulled out a pinkish orb with a long segmented tail. "A sea animal. It has ceased to function. I will return it to the biosphere for recycling."

"Mind if I take it back to the Menagerie?" asked David.

Romeo touched the ground and pulled up a glob of silver Europan matter. He formed it into a bubble around the dead sea animal and extended it to David. "For what purpose?"

"Thought I'd use it to play around with the DNA scanner in the Menagerie."

"That activity is unnecessary. The nucleotide sequences of all animal life on Europa are recorded in the database," Romeo said.

David shrugged. "I'm bored."

# Chapter Four

David waved as Al and Bet sped away on their Aquaskis with Romeo and Juliet riding shotgun. When they disappeared over the horizon, he frowned and let his arm fall to his side. Most days he awakened hoping to find that being on Europa was just a bad dream. He wanted to enjoy Europa like Pam did. Everything about Europa worked for her. The Bubble City was her Emerald City of Oz. The twins didn't know any better. Unlike Pam or his kids, he greeted each day increasingly desperate to return to Earth.

To make matters worse, Pam's favorite Earth movie was *Jurassic Park* in all its iterations. She watched at least one of the movies every week, or whatever amounted to a week on Europa. When she realized she could use Europan technology to resurrect living dinosaurs, and not the CG version, the temptation proved irresistible. In the movies, invariably some of the toothy beasts escaped and ate people. The thought of the same thing happening in his simulated neighborhood kept David awake at night, especially after Pam resurrected her first Tyrannosaurus Rex. To settle his nerves and keep him from going crazy, David needed to get away from Europa and go home, at least for a visit. He came up with a plan, which was why he was on his way to the Menagerie. Otherwise, he wouldn't go near the place.

He trudged along the simulated country lane with the artificial sun warming his back, stopping to inhale the fragrance of honeysuckles that weren't real. Along the way he encountered some of his wife's creations, a herd of massive herbivore dinosaurs. "You guys should be bones mounted in a museum," he muttered. He wanted to throw a rock at them, except the rocks weren't real either. Like everything else on Europa, except remaining sane, resurrecting extinct animals was easy to do. The raw material, fossilized bones, could be found on Earth either buried in the ground or majestically posed in museums. Earth paleontologists had already discovered that some fossils contain preserved fragments of DNA and proteins. Those fragments could be reverse engineered into nucleic acids, but not nearly enough to stitch together a complete dinosaur genome, which was why Earth zoos didn't have live dinosaurs on display. In *Jurassic Park,* the dinosaur's DNA came from the stomachs of mosquitos trapped in amber. In theory, this could have provided a more intact genome if the mosquito had bitten a dinosaur just before getting stuck in tree sap, and if the mosquito hadn't already digested the dinosaur's blood. In *Jurassic Park,* the missing Tyrannosaurus Rex gene sequences were borrowed from similar animals, like reptiles and frogs, which wasn't possible in real life.

Earth scientists knew that a bird, the modern descendant of dinosaurs, still contained the genes to make T-Rex teeth. Thankfully, for canaries, the genes for T-Rex teeth were switched off. The Europans could turn the rest of the T-Rex genes back on again. They could manipulate DNA to make a saber tooth cat out of a modern day tabby, or a dodo bird from a parakeet. Once Pam had mastered the art of gene manipulation, the Menagerie became a real life Jurassic Park filled with scores of interesting critters, or terrifying depending on your point of view. Pam had kept her resurrected prehistoric animals in habitats enclosed by invisible force fields. David found the invisible fences especially unnerving. He shuddered as he remembered Juliet suggesting that Pam resurrect extinct animals from other planets too. He hoped she hadn't heard.

He continued along the path towards the Menagerie doing his best not to lapse into a full-blown depression. His mood had been darkening for weeks. Pam noticed him moping around and diagnosed it as a combination of cabin fever and homesickness. In time he'd get over it, she kept reassuring him. David reminded her more than once that the "cabin" in his supposed cabin fever was an illusion projected inside a force field bubble populated by immortal silver robots. Pam's resurrection of living fossils that shook the fake soil as they lumbered about made their habitat even more surreal. As far as David was concerned, Lewis Carroll had to have been a Europan.

He knew that he needed Pam's buy-in to go home. Unfortunately, Europa didn't offer the usual ways a man could ingratiate himself with his wife. Flowers wouldn't work. They'd be fake and she could create her own in endless variety in the blink of an eye just by saying *flowers* aloud. He couldn't wash the dishes or take out the trash either. Romeo and Juliet handled most of the chores. He hoped Pam would see his participation in her hobby as the Earthly equivalent of taking ballroom dancing lessons.

David continued walking until he saw the simulated building housing the Menagerie and then slowed his pace. Pam thought it was funny that she'd designed the place to look like the entrance to Jurassic Park. He didn't. After forcing his face into a smile, he entered the Menagerie and found Pam seated in front of a three-dimensional hologram of a Velociraptor. "You wouldn't actually make one of those...would you?" he asked.

"Why not?" Pam replied.

"Don't you remember what those guys did in your favorite movie?"

Pam waved her hand and the image of a Velocirpator disappeared. She pointed at the bubble with the dead sea creature tucked under David's arm. "What's that?" she asked.

"Road kill from an aquaski. Thought I'd join you in the lab, if you don't mind some company." He held up the bubble. "I'd like to start with something simple till I get the hang of the resurrection game."

Pam's serious expression changed into a big grin. "That's great, honey!" She'd been encouraging him to find a hobby as a distraction. Her first attempt, exploring Europa on aquaskis with the twins, lasted three days. The twins never stopped. David loved astronomy, so Pam next suggested that he explore the Europans' astronomical database. It contained a library of vids from the entire galaxy collected during the Europans' millennia of space travel. After nosing around Venus for an hour, David changed channels to Monday Night Football and became more depressed. Pam didn't need a doctor to make the diagnosis—David was homesick with home four hundred million miles away. She had no idea what to do about it, or who to ask for advice. Discussing emotions with the Europans was like talking to a doorknob—which was actually possible on Europa.

She was thrilled with David's unexpected interest in her new hobby. "Don't start with the water blob...start with something more interesting, honey, like an Allosauras tooth. Allosauri were awesome."

"Why do all your projects have big teeth?" David asked. "What's wrong with bringing back simpler critters like...British Large Coppers?"

"What's a British Large, *whatever*?" Pam asked.

"An extinct butterfly," David replied.

Pam was afraid to say or do say anything that would give him an excuse to stop. "Okay, put your dead pink whatever in the DNA scanner and I'll show you how to use it."

"Don't have to. Everything on Europa has a talking manual."

Pam forced a smile. "I'll check on you later. Have fun!" She walked out the back door to the dinosaur habitat.

"How about a teddy bear? Would you like that better?" he called.

"Already have a couple of *Arctodus simus* in habitat 32," Pam yelled back.

"What's that?"

"Short-faced bears. They weigh about 1500 pounds each, but they're still growing." Pam's voice trailed off.

"Don't worry. I won't break anything," David shouted after her. "I want to, but I can't because everything on Europa is effing unbreakable…and silver."

David placed the bubble with the sea creature beside the scanner and sat down. To know how to operate the DNA scanner, all he had to do was ask it. To David, this felt like having a conversation with a washing machine. Maybe Steve Jobs was a Europan too.

"How do I analyze this animal's DNA?" he asked the scanner.

A compartment appeared in the face of the instrument that was otherwise a featureless silver box. "Deposit the specimen inside," the scanner said. David shoved in the pink blob. Within seconds, the smooth face of the scanner changed to a vid screen displaying the image of double helixes racing by too quickly to see.

David thought for a second. "Compare the sample's genes with my DNA. Show any sequences in common."

Double helixes streaked past again, so quickly the images made David dizzy. "Let's try this differently," he said. "How many genes do I have?"

"19,599."

"How many genes does the pink blob have? Wait… How many genes does it have in common with me and Pam?"

"The sample's genome contains five hundred and seventy-five genes in common with you. Pamela's nucleotide sequences are not available."

He leaned back. "Why not?"

"That information is not available."

"Tell me why."

"That information is—"

"Stop." Must be some kind of glitch, David thought. He found the thought of a malfunction of anything on Europa satisfying. He'd tell Pam to check it out, maybe gloat a while. He said "clock" and glowing numerals that read 5:30 pm hovered before his eyes. The Europan day lasted eighty-five hours, but Pam insisted on following a twenty-four-hour fake Earth day in their habitat. She thought it would help to make David feel more at home and put the twins on a schedule. Probably made the dinosaurs happy too.

Romeo and Juliet served dinner at six pm. David wouldn't admit it, but he actually enjoyed the simulated meatballs and spaghetti Juliet prepared the night before. Her cooking was definitely improving. "I'll deal with you later," he said to the scanner. He chuckled, still enjoying the thought of anything malfunctioning on Europa and started home for dinner.

He returned to the Menagerie the next day with a hair from Pam's hairbrush and placed it inside the scanner. "Analyze the sample's genome," he said, holding his breath.

DNA sequences flashed past. "Completed," reported the silver box.

"How many genes in the sample?" David asked.

"21,455."

David's knees threatened to buckle. "Are you sure?"

"Errors are—"

"Stop! How many genes in common with me?"

"575."

"How many genes in common with the dead sea creature I analyzed yesterday?"

"20,711."

"Shit," David muttered.

"That command cannot be executed."

David returned to the house and slumped in front of the vid screen. Pam's DNA analysis had to be incorrect—except he knew it couldn't be. Everything on Europa worked freaking perfectly. He couldn't ask Pam about the discrepancy with her DNA. He already knew what Romeo and Juliet would say. *What if the talking box is correct,* he wondered? He knew his own wife…didn't he?

In truth, there were things about Pam David tried to overlook. For example, Pam had been eager to make the Choice and relocate to Europa even if it meant leaving with Mickey and not him. She'd seemed downright anxious to return and had repeatedly badgered Mickey to make up his mind while the others were preoccupied with David's brother being shot and his mother's overdose. David had dismissed it as Pam's understandably enthusiastic reaction to being able to use her legs normally on Europa, but it still bothered him.

When Mickey had declined the Choice and David had accepted, Pam then agreed to relocate to Europa with him. Besides loving Pam and looking forward to making a life with her, back then David didn't mind leaving Earth. In some ways it was a relief to get away. His father didn't have any use for him, his mother overdosed and disappeared, and his brother Jake was on his way to jail for armed robbery, provided he survived being shot. Except for Mickey, David didn't have any big reason to stay.

His life pre-Europa hadn't been all miserable. He smiled as pleasant memories played before his eyes just like the DNA sequences on the scanner—riding his bike into the wind, his first kiss with Pam, and spending hours in the backyard with Mickey looking through Mickey's telescope. He laughed out loud when he remembered the night they saw the red orb of Mars and mistook it for a UFO. A year later, they took a wild ride to the moon in a real flying saucer, and soon after toured space between Earth and Jupiter.

David sneered at the scanner. "Hey, Mister know-it-all-box, I explored the solar system in a flying saucer. You're stuck on the shelf like a toaster."

"Leaving this location is unnecessary," the scanner said. "The Europan database contains files on every celestial body in the galaxy. State the quadrant of the galaxy you wish to explore."

David knew it wasn't possible, but the box sounded sarcastic.

"I don't talk to appliances."

A touchpad bubbled into existence below the screen. "According to the Earth database, homo sapiens may prefer a more primitive tactile interface."

David thought the word "primitive" sounded louder than the other words. "You want to play rough? Show me every habitable planet in the galaxy the Europans visited and choke your circuits on it."

Images flashed by in a blur of color—solar systems, inhabited planets, strange-looking aliens. Watching made David dizzy again, but he found it too fascinating to stop. "Slow down, you silver hunk of junk."

"Specify display rate." A list of numbers appeared. David had no idea what they meant, so he picked the lowest one.

Images whipped by more slowly now, but still too quickly for him to catch any of the details.

"Stop." He leaned forward. The vid screen displayed a city constructed from crystal spires hovering in diaphanous green clouds. "Holy crap. Look at that." He wouldn't give the scanner the satisfaction of knowing that he was into it now. "Narrow the search to within ten light years."

"At the transfer rate specified, the astronomical files requested will require forty-two Earth days to be reviewed by the primitive hominid brain. Do you wish to remain stationary for that period of time and risk blood clots, or refine your search?"

David felt certain the box was mocking him, but he was too curious to stop. "Restrict search to astronomical objects in this solar system, planets only. Convert coordinates to names from the Earth database."

A new list appeared with every planet in the solar system, plus three additional spheres with numerical designations.

"Are you sure the three objects without names are planets?" David asked.

"According to the standard definition, an object with sufficient mass to orbit a star, assume a round or ovoid shape, and clear smaller masses from its orbit is a planet."

"Why don't my people call them planets?"

"Earth science is primitive compared to…"

"Never mind." David remembered seeing the red dot of Mars in Mickey's telescope. "Show me what you have on Mars." Another list appeared, this time with thumbnail pictures. Because the NASA rover still plodded along, he found some of the features familiar. "Scroll down. Stop." His pulse started pounding. "Resume slowly." More pictures flowed by. "Stop. Son of a seagull." The image on the vid screen showed the unmistakable structures of a city. "When was that video taken? Specify in Earth-years."

"Two hundred thousand Earth-years ago," the scanner replied.

"There were real live Martians with cities two hundred thousand years ago?"

"The pre-industrial Martian civilization ceased to exist nine hundred eight thousand and two Earth-years ago."

"Were there any survivors? Did they go somewhere else?"

"No."

David felt a sense of dread. "What happened to them?"

"The Martian civilization was destroyed by high-energy proton beams."

"They had a war and killed each other?"

"No."

"Then how…" David began. Before he could finish his question, Pam walked in and he quickly closed the vid screen. Seeing her suddenly made him feel uneasy.

"Who were you yelling at?" she asked.

"Watching a football game. Guess I got carried away."

"You were watching TV on the DNA scanner? I thought…"

"It's an important game."

"You should see the Dodo Bird chicks that just hatched," Pam said, smiling. "So cute!" She studied her husband's face. "Are you sick?"

"Can't get sick, neither can you with those pesky little nannites swimming around in our blood."

"Okay, what's wrong?"

David looked away. "Nothing."

"Don't lie to me."

"I don't know."

Pam already knew what was on David's mind. She sat beside him and took his hand. "Yes you do. Spit it out."

David struggled to find something evasive to say, but it just came out. "I want to go home." The emotion burst from him like an erupting volcano. "I want to see my mom, show off the twins, see my dad, hell…even see my brother!"

Pam knew that David's funk had been teetering on a full-blown depression and she was frantic to do something about it. If going home for a visit was the only cure, she'd find a way to make it happen. "Don't forget Mickey," she added.

"Yes!" David shouted. "I want to see Mickey."

Pam looked in his eyes now brimming with tears. "You're seriously homesick, aren't you?"

He nodded.

"I miss Vic too," Pam said. There were things she couldn't do on Europa, like girlie-talk. Bet was three years old going on thirteen, but her precociousness had no Earthly frame of reference. Bet had no idea what going shopping meant, or getting her hair done. She didn't have hair yet, and there were no malls on Europa. And Juliet was…well, Pam wasn't sure what Juliet was anymore.

David jumped to his feet. "Ernie said we could visit someday. What's wrong with now?"

Pam bit her lip. "It's not that easy."

"Why not? They know we'll come back. Al and Bet were born here." *Oh my god, the kids,* David thought. *Pam's their mother. That means...*" With his anxiety level rising, David left the room.

"Where are you going?" Pam asked.

"To get a glass of water," David called from the kitchen. "Want anything?"

"No thanks."

David doused his face with water, dried himself off, and returned to the living room. "What's wrong with going back now?"

"I suppose we could ask Unit One." Pam paced around the room. "If we do go, somebody will have to feed the animals...and the lemon harvest is almost ready for picking."

"I'm sure the Europans would be happy to help out while we're gone. They're always looking for something to do."

"Romeo and Juliet can handle it," Pam said.

"Can't be them. The twins won't go anywhere without them."

"You're right. I could train a few of the other Euorpans."

"Don't have to. They're omniscient. They already know everything."

Pam smirked. "Watch them walk underneath the brontosaurus after feeding time and you'll change your mind."

David heard scratching sounds followed by the sound of something crashing into the wall. "What was that?" he asked. He looked towards the doorway leading to the dining room and shouted, "Run!"

Pam remained on the couch seemingly unconcerned.

David ran back to her. "We have to get out of here!" he shouted.

Pam stared back at him. "No we don't."

A saber tooth cat the size of a Great Dane skidded through the doorway, lost its footing on the slick simulated hardwood floor, and slid into the wall collapsing in a heap.

"Sit down, honey," said Pam. "It's only Micetro."

The saber tooth cat stood and gingerly walked towards them.

David looked at the cat, horrified. "It's a..." he stammered.

"It's a hybrid, honey, part saber tooth and part common house cat with a dash of cocker spaniel." Micetro rolled over at David's feet exposing his belly with his tongue hanging over one of his tusks.

David shrank back. "Why?"

"The kids wanted a pet. He wants you to rub his belly."

"Where does *it* sleep?"

"His name's Micetro, not *it*, and he has his own bed."

"Where?"

"Al's bathroom. Be careful going in there. The saber tooth part of him hasn't figured out the litter box yet."

# Chapter Five

David and Pam walked hand in hand to the tube connecting their habitat to the city center. David had a new spring to his step. An amorphous pedestal of silver projected from the ground near the tube's entrance. The twins called the transportation pedestals "lumps." First Pam, and then David touched the lump, and it flowed around them solidifying into a teacup shape with contoured seats and a clear bubble cover.

"Reminds me of the ride at Disneyland," David said.

"Your nostalgia for Earth knows no bounds." Pam spoke to the teacup, "Take us to Unit One." The teacup sped through the tube towards the city center.

"Ever wonder why Unit One's the only robot dude without a letter in front of his number?" David asked. Romeo and Juliet were officially known as R131 and J262.

Pam smiled. "He's the only *One*...get it?"

"Ha ha. I'm going to ask him about it."

"Maybe now's not the best time to piss him off," Pam said.

"*It* is a computer. No emotions. Can't get pissed off."

"Honey, we need Unit One's approval to leave. Don't antagonize him."

"What do you want me to do?" David asked.

"Try practicing your smile with your mouth closed."

The teacup dissolved leaving them on a platform in front of Unit One's structure at the city's center. Unit One's quarters were at the very top. One appeared to be in charge of everything on Europa. David once asked Romeo to describe the Europan hierarchy. "If everybody is networked to everybody else, the actions of individuals become subordinated to the group," Romeo had explained. David interpreted this as a fancy way of saying that if everybody knows your business, better keep changing your underwear.

They rode an elevator to the top floor and stopped in front of a blank wall. None of the city's structures had doors or even addresses. Pam held up her palm, her disc blinked twice, and an opening appeared in the wall. Doorbells weren't necessary either. Europans didn't wear clothes or engage in sex. Opening the wrong door by mistake wouldn't be a problem.

Unit One stood stationary in the center of a featureless circular chamber without windows. He looked the same as a transportation lump, except with a panel of flashing lights.

"You are well," remarked One in their heads. It wasn't a question.

"Physically," David said using his vocal chords.

"Explain."

"We need to visit Earth," he replied.

Pam jumped into the conversation. "We would *like* to visit our families."

One oozed up from the floor until it towered over them. "Are your needs not being met?" One used its audible voice.

David shrank back. "Yes."

One's lights flashed faster.

"He means no!" Pam said.

"Explain."

Pam elbowed David, a signal to stop talking. "It's a hominid thing," Pam said. "We need to revisit our biological parents from time to time…to renew."

"What do you renew?" asked One.

Pam thought quickly. "Our connection."

"This requires physical proximity?"

"Yes!" David shouted.

"Leave now," said One.

"That's it? You just send us away?" David exclaimed. "You heartless…"

"Europans do not have hearts. Internal circulation is irrelevant."

"Won't you at least consider our request?" Pam pleaded.

"Reconsideration is redundant," One replied.

"If you want us to keep breeding, you better keep the livestock happy," David said. Pam gawked at him.

"You may leave," One repeated.

Pam clamped her hand over David's mouth. "Leave you, or Europa?"

"Your auditory processors are in need of realignment," One replied. "See to it before your departure." Legs sprouted from One's torso and it flowed toward the portal.

David turned to Pam. "Did he say we could go home?"

Pam blinked. "Sounded that way."

# Chapter Six

The twins sat on the bed in Al's room with Micetro asleep on the floor. Al looked glum. Bet's expression radiated defiance.

Romeo and Juliet glided into the room. Juliet dropped an empty silver bag on the bed. "You should rejoice," Romeo said. "Visiting a backward planet will be an educational experience."

Juliet spoke to Romeo on a private channel. "You should not refer to Earth as a backward planet."

"Why?" Romeo replied.

"Pamela and David are from Earth."

"Why restate a known fact?"

"I have observed that earthlings sometimes exhibit a trait called loyalty," Juliet replied.

"Explain."

Juliet's lights flashed pink and white. "They can feel a protective affiliation to a person, place, or object."

Romeo's lights flashed back, his a shade of red. "I am loyal to you," he said.

"I am loyal to you too," Juliet replied. One of her tentacles snaked around what might be considered Romeo's waist.

"Ah-hem!" Bet cleared her throat.

"Your parents wish to exhibit you to their parents and to their higher level friends named Mickey and Vickie," Juliet said, out loud. Her lights changed to her usual mixture of colors.

Bet scowled. "Why bother? We see them all the time on the vid."

"They wish physical contact," Juliet replied.

"Why?" Bet persisted. She eyed Romeo draping a tentacle over Juliet's shoulder, or the closest thing a Europan had to a shoulder.

Romeo retracted it. "Humans require periodic physical contact for…" Romeo thought for a microsecond, still a long time for a Europan "...optimal operation."

Red lights sparkled across Juliet's face.

David and Pam were in their bedroom. "I'm a little nervous about seeing everybody again," David confessed as he lay on the bed watching her pack.

Pam looked up. "Why?"

"A lot of things have changed in the past five years...mostly us."

"We're still the same two people, just enhanced a little."

"Sure."

Pam frowned. "You make us sound like freaks."

"Maybe we are."

"Are our two best friends freaks? They're enhanced too."

"But the Europans continued messing with us," David persisted. "Are we sure we know what they did? Maybe I'm not David anymore." *Here it goes,* he thought. "Maybe you're not really Pam."

Pam put her hands on her hips. "What's that supposed to mean?"

"Maybe they did things to me that are different than what they did to you."

"Duh! Of course they did," Pam exclaimed.

"You knew about it?"

"Seriously? I'm a woman and you're a man. My enhancements *have* to be different than yours."

David slapped his forehead. "Of course. That explains it."

"Explains what?"

David changed the subject. "You're right, Mickey and Vic look the same, except more mature."

"We look the same too...except for a few cosmetic changes." Pam drew back her shoulders. "I've changed from a 32A to a 34C." She studied David's expression. "You like my enhancements, don't you?"

"I love them…I mean your enhancements." David blushed. "But you were beautiful before."

Pam smiled. "Ten points, honey." She picked up a photo of Vickie. "I never liked her hair. I still can't decide if it's cranberry or fire engine red."

David was feeling better. "What's the matter with red?"

"Looks unnatural, like Ronald McDonald. Blonde's more her style." Pam ran her fingers through her hair. "Are you tired of my hair?"

"No."

"I could add some blonde streaks to jazz it up," Pam said. "What do you think?"

"I think you need some private girl-time with Vickie to discuss all your fashionista stuff." He gathered Pam into his arms.

"Shopping with Vickie would be fun, or girl talk at Starbucks over a café mocha with whipped cream." She sighed. "You're right. It's not the same talking over the vid screen. But hanging out with them in person again will be a little weird, at least at first."

"Admit it. You're nervous about seeing everybody too," David said.

"It's true, we're not the same as we were before—and not just how we look." Pam reflected for a moment. "But are the changes in us the result of what the Europans did, or what happened to us after—because we're living on Europa?"

"That's the old heredity versus environment argument…or in our case, *fake* heredity."

"Fake heredity? What do you mean by that?"

David felt anxious again. "They fiddled with our genes. Are we still *you* and *me*?"

Pam withdrew from his arms. "They helped us adapt to our environment."

"You're saying we've become weird because of this crazy

place."

She punched his shoulder. "Stop saying we're weird!"

"What about the kids?" David asked.

"What about them?"

He chuckled. "Those two are *seriously* weird."

"Stop it."

"Oh yeah? Try seeing them as an earthling would. No hair, three Earth-years old but already looking like teenagers, not to mention off the chart IQs."

Pam frowned. "I see what you mean."

"This trip could be rough on them," David continued.

"They can handle it."

David smirked. "I was referring to the people of Earth."

"Not funny. I could program their scalps to grow hair. That should help them blend in."

"You're not listening."

Pam looked distressed. "Yes I am…I want them to blend in, but I don't know what to!"

"It's more than their appearance I'm worried about," David said. "Imagine our little darlings with a whole new world to find trouble in."

Pam bit her lip. "You're right. I better talk to Romeo and Juliet."

"Good luck with those two." David thought about going home and burst into a smile. Figuring out Pam's unusual genome could wait. Then he remembered Mars.

# Chapter Seven

The room was dark, except for flickering light from the television. Vickie sat beside Mickey on the couch looking at the screen. "What are you watching?" she asked.

Black and white images played across Mickey's face. He didn't reply.

Vickie watched for another moment. "It's an old sci-fi flick with a guy in a rubber suit."

Mickey continued staring at the screen. "It's *The Day the Earth Stood Still.* Watch. You might learn something."

Vickie sighed and sat back. "Three minutes, buddy, then we're outta here."

*The flying saucer settled on the White House lawn. As a frightened crowd of earthlings held its collective breath, a ramp extended and a humanoid figure dressed all in silver descended. "We have come to visit you in peace and with goodwill," he announced. He extended his hand to reveal a gift intended for the US President, a silver sphere. The background music stopped, heightening the tension. In the silence, a shot rang out and the figure in silver slumped to his knees. Behind him a menacing-looking silver robot appeared in the flying saucer's doorway. A shield lifted up from its face revealing, instead of eyes, a pulsing orb of light.*

"Remind you of anything?" Mickey asked.

Vickie ran her fingers through Mickey's hair. "Let's watch a *real* movie, something a little steamy," she whispered, near his ear.

Mickey left her on the couch and moved to the window. He stared down at the street. "They're always watching," he said. Night and day, people waited in the street below straining to catch a glimpse of them—paparazzi, curious passersby, and increasing numbers of Sphere Cult members waving signs.

Vickie joined him at the window. "Doesn't bother Brad and

Angelina. Why should it bother us?" She nibbled at his ear. "You need a change in scenery. Let's go to a hotel."

Mickey turned away from her. "What's the point?"

"Why are you pulling away from me? Most men find me attractive." Vickie straightened her dress and stormed out of the room.

A pane of bulletproof glass separated Mickey from a world he no longer felt part of. He pounded his fist against the glass causing a spider web of cracks and setting off an alarm. Seconds later, he heard his Secret Service detail pounding on the door. "I'm all right!" Mickey shouted. "Go away."

"Are you sure, sir?" a man asked through the door.

"Yeah. Everything's fine. Dropped something."

The alarm stopped blaring.

Vickie came running into the room and saw the window. "What the fuck?"

She found him with his chest heaving. "I'm sorry," Mickey said.

"You know what, honey, you need some serious help."

"Can't get sick anymore. Neither can you."

"I know what's wrong. You're so fucking jealous of Davie, you can't see straight!"

"Wait a minute, Vic. That's not fair."

"And you're too damn immature to deal with it."

Mickey scowled. "Leave me alone."

"With pleasure, asshole." Vickie thrust her middle finger in his face and slammed the door shut as she left the room.

Mickey winced. *Maybe Vickie's right,* he thought. Except for joining Ernie at Sphere encounters, he rarely stepped outside their apartment. When Vickie left for work in the morning, he locked the door and closed the shutters. All his neighbors were Secret Service agents, never great conversationalists, or they were international spies trying to steal the Sphere. After five years of foiled attempts, the mayhem was tapering off. Too bad,

Mickey thought. The foreign agents were much more interesting than the government guys, but they never stayed around very long.

Vickie had recognized Mickey's growing depression and had kept encouraging him to cheer up. Couldn't he see all the wonderful things happening, she'd argued? Antarctica had stopped melting. The Sahara desert had stopped receding. No more earthquakes were shaking Japan. Thanks to the Sphere, the whole world was becoming more orderly, fresh and clean, and in some ways unrecognizable. Several familiar icons of civilization were either gone or on the way out. In North America, electric trains were replacing the network of highways synonymous with wealth. It meant no more high-powered muscle cars and exotic foreign sports jobs plying the roads, but no more rush hour traffic or road rage either. Wasn't that better? Energy had become free, clean, and plentiful. Food and medical care were more abundant too because of the information extracted from the Sphere. Mickey knew he should be happy about all the changes, but he wasn't.

He found her in the kitchen. "Can we start over?" he pleaded.

"From where?" Vickie snapped.

"From where you said let's go to a hotel," Mickey replied, forcing a smile. He reached for her, but she pulled away. "Come on, Vic. Don't play hard to get."

"You forgot how to play."

"Remember when you wouldn't walk on the same side of the street as me?" Mickey asked.

"I had the right idea."

"Jesus, Vic, can you tone it down a little? Can't you see I'm trying to apologize?"

She looked away.

"I have something to ask you," Mickey said.

Vickie rolled her eyes. "It took you long enough."

"What?"

"You can skip the part about getting down on your knees."

"There's something I'd like to know first," Mickey said.

"Before you propose to me, or before you apologize?"

"Would you have gone to Europa with me if I'd asked you?"

Vickie looked surprised. "Wow. Not where I thought you were going with this." She sighed. "Honest answer—I don't know. I was falling for you…I'm sure of that. But at seventeen and from a broken home, I didn't know jack shit about life. I was seriously confused before I took a ride in a flying saucer. After that, I didn't know what to do."

"It's okay, Vic. I'm not offended," Mickey said. "I wouldn't have gone either."

"Everybody knows that. It's time you realize it too." Vickie's jaw muscles tightened, never a good sign. "Since this is about you apologizing and not proposing, here's the deal. I'll accept your apology on one condition—you stop being so damn morose! You have ten seconds to decide before things get really unpleasant and I totally lose it."

"Ten seconds? The Europans gave us ten days."

"Nine, eight… "

He got down on his knees. "Okay, I apologize! Which hotel do you have in mind?"

# Chapter Eight

## Cheyenne Mountain, Wyoming
## Headquarters of the DIA

General Westlock sat behind his desk smashing grapes with the butt of his pearl-handled Colt 45 replica. "I won't be defeated"—he smashed a grape—"by a guy who drained outboard motors for a living"—he smashed another grape and it spattered his shirt—"and speaks to an alien grapefruit." He glared around the Control Center, causing his analysts and support staff to cringe, and focused on his adjutant, Major Latham. "Where's my new op to steal the Sphere?"

Latham spun around in his chair. "We've been trying to capture the Sphere for five years, Sir. Nothing works. We're out of ideas."

"When I want excuses, I'll order them!" Westlock squashed several more grapes on his desk.

"But, Sir, Ernie is surrounded by his own personal force field and talks to flying saucers through his television set. Nobody can get near him."

"He's a boat mechanic, and by God, Latham, there's only one flying saucer… Where is that damn UFO?"

"Back on Europa…isn't it, Sir?"

The general gestured at a bank of equipment. "Where are we, soldier?"

"In the Control Center?"

"What do we do here?"

"Spy on people, run black ops, that kind of thing?"

"For whom?"

Latham scratched his head. "Sir?"

"For America! That's why we have all this shit, the world's best spy equipment. Cost the taxpayers billions of bucks.

Satellites, sensors, spy planes, every electronic gadget available, and you can't tell me where one goddamn flying saucer is?"

"No."

General Westlock sighed. "Do you know where the Sphere is?"

"Everybody does. Ernie has it."

"I want it."

Latham lowered his voice. "What's wrong with leaving it with Ernie? I mean…it's changing the world."

"I noticed," the general grumbled. "But there's still time to change it back."

"No famine, no disease…pretty soon there won't be any war." Latham sounded hopeful.

"You're a soldier, Latham. You need wars."

Latham looked down. "Yes, Sir."

"I'm worried about you, Latham. You're beginning to sound like a Cult wacko. Damn weirdoes are everywhere now, going door-to-door, handing out leaflets with little plastic Sphere key rings that light up. They're like Mormons with penlights." The general glared down the row of analysts seated in front of their computer screens in the darkened Control Center. "Listen up!" he shouted. "You join the Cult, you turn in your uniform!" One analyst hid his Cult key ring in a drawer and eased it closed. The general turned back to Latham. "Here's your new op, soldier. You're going to kidnap Mickey's parents. We'll trade them for the Sphere."

Latham's face blanched. "We don't do that kind of thing…do we?"

"It's war, for chrissake! Besides, we're not going to hurt them, just use them as bargaining chips to make that traitor boat mechanic hand over the Sphere."

"But, Sir, Ernie will stop us just like he always does."

"Mount a diversion. Improvise. You're wearing a uniform, do something military. This time we have the element of surprise.

Nobody thinks we'd stoop to kidnapping senior citizens."

"The Russians tried kidnapping Vickie," Latham said.

The general sneered. "Could have told the Ruskies that wouldn't work. She's got one of those palm gadgets that connects her to the Sphere. Mickey's parents don't have the damn things."

"The Saudis tried bribing Ernie when they still had oil money." Latham sounded increasingly flustered. "The Chinese are still trying to hack into the Sphere. Nothing works."

"You're kidnapping Mickey's parents. That's an order!"

"But..."

"It's still freezing in Alaska, Latham. The Sphere hasn't changed that. Snatch Mickey's parents or start packing for the snow." The general stormed out.

Latham slumped in his chair. "I don't think I can do it."

"Maybe it's time to get out," said the analyst sitting next to him. "Hell, maybe it's time for all of us to get out. Who needs this shit? Besides, war is becoming obsolete." He gestured around the room at all the high-tech equipment. "So's all this stuff."

"You're thinking of quitting?" Latham asked.

"It's crossed my mind," the analyst replied.

"What would you do?"

"Take off this uniform and get a regular job."

Latham edged closer. "Doing what?"

The analyst shrugged. "That's the problem. Almost went to medical school. Now, what's the point? The cure for everything's posted on the net—SphereMD.com. Don't need lawyers, cops, scientists, or auto mechanics. All anybody needs these days is Internet access."

Latham frowned. "Yeah."

"I always wanted to be a painter," the analyst said.

"There you go. Now's your chance."

"I'm color blind."

"The cure's probably posted on the Internet."

"Yeah, but I can't draw very well either."

Latham nodded, and neither of them spoke for a moment.

"Haven't seen your buddy Frankel in a while," the analyst said. "What's he doing these days?" Air Force Major Daniel Frankel had been instrumental in thwarting the general's plan to capture the flying saucer after it brought Mickey and his friends back from Europa before the Choice. The general would have shot Frankel for insubordination had Melanie Dilman not been broadcasting the event live.

"Haven't seen him," Latham replied. "He makes himself scarce when Westlock's in town."

# Chapter Nine

## London

Frankel ducked under the building's eave and shook out his umbrella. The structure appeared to be an ordinary brick walkup from the outside, one of several walkups lining the street. The décor inside suggested a swank hotel including dark wood, leather couches, and classic artwork.

Once inside, Frankel stood at the desk with his hands up and submitted to a retinal scan. His tradecraft identified several potential threats in his immediate vicinity – the muscular bellhop, a guest reclining on a couch with the outline of something in his vest pocket shaped like a gun, and a petite Asian receptionist who could probably kill him with one hand while eating sushi with the other. She offered a key. "Cocktails in Conference Room One at 7 p.m. sharp, Major. Evening attire."

"Last minute trip for me. I'm afraid I didn't bring anything," Frankel replied.

"You'll find something suitable on the bed." The receptionist batted her eyelashes. Her face reminded Frankel of a cobra's. "Don't be late."

Frankel took the key. "Thank you," he said. She pointed towards an elevator at the back of the foyer.

The elevator door closed and the car began ascending. Frankel couldn't see any control buttons or display that indicated how far. He estimated he was on the third floor when the door opened.

Frankel's room overlooking Piccadilly Circus had sumptuous Victorian-style furniture and expensive prints on the wall depicting English hunting scenes. The bed, an oversized canopy with satin pillows fit for a king, had a tuxedo laid out on the bedspread—Savile Row custom tailoring in his size with all the accouterments. After a glance at the clock, Frankel selected an exquisite bottle of champagne from the minibar and took a glass to the chair near the window.

At precisely seven o'clock, the elevator door opened and Frankel, now impeccably dressed, stepped inside. When the car reached its undisclosed destination somewhere below, he stepped into a small vestibule facing an unmarked door. A video camera mounted on the wall panned towards him. He ignored it and waited without looking at his watch. A half hour later, the inner door opened revealing a conference room with a long table. Frankel had the sense that every chair was occupied, but he couldn't see clearly because of a bright light shining directly at him.

"Do come in," said a voice from the far end of the table. He squinted into the glare trying to see the two people seated nearest him, a man and a woman both formally dressed. He thought the woman looked familiar. Sensing his interest, she swiveled her chair away from him.

"The debacle at the UN was embarrassing," the familiar voice said.

Frankel focused in that direction. He could see a man's hands resting on the table, but nothing more. One hand had a ring with a large orange stone. "Direct attacks on Ernie and the Sphere won't work."

"Sergeant Ernest Santos, US Army Rangers retired. Explain how a man whose most recent position was as a handyman at a fisherman's resort ends up in possession of the Sphere? Could he be more than he seems?"

"We've checked him out several times, and his dossier's clean—nothing unusual," Frankel replied.

The bejeweled man sat silently for a moment. "I have new orders for you, Major. You'll arrange for your associate Major Latham to join the Cult."

Frankel stifled his surprise. "Latham is career military. He'll never join the Cult. It's full of weirdoes and misfits."

"*We* are the Sphere Cult." The words echoed off the walls. "See to it that Major Latham becomes a member. Is that clear?"

Frankel blew out his breath. "It won't be easy."

"You'll find a way." Frankel found the obvious menace in the voice chilling. "One other matter. General Westlock is planning another operation to seize the Sphere. This one's better conceived than his usual escapades."

"What do you want me to do?" Frankel asked.

"If the fool succeeds, relieve him of the Sphere."

"The general isn't too fond of me. What if he won't add me to his team?"

Frankel heard the scraping sound of a chair pulling back. A moment later, a man in a black tuxedo stepped through the glare and extended an envelope. "This should take care of it," the Vice President said.

# Chapter Ten

A van marked "Tom's Plumbing" stopped in front of David's old house, the only house on the block covered with a transparent blue force field.

Boris leaned back in his seat. "Are you ready, comrade?"

His partner Viktor stared through the windshield. "*Comrade* is dated. It makes us sound like KGB."

"We *are* KGB." Boris checked the rear view mirror to make sure they weren't being followed.

"But nobody knows that," said Viktor.

"We do."

"But we don't tell anybody," Viktor added.

Boris sighed. "Let's go."

They walked nonchalantly to the rear of the van. After a quick look around, Boris unlocked the doors and leaned inside. The interior of the van contained a small arsenal and two metal toolboxes. Boris checked two silenced automatic pistols and put one in each toolbox. He handed one to Viktor, picked up the second one, and closed the van's doors. "Do you remember the plan?" he asked.

"Da. We steal the Sphere," Viktor replied.

"Before that. How do we gain access?" Boris held up his toolbox as a reminder.

"We are plumbers who have been invited to fix the water heater." Viktor paused. "It is bad plan."

"Why?"

"I don't know how to fix water heater. I only know how to kill people."

Boris struggled for control. Since the demise of the old USSR, budget constraints had severely limited the KGB's training efforts. Viktor was an example of the new KGB. "We do not fix the water heater," said Boris, trying to be patient. "That is our ruse for gaining entrance."

"If we do not fix water heater, why do we carry heavy toolboxes?" Viktor asked.

"To hide our guns!" Boris hissed.

Viktor nodded. "Da. That is good plan."

Boris glanced up at the sky. He had six months until retirement. "Let's go."

They carried their toolboxes to the edge of the force field. Boris pushed the red button on a call box mounted nearby.

Ernie was relaxing in the den watching his favorite fishing show. He saw a window open in the corner of his television screen with an image of Boris and Viktor and leaned forward for a better look. Scrolling text underneath identified the two men as KGB agents. The guns inside their toolboxes, as well as other sundry weapons concealed under their coveralls, appeared highlighted in red. "Time out for a little fun," Ernie said. He paused the fishing program and activated the intercom. "What can I do for you boys?"

"We are here to check the water heater in your fine house," Boris replied in heavily accented English.

"Why? It's brand new," Ernie asked. He had no idea how old the hot water heater really was.

Viktor shrugged and took one step back towards the van. Boris stomped on his foot, stopping him. "Which is why your fine machine should be checked! It may be out of…adjustment." Boris smiled into the video screen on the callbox.

"I shower every day and the water temperature seems fine," Ernie replied.

Boris thought quickly. "The service is free."

"Well, in that case," Ernie said, stifling his laughter. "Hang on while I lower the force field."

Boris winked at Viktor.

Another van was parked halfway down the block. Fancy writing on its side read *Sally's Catering, Italian our specialty*. An FBI agent inside the van focused on Ernie's house with his binoculars. "That's one of the KGB boys, Boris something-or-other."

His partner took a bite of his Big Mac. "This artificial meat sure tastes real."

"Did you hear what I said?"

"Two more KGB guys are about to get busted by Ernie. So what?"

"The FBI's still paying us. Phone it in."

An opening appeared through the force field's blue haze. Boris nodded to Viktor, and they walked to the front door carrying their toolboxes. Boris rang the doorbell. When Ernie opened the door, Boris extended a business card. Viktor smiled and held up his toolbox.

Ernie glanced at the card. "Armand's Fine Wine? I thought you guys are here to check the water heater."

Boris snatched back the card and handed Ernie a different one. He forced a smile. "Brother-in-law's card." He kicked Viktor before he could remind him that he didn't have a brother-in-law.

"Come on in," Ernie said.

The two KGB agents entered the house. While Ernie had his back turned to close the door, Boris threw open his toolbox and withdrew his gun.

Ernie turned around, feigning surprise. "My goodness!" he exclaimed, maintaining a straight face. "Is this a robbery?"

"No," Boris replied.

"Yes," said Victor.

"No!" Boris shouted. "We are here to take the Sphere. You will hand it to me, please." He held out his other hand.

"You're not here to check the water heater?" Ernie asked. "Too bad. I think the water pressure might be a little low."

"The Sphere!" Boris shouted, brandishing his gun.

Viktor looked around the entryway. He pointed at a small statue sitting on a table. "I will take that too." He glanced at Boris. "So local police will believe this is robbery."

Boris shook his head.

"Hate to tell you boys, but your guns don't work anymore," Ernie said, smiling.

"Russian weapons never fail." Boris pointed his gun squarely at Ernie's chest.

"Try it," Ernie suggested.

Boris looked perplexed. "You want me to shoot you?"

Viktor came up beside him with the statue under his arm. He had an evil gleam in his eyes. "Allow me, Tovarich."

"Works for me," Ernie said.

Boris wiped his forehead.

"You boys mind speeding this up. I'm missing my favorite fishing show," Ernie said.

Boris pointed his gun at the wall and pulled the trigger. Nothing happened. He tried several more times with the same result. Viktor aimed his gun at Ernie, smiled and pulled the trigger. When nothing happened, he pulled a knife hidden under his coveralls. The knife oozed through his fingers like molasses.

Ernie removed the Sphere from his pocket and extended it to Boris. "Is this what you boys came for?" The little globe swirled with storms of color like a psychic's crystal ball.

Boris stared at it, wide-eyed.

"Catch," Ernie said. He tossed it to Boris.

Boris caught the Sphere, now blazing with bright orange light, with both hands, beamed triumphantly at Victor, then yelled "Blya!" He threw the Sphere towards Viktor who snatched it out of the air with one hand, then shouted something worse and promptly dropped it on the carpet.

Ernie picked up the Sphere and its angry color quickly faded. He extended it to Boris again. "Sure you boys don't want it?"

Viktor stared at his hand covered with blisters. Boris's face contorted with rage. "We take you instead!" he yelled. He lunged for Ernie, but before he reached him a loud *pzzzt* sound assaulted his ears and he flew backward onto the carpet. Victor glanced at Boris dazed on the floor and began backing away.

"You guys mind letting yourselves out?" Ernie said. "And don't forget to leave the statue."

Boris scrambled to his feet and ran to their van with Viktor close on his heels. The KGB van accelerated down the street passing the FBI's van. One of the FBI agents scratched a checkmark on a pad. "That's five attempts for the Russians. Ties them with the North Koreans."

"Who has the record?" the second agent asked.

"The home team, nine attempts and still no cigar."

# Chapter Eleven

Frankel slammed his locker closed.

"Having a bad day?" asked one of the NORAD technicians changing in the locker room.

Frankel lied. "Broke up with my girlfriend. Kind of messy."

"Take it from a guy who's been married four times," the technician said, "a bachelor is a guy who didn't make the same mistake once."

Frankel guffawed. "Heard that one before." He stood in front of the mirror and finished buttoning his uniform coat.

"Come on, Major. Everybody knows you're a player. You'll have another gal sitting on your lap by Saturday night." The technician left the locker room.

Frankel stared at himself in the mirror. He still felt uneasy about his meeting in London. It wasn't about the latest operation to steal the Sphere. Sphere operations were nothing more than grown men playing games they couldn't win. He was upset about getting Latham involved. The two of them didn't hang out and never spoke outside of NORAD, but in an odd way Frankel liked him. The thought of Latham being dragged into his monumental mess made Frankel uneasy, like a lot of things lately.

Frankel put his lunch tray down across from Latham and sat down. "Is it my imagination, or are you looking glum?"

"Heard you were away on leave," Latham replied. "Where'd you go?"

Frankel speared a wedge of pineapple. "Hawaii. Anything interesting happen while I was gone?"

"Nope."

Frankel popped the pineapple into his mouth and started munching. "No super-secret black ops launching in the middle of the night?"

"None of that shit happens anymore," Latham grumbled. "Fucking boring around here."

Frankel lowered his voice. "I'm going to a Sphere Cult meeting tonight. Want to come along?"

Latham looked surprised. "You're getting into that shit?"

"A lot of people are."

Latham sneered. "They're a bunch of kooks with too much time on their hands."

"No, lots of them are normal people like you and me."

"I'm not into religion, and by the way, neither of us are normal."

"The Cult has nothing to do with religion," Frankel said.

"Get real. Of course it does."

"What are you afraid of?" Frankel asked.

Latham bristled. "Nothing."

Frankel pulled on his uniform lapel. "See these things we're wearing? We kill people for a living. You happy about that?"

"I thought we were protecting America."

"There aren't any more wars."

Latham looked down. "Yeah."

"Come with me tonight. The food's always good at the meetings. If you don't like what you hear, you had a nice meal. What's the big deal?"

"Okay…but don't tell anybody," Latham whispered.

Frankel held up three fingers. "Scout's honor."

Frankel opened the door to the restaurant, but Latham hung back. "Not sure about this," Latham muttered.

"They're not going to light candles and paint a pentagram on the floor," Frankel scoffed.

Several normal-looking people nodded at Frankel as they entered the restaurant. Frankel held the door and gestured for Latham to follow him inside. After peering through the door to make sure he didn't recognize anybody, Latham followed him.

Well-dressed men and women engaged in conversation at tables with white tablecloths and cloth napkins. Latham and Frankel took a table near the back corner. "I'm not writing any checks," Latham whispered as he fidgeted in his chair.

"They don't ask for money unless you want to buy a key ring." Frankel placed his on the table.

Latham smirked. "Does it come with a Happy Meal?"

"Remember, you can leave any time you want."

A man wearing a hand-tailored Italian suit entered the restaurant, nodded to a few people and took a seat by himself. The room quieted.

"Who's he?" whispered Latham.

"The leader," Frankel replied, keeping his voice down.

"What's his real job when he's not hustling for the Cult?"

"He's not hustling anything…he doesn't need to. Do you know anything about art?"

"The Mona Lisa has a weird smile?"

Frankel flicked his eyes toward the speaker. "That's Paul Rudnick."

"Never heard of him," Latham replied.

Frankel smirked. "Seriously? His name's on the façade of the Museum of Modern Art. You need to get out more. "

"I haven't had the time to stroll through museums or attend the opera. I've been too busy protecting our country."

"From what?" Frankel sneered.

Latham looked away.

"I'll give you a hint. Ever heard of the Butte Big Rigs?" Frankel whispered.

"NFL," Latham replied. "First place in the Mid-West Division. Why?"

"He owns them."

Latham looked impressed. "*That* Rudnick?"

"Bingo."

A tall, reed-thin man with an aristocratic air, took a sip of water and stood. "Good evening everyone," Paul Rudnick said, smiling warmly. He was greeted by murmurs of acknowledgement. "I see some new faces tonight." He nodded towards one of the tables, and then at Latham who squirmed in his seat. "This fills me with happiness *and* pride. Happiness because, with more good people joining us, we can do the job that so desperately needs to be done even faster. And pride because nothing could be more important than what we do." He paused surveying the room. "I'll ask our regular members to forgive me for making a few introductory comments to the new people I see here tonight." He looked directly at Latham. "We've finally entered an age when lines on a map dividing us are meaningless...so are skin color, language and religion. None of that matters anymore."

"If he says it's because of the Sphere, I'm leaving," Latham whispered to Frankel.

Rudnick continued. "It's because there's enough for everybody now—enough clean air, clean water, food, and energy. The business of creating barriers to concentrate wealth is obsolete. Isn't it wonderful?" He held up his Sphere key ring and the room erupted with applause. Rudnick signaled for quiet. "But having the Sphere isn't like waking up on Christmas morning and finding gifts under the tree." The power of his voice continued rising. "First of all, the Sphere won't help unless we ask it the right questions. Even if we're smart enough to do that, the information inside is worthless unless we do something *worthwhile* with it." He paused for emphasis. "Make no mistake. The knowledge inside the Sphere isn't a gift. It's a great deal of work." He looked around the room. "I'm not religious, and never was. Never joined anything in my life, not even the Boy Scouts. But let me tell you, I can embrace a cause that heals the human race and our planet. I'll gladly spend my time thinking about what this world really needs, and when the Sphere provides the answer, I'll roll up my sleeves and work alongside you to make sure the knowledge is implemented for the benefit of every living soul. I think that's a helluva way to spend my life." The room erupted with applause again. "That's a helluva way for all of us to spend our lives! Who's with me?" Everyone except Frankel and Latham stood and started clapping. A few yelled, "Yessir, count me in!" and other rah-rah statements.

Frankel poked Latham in the ribs. "See, I told you." He stood and started clapping.

Latham studied the enthusiastic faces of the Cult members. He tried to fight it, but his personal demons were stirring. He hadn't had a good night's sleep in years. Nightmares from two decades in Special Ops kept waking him up sweating and afraid. In recent months, those memories had begun stalking him into the light threatening his sanity. They were pounding on his psyche now. Was it because of Paul Rudnick's speech? He began to wonder if joining the Sphere Cult could send his demons away and finally let him rest. Instead of walking away, he rose to his feet and started clapping.

# Chapter Twelve

Vickie couldn't decide whether to find Mickey and try to talk sense into him, or to leave him alone and let his emotions play out. After several orbits around the living room, she decided to do what most women do in this kind of situation—call somebody. She couldn't call Pam without sitting in front of Ernie's TV. Ernie gave her the creeps. She hadn't spoken to her father or her sister in two years and preferred to leave it that way. She cringed…her mother would probably be available.

"Hi, Mom," Vickie said into the video phone. She forced a smile and maintained an even tone to her voice.

Her mother sounded breathless. "If I have to give another interview, I swear I'm going to keel over!"

"That's nice. Mother…"

"The Channel Seven News anchor woman is writing a book about me…Melanie something-or-other."

"Dilman. Melanie Dilman," Vickie corrected.

"She asked me a thousand questions about…well, everything."

"Mother?"

"I've been meaning to tell you. You could use a little more pizzazz in your wardrobe. You don't want to look frumpy in front of the cameras."

"Mother?" Vickie interrupted.

"Yes?"

"I'm not a star."

"Of course you are. You're *with* the boy who passed the Test."

"His name is Mickey, and he's not a boy."

"When are you two *adults* getting married? Everybody keeps asking me." Marie's voice sounded conspiratorial.

Vickie sighed. "I don't know."

"You can trust me."

"Can we talk about something else?"

"I don't have a lot of time, dear. I need to get ready. I'm the guest of honor at a DAR meeting tonight."

"DAR?"

"Daughters of the American Revolution."

"Your parents arrived in a ship, but it wasn't the Mayflower."

"Is that any way to talk to your mother? Who bathed you? Who…"

"Catch you later, Mother." Vickie ended the call and sighed. "One person to go." She dialed her phone.

"Hey, Vic," Ernie answered.

"Have you talked to Mickey lately?"

"I did a couple of hours ago," Ernie replied. "He wasn't in the greatest mood."

"I know. Any ideas how to cheer him up?"

"He said he's going fishing. That always works for me, although I haven't done much lately. This saving the world stuff is real time-consuming."

"Any idea where?" Vickie felt certain she already knew.

Ernie's grin widened. "The sweetest place this side of heaven—Twin Lakes Resort near the little town of Bridgeport California. His folks are up there too."

"How nice," Vickie muttered.

"Doing a little fishing with his dad, eating his mom's High Sierra burgers…that'll cheer him up." Ernie studied Vickie's face. "That's what you want, isn't it?"

Vickie forced her own smile. "Sure."

"Want some advice from old Ern?"

Not really, Vickie thought. "Sure."

"Let Mickey do this his way. He'll be okay."

"Thanks." Vickie terminated the connection. "Enough of this bullshit." She put her silver palm disc on top of the phone and shouted, "Find Mickey."

The phone's screen showed Mickey's location at the town of Independence, California, population seven hundred fifty-one. To Vickie, Independence looked like a sleepy little town in the middle of nowhere. According to the map, the city of Bridgeport, the county seat, was only one hundred thirty-two miles farther north, and Twin Lakes Resort eleven miles above that. Why had he stopped in Independence, she wondered? She remembered him mentioning something about a bridge over a creek. She grabbed her purse.

# Chapter Thirteen

Mickey stood at the center of the wooden bridge over Independence Creek staring down into the water. He felt as if he'd awakened from a bad dream. For the first time in months, he knew what he needed to do. The irony of it forced him to smile. The world celebrated him as a hero because he passed the Europans' Test, but he knew the Test was a lie. He'd soon be a real hero for exposing the truth, yet was certain to be vilified for it.

He looked up and saw Vickie approaching the Secret Service perimeter. He wasn't surprised she came. That's why he loved her, now more than ever.

She stepped onto the bridge. "Is this the bridge you told me about?" Vickie asked. "Not exactly the Golden Gate."

"Sometimes there's more to a thing than what meets the eye…like cheese," Mickey replied.

Vickie leaned against the rail. "What the hell does that mean?"

"Cheese is cow's milk gone sour. Looks bad, sometimes smells bad, but a cob salad dies without it. Now do you understand?"

Vickie chuckled. "No."

"Why'd you follow me?" Mickey asked.

"Because I'm worried about you, asshole."

"Sorry. I needed some alone time to sort things out."

"The library's closer to home," Vickie said.

"Let me tell you about this old bridge," Mickey began.

"There's a limit to the amount of cheesie philosophy I can swallow in one day," Vickie said, sounding annoyed. "Your sidekick Ernie already gave me an earful."

"You never call Ernie."

"The bridge?" Vickie prompted.

Mickey looked down into the water again. "I've stood on this bridge with my dad every year that I can remember." He sighed. "Doesn't matter if the wood's cracked or the paint's chipped, part of me never leaves this place. Does that make sense?"

"You're talking about tradition, not cheese. Sometimes things change because they have to."

"You're wrong, Vic. Some things aren't supposed to change."

"Ever hear of the Dark Ages, or how about the Europans? They stopped changing and nearly became extinct."

Mickey's expression darkened. "That's the way they're selling it to us."

"Please Mickey, let it go," Vickie pleaded.

Mickey glanced towards the Secret Service perimeter. "It's a fairy tale, and I was too busy being a hot-shot celebrity to realize it."

"What difference does it make? The world's changing for the better. Isn't that what matters?"

Mickey caressed her cheek. "No matter what happens, promise me you'll keep believing in me."

"I think you're nuts." Vickie nestled in his arms. "But I still love you. Now come home before I kill you."

Mickey kissed her and started for the parking lot. "I have to finish what I started."

Vickie hurried after him. "Finish what?"

"The damn Test! It isn't over."

She caught up with him. "You're not making any sense!"

"I have to go back and finish it, Vic, once and for all."

"Go back where?"

Mickey pointed towards the snowcapped mountains in the distance. "There. Where it began."

Vickie looked angry. "I know what this is really about. You're afraid of getting married and you're running back to your parents like a scared little boy."

"This isn't about them!" Mickey exclaimed.

Vickie wiped a tear from her eye. "I should be the center of your life now."

"This isn't about you either."

"I know. ...I won't be there when you get back." She pushed past him and walked away.

# Chapter Fourteen

The modular train line hadn't reached Twin Lakes Resort yet. This forced Mickey to lease a conventional car in Bridgeport. He found it exhilarating to be in the driver's seat again with his hands on a real steering wheel and his foot on the accelerator. Before ascending into the mountains, the road out of Bridgeport passed through gently rolling ranchland crisscrossed with fences and grazing cattle. The livestock paid no attention to the mile-long line of vehicles following Mickey like a multi-colored snake. Mickey's entourage included four black SUVs with his Secret Service detail trying to keep up with his speeding car.

Mickey pulled off the road and got out of his car near two future Big Macs mooing balefully across the barbed wire. The lead SUV stopped a short distance away and several Secret Service agents wearing dark suits and glasses jumped out. Mickey smiled when he remembered Ernie's description of Secret Service agents as "Dudes in Black."

"Can I help you?" asked one of the agents.

Mickey pointed at the stationary line of vehicles clogging the road. The paparazzi were out of their cars aiming cameras with long lenses at him. "Keep them out," Mickey said.

The agent looked perplexed. "Out of where?"

Mickey pointed towards the snow-capped mountains that cradled Twin Lakes Resort. "There."

"I'm not authorized…" the agent began.

Mickey crossed his arms over his chest. "Then turn everybody around."

The agent scratched his head. "Why?"

"I'm going by myself, or everybody goes home."

"I can't let you go anywhere without your Secret Service detail, Sir."

Because of the Europan nannites in is blood and his

connection to the Sphere, Mickey didn't need protection. "I'll allow two cars to come with me," he said.

The agent spoke into his lapel mic, listened to his earpiece, and then turned to his associates. "The first two units go with Mickey, the other two stay here and set up a roadblock."

One of the other agents pointed at the line of cars. "What do we tell *them*?"

"Photograph the cows."

Mickey's car rounded the final curve, and he saw the lake for the first time in five years. He stopped the car at the side of the road and turned off the motor, then rolled down the window so he could hear the wind whispering through the pines. Thanks to the new weather control system, rainfall had been ample and the weather calm. Unlike the years of drought, the lake looked full. Mickey knew fishing would be good. Maybe his dad would finally catch "the big one." After a few moments of pleasant remembrance, Mickey's thoughts turned to his best friend half way across the solar system. Being at the lake without Davie felt like standing on the bridge without his father. He rolled up the window and started the car.

Mickey walked up the steps to the cabin his family always rented and opened the door. "Hey, Mom," he said.

"Mickey!" Jerry exclaimed. "We didn't know you were coming." She smothered her son with a hug and pulled out a chair for him at the table. Then she stepped back and gave him the once-over. "Doesn't Vickie feed you?"

Mickey smiled. "Vic's idea of cooking is buttering the bread."

Max walked out of the bedroom wearing his fishing vest. He burst into a smile when he saw his son. "What are you doing here?"

"Hey, Dad," Mickey said. "Had any luck?"

Max sat across from Mickey and picked up a fishing lure. The table was piled with all manner of fishing paraphernalia—flies, lures, hooks, sinkers, and several jars of Power Bait. Five fully rigged fishing rods leaned against the wall. Max always brought along spares. "Caught a few little ones," Max said. He put down the lure. "One of our Secret Service guys caught a six pounder the other day." He shook his head. "Can you believe it? He didn't even know how to bait his hook."

"Beginner's luck." The smile faded from Mickey's face.

Max glanced at Jerry. They often communicated without words.

"Everything okay with you and Vickie?" Jerry asked.

"Yes." Mickey answered too quickly.

"How long can you stay?" Jerry asked while hiding the concern in her voice.

Mickey composed himself. "Couple of days."

"Heading out again with Ernie and the Sphere?" Max asked.

"Something like that."

Max grabbed two fishing rods. "Let's go."

Mickey smiled at his father. "It's been awhile since I dunked a line."

"Like riding a bike," Max said. "It'll give us time for a father-son chat." He picked up a jar of bright pink Power Bait which looked like Play-Doh infused with glitter. "Unless we're too busy reeling 'em in."

"If you bait your hooks with that pink disco bait, you'll have plenty of time to talk," Jerry said. "Any self-respecting trout won't go near it." Actually, fish grown in a hatchery went wild for the stuff. The few native trout left in the lake looked at it and laughed.

Mickey watched the tip of his fishing rod and waited for signs of a bite. Trying to be inconspicuous, his Secret Service agents pretended to fish twenty yards down the bank. They were the only people wearing black suits above ground within fifty miles.

"Something's on your mind," Max said. "That's why you came up here, isn't it?"

"Not sure I can do this anymore," Mickey replied.

"Do what?"

"The whole Sphere thing."

"Do you have a choice?"

"Interesting question. Did I ever?"

"You lost me," Max replied.

"The Europans' Test was rigged," Mickey said.

Max looked surprised. "Why would they do such a thing?"

"Don't know yet."

"What does Ernie have to say about it?"

"He works for the Europans."

Max reeled in his line. "What about Davie?"

"We haven't talked about it. He's too busy with Pam and the twins to think about much of anything, not to mention being four hundred million miles away."

"Are you and Vickie *really* okay?" Max asked.

"Yes, and please stop asking me."

"Then get married and start your own family." Max's glob of pink Power Bait remained pristine on his hook. He changed it for a glob of bait the colors of Neapolitan ice cream and recast his line.

Mickey frowned. "It wouldn't be a marriage, it would be a coronation."

"Then why don't you elope?"

Mickey pointed at his Secret Service detail. "Hard to slip away with those guys following me like hound dogs."

"If you didn't come up here to tell us you're getting married, and you're not here to go fishing, why did you come?" Max asked.

Mickey looked towards the marsh. "I haven't been up here for a while. Thought I'd look around, maybe check out the marsh again."

"It's been five years," Max said. "There's nothing there now except mosquitos. The flying saucer left a long time ago. Ernie's gone too." Max studied Mickey's face. "You're not here because of nostalgia. I think you came back to find something you lost."

Mickey chuckled. "You mean my mind?"

"Your way." Max squeezed his son's shoulder. "Most men face this moment at some point in their lives. Coming of age, becoming a man—lots of names for growing up. Sometimes you have to retrace your steps to find the right path."

"Want to come with me?"

"You've got to take this journey by yourself," Max replied. "Besides, you know how much I hate mosquitos."

Mickey followed the growl of outboard motors to the resort's marina where he and David first met Ernie. Along the way, he stopped to savor the aromas wafting from the Lodge's rustic restaurant. Since being enhanced by the Europans, his nervous system instantly analyzed the chemical composition of everything in his environment. He preferred his original taste buds, the ones that enjoyed cheeseburgers and French fries without knowing how much linoleic acid they contained.

Everyone he encountered looked happy—kids with fishing poles, dads with coolers full of cold soft drinks and snacks, moms walking dogs. He remembered what it felt like to be one of them, and something his dad said the first time they went fishing together—a boy walking beside his dad with a fishing pole has more riches than the world's mightiest king. It didn't make sense to him then, but it did now.

Beyond the marina, a foot-worn trail led along the edge of the lake towards a forest of reeds waving in the breeze. Five years before Mickey and David were hiking through the marsh on the way to Horse Tail Falls when Mickey fell into a hole and started the Europans' Test. That Mickey didn't exist anymore—part of the price paid for a better ozone layer and a cure for cancer.

He started into the maze of reeds, and after several twists and turns of the path, he lost sight of the marina. The sun beat down on the back of his neck and he batted away a mosquito. Perhaps because of his enhanced hearing, he thought the cicadas seemed louder than he remembered with a more strident cadence. He stopped and kicked at the dirt. "Stop laughing at me!" he shouted.

"Are you lost?" a voice asked from behind him.

Mickey spun around expecting to see his Secret Service detail. Instead, he saw an older man perhaps the same age as his father. The man had gray hair and a suntanned face, and he carried a fishing rod and wore the clothing of a fly fisherman. Mickey thought the man looked familiar. "I know where I'm going," he replied.

The man extended his hand. "Stevens is the name. Heading up to the falls?"

"Not today."

"I hiked up there this morning," Stevens continued. "Pretty scenery, but didn't have any luck." He wiped his brow with the back of his hand. "Hot today." He opened his creel and pulled out a can of soda. "It's still cold if you want it. I've got another one."

"Thanks." Mickey popped open the can and took a swig.

"You're the kid who passed the aliens' test, aren't you?" Stevens asked.

"Thanks for the drink," Mickey said as he stepped away.

"Your friends back there won't have any problems with me. I'm a cop too."

"Next time try fishing the lake on the side near the highway." Mickey started back towards the marina.

"You're not the only one who doesn't trust the Europans," Stevens said.

Mickey stopped and turned around. The sun was behind Steven's shoulder forcing Mickey to shield his eyes.

"The Sphere's a Trojan horse," Stevens continued. "Surprised nobody sees it."

"Why do you say that?"

"Met any kids lately filling out their college applications? Thomas Moore was right. Utopia is a bad idea."

Mickey took a step closer. "Who are you?"

"I told you, I'm a cop. Here's a question for you. What's the very first choice you had to make when all this Europan stuff started?"

"If you know who I am, you already know the answer."

Stevens looked into Mickey's eyes. "Was it the Choice everybody school kid knows about, or when you decided to step into that flying saucer the very first time, before you met any Europans?"

"Never liked riddles," Mickey replied.

"If you're looking for answers, I'd go back there," Stevens said.

"What makes you think I'm searching for anything?"

"Because you haven't been back here in five years...until now."

"Who the hell are you?"

"The Griffith Park Observatory is holding a symposium on Europa next weekend. Maybe I'll see you there." Stevens walked past Mickey towards the marina passing two secrets agents who came jogging up the path. The agents watched Stevens until he disappeared behind the reeds. One of the agents had a camera with a telephoto lens and a satellite phone.

"Who was that guy?" Mickey asked.

"A police captain from your old home town. He checks out...except we're still trying to figure out how he got past us." The agent looked embarrassed. "Do you want us to bring him in for questioning?"

"No, "Mickey replied. "Anybody hungry? My mother makes a mean High Sierra burger."

The agent looked relieved. "Count me in." The other agent nodded.

# Chapter Fifteen

General Westlock sat brooding in his office. He did a lot of that lately. Most of his best analysts had turned in their uniforms with nobody lining up to replace them. Latham had been acting weird too. Westlock felt certain it had something to do with him palling around with Frankel. The general blamed Frankel for botching the capture of the Europans' flying saucer the first time around and making him look incompetent on international television. He was sure it cost him his sixth star, one more than his idol Patton. Adding insult to injury, Frankel was back on his staff again by direct order of the Vice President. The general planned to deal with Frankel later, starting with posting him to Antarctica. He had more pressing matters to deal with now starting with saving America from the Sphere. He'd straighten Latham out later too.

"Latham!" the general yelled.

"Yes, General?" Latham didn't snap to attention as quickly as he used to.

"Is that a stain on your uniform, soldier?"

Latham looked down. Some of his tuna sandwich hadn't made it to his lips. "I believe you're right, General. Sorry about that."

"Sorry about that, *Sir*!"

"Right."

The general's face turned bright red. "What did you say?"

"Right…Sir." Latham turned and smirked at Frankel who sat at the next workstation.

"Where's my operational plan, mister?" Westlock demanded.

"What plan?" Latham asked.

"Operation SCS."

Latham looked puzzled. "SCS?"

"Senior Citizen Snatch, you idiot!"

"Oh, that one."

The general pounded his fist on the table causing Latham's Cult key ring to hop off and fall on the floor. It landed near the general's foot. He kicked it away. "I expect that plan on my desk by 0900."

"0900. Got it," Latham replied.

"Got it, *Sir*!" the general bellowed.

"Right."

"Oh, for the love of…" The general stormed out.

Frankel handed Latham back his Cult key ring. "What are you going to do?" he asked.

Latham popped the key ring back into his pocket. "Delegate."

"To whom?" Frankel asked.

"Special Ops. Still plenty of crazies looking for work over there."

"Aren't you Special Ops?" Frankel reminded him.

"I'm the Special Ops *officer* now. My job is to delegate. Somebody else does the actual sneaking around and shooting." Latham picked up the phone. "Get me Team Thirty-six." He blocked the phone's video screen with his hand. "Those boys love this kind of shit."

"Yeah?" responded the soldier on the video screen. He yawned.

Latham stared at the phone. "Who are you?"

"Who are you?" the soldier asked.

"Excuse me," Latham demanded.

The soldier smirked. "How can I excuse you if I don't know who you are?"

"I'm your superior officer!" Latham shouted. At least for the moment, he was back into military shtick.

"Oh," the man replied.

*"Oh?"*

"I get it…oh, *Sir*."

Latham covered the phone's screen again. "Can you believe this asshole?"

Frankel shrugged.

"Where's the meeting tonight?" Latham asked Frankel, still with his hand over the phone.

"That Italian place on Third" Frankel replied. "I hear it's pretty good."

"Can you pick me up?"

Frankel nodded.

Latham took his hand off the video phone's speaker. "Have you been briefed on Operation SCS, soldier?"

"I thought it was a joke," the soldier replied.

"It's not a joke, it's an order. I need an OP by 0830. *Do I make myself clear*?" Latham shouted.

"You're serious?"

Latham put his hand over the speaker. "Can you pick me up a little early, say half an hour? I need to drop off my dry cleaning on the way." Frankel nodded. "0830 soldier!" Latham shouted into the phone. He broke the connection and looked at Frankel. "I love seafood. Do they have Cioppino?"

"You had tuna for lunch," Frankel replied. "You're still wearing it."

Latham looked at the stain on his tunic. "I'll order eggplant."

Frankel sat in the stall in the men's room with a hidden telephone behind the toilet paper dispenser. He peered out the stall's door, and when he was certain he was alone, he secured the door and placed a call. "The operation is called Senior Citizen Snatch," he whispered.

"At least that fool has a sense of humor. Who are the senior citizens he's trying to snatch?"

"Don't know yet. The general keeps me out of the briefings."

"Are you progressing with your recruitment of Latham to the Cult?"

"Yes. We're attending another meeting tonight."

The line went dead.

# Chapter Sixteen

Lieutenant Peterson hung up the wall phone and faced four partially uniformed men playing cards. The tattooed men had physiques suggesting they worked out regularly, the kind of men who deliberately parked their cars in dark alleys hoping somebody will try to steal them. "Gentlemen, we have a mission," Peterson said. "Assemble the rest of the team."

One of the men threw down his cards. "My luck sucks."

"So do your arm pits," laughed another member of Seal Team Thirty-Six. He spread his cards on the table. "I got three deuces. Read 'em and weep, ladies."

"Beats me," said a third man throwing down his cards.

The first man stared across the table at the lone remaining player. "I'm waiting, Ralphie. What you got?"

"Guys," said Petersen.

Master Sergeant Ralph Jenkins of ST36 sneered at his bunkmate Sergeant Fred, *Freddie*, York and laid out his cards one at a time. "Looks like four madams to me. Pay up, and I don't take credit cards."

"Guys!" Petersen shouted.

"Let me guess," York said. "You want us to make another attempt on the Sphere. That's all we do these days." He started raking in his chips. "Might as well save the trouble and phone in our Mia Culpa."

Jenkins cocked an eyebrow. "You have her phone number?"

"Who's phone number?"

"Maria Culpa. I hear she's hot."

York stared back at him.

"We're not going after the Sphere," Petersen said. "We have a different mission." All four Seals looked up. "We've been ordered to kidnap Mickey's parents."

Ralph chuckled. "Yeah, right."

Petersen shook his head. "This isn't a joke. We need a plan by 0800."

"A plan for what? How to land on our asses gracefully?"

# Chapter Seventeen

Latham straightened his uniform jacket and opened the door to Seal Team Thirty-six's ready room. The twelve members of the Team were sitting in captain's chairs. Nobody stood to attention. Latham went to the whiteboard and spun sharply around. "At ease," he said. Already completely at ease, the Seals ignored him. Latham tapped the board covered with columns of numbers. "Is this the O.P. for Senior Citizen Snatch?"

"Poker winnings," somebody muttered. A few of the men laughed.

"But don't look for York's name. He ain't won shit," Jenkins said. He slapped York on the shoulder.

Latham didn't appear amused. "Maybe you didn't hear me the first time, gentlemen. I said, where's my O.P.?"

Lieutenant Petersen got to his feet and saluted. A head taller than Latham and quite a bit beefier, he was one of the smaller men in ST36. "Don't have one, Sir."

Latham stared up at Petersen trying to appear intimidating. "Why not?"

Petersen shrugged. "Because it's impossible."

The door burst open and General Westlock strode into the room. Petersen yelled "'Tention!" and the Team members jumped to their feet. The general glared first at Latham, and then at Petersen. "Where's my O.P.?"

A poker chip fell off the table and clattered to the floor.

Petersen stood ramrod straight. "Don't have one, General, *Sir*!"

The general got right into his face. "Why not, *Private* Petersen?"

Petersen's lips pulled pencil thin and he stared straight ahead. "Couldn't come up with anything that would work, *Sir*!"

The general strolled along the line of Seals stopping to glare into each man's eyes. "I see," he said. "We must be in the wrong ready room, Latham. These men aren't Seals, they're something else…maybe cub scouts?" A Seal standing in front of the general sneered, but didn't say anything. "Not cub scouts, *girl* scouts!" the general shouted. He was nose to nose with the man. "How much are your cookies, *little girl*?"

The Seal looked ready to explode.

The general walked to the door with Latham trailing after him. "One hour, ladies," the general said over his shoulder. He slammed the door.

Petersen turned to his men. "We better come up with something." A chorus of blank stares greeted him. "Okay, what kind of reconnaissance assets do we have? Do we have any drones in the air? How about locals we can recruit as spies?"

"We don't need reconnaissance. Just turn on the TV," one of the Seals said. "Ernie's people can't take a crap without CNN interrupting their regular programming."

"Then some guy on Twitter tweets what brand of toilet paper they used," York added. Jenkins slapped him on the shoulder and whispered, "Good one."

"Stow it, York!" Petersen pounded the table. "We need a diversion, something to draw Ernie and the Sphere away so we can make the snatch."

"We could set a house on fire," York suggested.

"Yeah," Jenkins chimed in. "I saw that in a *James Bond* movie. We'll pretend we're firemen so we can clear everybody out, and then…"

"That was Bruce Willis," interrupted another Seal. "He always does shit like that in his movies."

"He always ends up all cut up and bloody too. Dude needs a transfusion halfway through every freakin' movie."

Petersen frowned. "Come on, guys. How about something a little less obvious?"

"I know," Jenkins said.

# Chapter Eighteen

The twins stood at the base of the ramp with Romeo and Juliet. Al wore his usual silver jumpsuit and seemed relaxed. Bet wore an environmental helmet, completely opaque except for a small slit in front of her eyes.

"I don't want to go," Bet moaned.

"Mistress Bet," said Juliet, "you may remove your helmet. There is no need to maintain atmospheric containment within the flying disc."

"No. I won't let anybody see me like this," Bet said.

"Why not?" asked Juliet.

"I have fur on my head…like a rat!"

"Your parents have chosen to retain their hair," Juliet said.

"They still listen to music made by scratching on strings," Bet whined.

Pam and David stood off to the side talking to Unit S119 who would be in charge of the Menagerie while they were gone. "The feeding schedule is posted under the file name DEA 1," Pam instructed.

David glanced at his wife. "DEA?"

"Dino's Eat A lot," Pam replied. She resumed talking at a rapid pace. "Keep the temperature in the Jurassic enclosure at thirty-seven degrees Celsius and the humidity at eighty percent."

"Your requirements for the Jurassic and Cretaceous habitats are accessible on the central data net," S119 said. "There is no need to restate the parameters."

Juliet heard the exchange and moved closer. "Mistress Pamela is human," she sent to S119 on a private channel. "Repetition is a human trait."

"The Pamela unit is no longer human," S119 replied out loud. It started moving towards the menagerie.

Pam whipped her head around. "What did 119 say?"

"Nothing," David replied.

"We'll see about that," Pam snarled.

David grabbed her by the arm. "Who cares what 119 says? You're nervous about going home and it's making you edgy."

"You're right," Pam agreed.

"I am too. It's like going to the class reunion knowing you've gained a few pounds."

"I have not!" Pam exclaimed.

"That's not what I meant. You've never looked more beautiful."

Pam felt her waistline. "I could program my nannites to take off a few pounds."

The twins stared at them, Al now with a scowl on his face, and Bet…they couldn't see her face.

Pam looked at her daughter and struggled not to laugh.

"What's so funny?" Bet demanded using her helmet's radio voice.

David started chuckling. "You look ridiculous."

Bet stamped her feet. "I hate all of you!" She bolted up the ramp. Juliet hurried after her.

"On second thoughts, I think I'd rather stay home," Al said.

Still laughing, David gestured toward Romeo. "Get him on board, please."

Romeo projected a tentacle around Al's shoulders. "Your mother has authorized a pre-flight snack of frozen bovine lactation fluid, flavored with Earth cocoa beans."

Al stared at his mother. "*Real* chocolate ice cream?" Pam nodded. "Cool!" he raced up the ramp.

"Mickey must be thrilled," Pam said, when they were alone.

"Couldn't find him," David replied. "Vickie said she'd tell him."

"Oh my god! Vic must be plotzing! What did she say?"

"She sounded excited, but kinda touchy too," David replied. "Reminded me of the old days."

Pam nodded. "Probably fighting with her mother."

David pointed at the flying disc. "Remember the first time we rode in one of these?"

"I remember Vickie screaming when a lump grabbed her."

"I remember Mickey getting space sick and puking in his helmet." David sighed. "Most of all, I remember the wonder of it all."

Pam nestled in his arms. "Are you *sure* they won't see us as freaks?"

The golden aura bloomed around them. "Never," he whispered in her ear.

"Why?"

"Because they love us, that's why. The twins on the other hand"—David shrugged—"those two are definitely weird."

# Chapter Nineteen

Mickey closed the door. He was relieved to see Vickie sitting on the couch until he realized that he couldn't read her expression—never a good sign.

"Hey, Vic," Mickey said, steeling himself. Vickie had two flavors of "angry"—a hurricane, and something Mickey called "taking evil," a slow boil with no end in sight. He preferred Hurricane Vickie.

"Have a nice visit with your parents?" Vickie asked too nonchalantly.

Mickey cringed. "Met a cop from Burbank who doesn't like the Europans."

"How nice," Vickie replied.

Mickey sighed. "We need to talk."

"*Now* you want to talk?" Vickie's voice rose twenty decibels.

Here it comes, Mickey thought.

"I'm going first!" Vickie yelled.

Mickey prepared himself for Category Ten. "Go ahead."

Vickie burst into a smile. "They're coming back!"

Mickey blinked. "Who's coming back?"

"Pam and Davie!"

Mickey's knees threatened to buckle. Vickie rushed into his arms and started pounding on his chest. "Oh my God! Can you believe it?"

Mickey looked dumbfounded. "Really?"

Vickie nodded.

"Oh my God!" Mickey exclaimed. He broke into a smile. "Woo hoo! ...We sound like idiots!"

"I know!" Vickie shrieked. She started to cry. "I miss Pammie so much...and Davie too."

"They're not the same any more. You know that?" Mickey cautioned.

"I know," Vickie replied. She took a deep breath. "They have the twins, and the Europans messed with their bodies more than ours. But they still look and sound the same, at least on TV."

"The twins. I forgot about those two. I don't suppose they're staying on Europa?"

"They're two cute little kids…our godchildren."

"That's like saying Godzilla is just a lizard," Mickey grumbled. Before Vickie could jump down his throat, he held up his hands in surrender. "They're two sweet little kids who are three years old, but already look like teenagers, and besides that—"

"Mickey," Vickie warned.

"When do they arrive?"

"In three days," Vickie replied, grinning ear to ear.

"Seriously cool." Suddenly Mickey's eyes had a faraway look.

Vickie studied his face. "You said there was something you wanted to tell me."

"It'll wait," Mickey said.

"You sure?"

Mickey headed for the kitchen. "Got anything in the fridge, something you didn't cook?"

Vickie raised her middle finger. "We're going over to Ernie's to make plans for their homecoming. He's ordering the food."

"Let me guess. Domino's Pizza?"

# Chapter Twenty

The Sphere lay on the kitchen table next to an empty Domino's Pizza box. Ernie looked at his watch and smiled. "It's official, ladies and gentlemen. They're on their way."

"So cool," Vickie said. "...Wait a minute. It takes less than an hour to get here from Europa. Why three days?"

"David said they were taking a short sight-seeing trip on the way," Ernie replied.

"Sight-seeing, what the hell does that mean?" Vickie asked.

"They're stopping on Mars," Ernie replied. "David wants to stretch his legs and take the family camping."

"What's wrong with Yellowstone Park?" Mickey asked.

Ernie shrugged. "Mars is on the way?"

Vickie took Mickey's hand. "Honey?"

"What?" Mickey seemed lost in thought.

"Davie's going to be here in three days. You're happy, aren't you?"

Mickey forced a smile. "Of course. Totally cool."

Vickie glanced at Ernie.

"They're landing on the White House lawn." Ernie smirked. "Could make quite a mess."

Vickie frowned. "My mother said everybody's who's *anybody* is going to be there. She's happier than a witch in a broom factory."

"Wonderful." Mickey let go of Vickie's hand.

"Don't worry, Mick, we've got front row seats," Ernie said.

"Where're they staying?" Vickie asked.

"Here, of course," Ernie replied. "This is David's old house. Mick used to live right across the street—right Mick?"

Mickey didn't answer.

"Mickey?" Vickie said.

"Yep, right across the street."

"Going to be more speeches than the Republican National Convention," Ernie said. He took a piece of paper out of his pocket and started reading. "First the President, then the VP, after that a Senator from each side, a few congressmen…the list goes on."

Mickey opened a second pizza box. "Pepperoni, anchovies and pineapple. Anybody want a slice?"

Vickie wrinkled her nose. "Gross."

"I'm looking forward to hanging out with their kids," Ernie said. He puffed out his chest. "I'm their official tour guide."

"They're bringing the twins' Europan nursemaids, aren't they?" Mickey asked.

"Yes…I forget their names." Ernie scratched his head.

"They don't have names, they have numbers," Mickey corrected.

"How do you plan on entertaining them?" Vickie asked. She kept her eyes on Mickey.

"Disneyland, Universal Studios Tour, Magic Mountain," Ernie replied. "I'll try not to scare them—no Matterhorn or Hyperspace Mountain."

"You're talking about them like they're two regular kids," Mickey scoffed.

"They are, Mick."

"Had a conversation with one of them lately? They're aliens," Mickey replied. "You think they give a crap who Mickey Mouse is?"

Ernie tossed the Sphere in the air and caught it like a baseball. "I can entertain them, just like I did you and Davie a few years back."

"You're probably right." Mickey took a bite of pizza.

# Chapter Twenty-one

Pam surveyed the saucer's interior. "It's been five years since we rode in one of these."

David rubbed his hands together. "Let's get this show on the road. Wait a minute. What's he doing here?" He pointed at Micetro asleep in a cocoon next to Bet.

"Micetro is Bet's service cat," Pam replied. "In case you haven't noticed, our daughter is developing a bit of an attitude. Micetro calms her down."

"Our daughter was born with an attitude," David said.

Pam turned to Juliet. "Where are you and Romeo going to sit?"

"Sit, Mistress?" Juliet replied.

"A place for you to park yourselves during the trip," David added.

"I will be the pilot and Romeo will augment," Juliet said.

"Saucers don't need a pilot," David said.

"All flying discs require a pilot," Romeo said.

David glanced at Pam. "Not the first two times we rode in one of these."

Lights flashed across both Europans' faces. "That is not possible," Juliet replied. "If you will be seated, we will prepare for departure."

David studied Juliet's face, then he and Pam reclined against their lumps and were quickly cocooned. Romeo and Juliet began melting into the floor, flashing lights and all, until both disappeared.

"Reminds me of the *Wizard of Oz*," David said.

"Take us to Earth," said Pam smiling, "and don't spare the horses."

"We did not bring any equine mammals on board the flying disc, Mistress," Juliet's voice said. "Was that an error?"

Pam chuckled. "Sorry, I need to remember to be more precise in my speech. Take us to Earth, please."

"Actually, I was thinking about taking a little side trip on the way," David said.

"Aren't you in a hurry to get home?" Pam asked.

"The White House shindig for our homecoming is not for another three days," David replied.

"I know, but I was looking forward to some private time with Vic and Mickey before the ceremony." Pam sounded disappointed.

"Wait!" Bet shouted. "We don't have to be there for *three more days*? I'm outta here." She stabbed at the white button on her armrest that should have released her from her cocoon, but nothing happed. "Hey!" she yelled. "Get me out of this thing."

"Watch your language, young lady. Hay's for horses," Pam said.

Romeo sent to Juliet on a private channel. "It appears that we erred when we did not bring equine mammals on board."

"The closest mammals in the Menagerie's inventory are two Mesozoic rhinoceroses," sent back Juliet. "Their dispositions are most unfavorable for confined spaces."

"You're not going anywhere, missy," David said. "Besides, I've got something exciting planned. Trust me; you don't want to miss it."

"What?"

"A camping trip," David replied.

"What's a camping trip?" Al asked.

"According to the Earth database," Juliet said, "camping is the process of traveling to a remote location with a small group, occupying a cloth-covered shelter, and cooking food over an open flame."

"Mom!" Bet shrieked.

"Sounds cool," Al said. "Where are we going to do your camping activity?"

"Mars," David replied. "We're stopping there on the way to Earth."

Everyone remained silent for a moment, except for Bet.

"You're joking, right?"

"I'm not," David replied.

"Honey, why Mars?" asked Pam, trying to sound calm in front of the children.

"Why Mars, or why a camping trip?" David replied.

"Both."

David cleared his throat. "I thought we could use some family bonding."

"Bonding is for polymers," Bet moaned.

"Mars has interesting ruins," David said. "I want to have a look."

"There aren't any ruins on Mars," Pam said, sounding surprised. "The NASA rovers and satellites have studied every inch of the planet and never found anything."

"Mars is a big place with lots of nooks and crannies the rovers could have missed. This is our chance to be real explorers, to be the first humans to set foot on Mars and discover a real lost civilization that not even NASA could find. How amazing would that be?"

"I'm in," Al said.

"Noooo," Bet whined.

"Okay," Pam said feigning cheerfulness, "but we didn't bring any marshmallows." To make David happy, Pam would do anything including a ridiculous side trip to Mars.

"Our inventory of supplies does not contain any plants in the Cucurbitaceae family that grow in a marsh," Juliet said. "Was this another oversight in our provisioning?"

"They're little white globs of sugar you roast on a stick over a fire and eat," Pam explained.

"But they have to be cooked just right," David added, "crispy on the outside and still gooey on the inside."

"I have located the reference for marshmallows," said Romeo. "Marshmallows are cellulose-sucrose resins formed into balls, suspended on sticks, combusted over an open fire and consumed."

"We can synthesize cellulose-sucrose resin from available materials, but there is insufficient oxygen on Mars for the process of combustion," Juliet said.

"We do have a small nuclear reactor," Romeo added. "Will that suffice?"

# Chapter Twenty-two

The disc landed near Mar's Great Rift Valley, the largest canyon in the solar system. In comparison, Earth's Grand Canyon was a ditch. David stepped onto the surface first, wearing a silver environmental suit with a yellow bandana tied to his arm.

Pam joined him. "Are you planning on making a speech like Neil Armstrong?"

David glanced around. "How about something like what Vickie shouted when we first encountered the Europans?"

Pam laughed. "That was classic Vickie."

"Where are the kids?"

"Inside arguing." Pam pointed at the yellow bandana. "What's the yellow bandana for?"

"I wanted to wear something that isn't silver for a change." David kicked the ground with his boot raising a plume of red dust. "I can't wait to sleep under a real sky."

"Without this little side trip, you would've been home by now pitching a tent in your old backyard with Mickey, farting and telling dirty jokes all night."

David looked towards the red horizon. "Does the way we've changed make a difference?"

Pam sighed. "Here we go again."

"Forget it."

"Spit it out," Pam said. "We both know you won't be happy until you do."

"Five years ago, four teenagers who didn't know any better set off a chain of events that hasn't stopped," David began. "Because of us, everything's changing on Earth and Europa. What if Mother Nature isn't happy about it?"

"Mother Nature? That sounds scientific."

"How about this? For every action there's an equal and opposite reaction," David continued.

"Now you're quoting Isaac Newton? Honey, you're all over the map."

David turned away.

"Let's start over, okay?" Pam sounded frustrated. "You wanted to come here, and this planet is as primitive as it gets. Do you feel better now?"

David faced his wife. "As a matter of fact, I do. There's nothing artificial here, just four-billion-year-old rock."

"Nothing artificial? Hmm...let me see. How about a flying saucer with a couple of aliens who can melt into the floor, or a saber tooth cat in cryo-sleep? I think something else is bugging you. Spit it out."

"Nothing's going on," David protested.

"Tell me what's really bothering you or we're leaving."

David knew it was hopeless to refuse. "Okay. I browsed around the Europans' astronomical database."

"Good for you. What's that got to do with anything?"

"There used to be Martians, a whole civilization full of them."

"Wow. You told us about the ruins, not an entire civilization. What happened to them?"

"They died out two hundred thousand years ago," David replied.

"That's a long time ago," Pam said.

"Doesn't that bother you?"

"Civilizations come and go. The human race was on its way to extinction until the Sphere arrived."

"We're not talking about climate change or an asteroid impact. They were wiped out by somebody with advanced weapons—high-energy proton beams."

"You're sure about that?" Pam asked.

"That's what it says in the Europans' database."

"How horrible! But, honey, that happened two hundred thousand years ago."

"How do we know whoever did it won't return?" David

asked.

"Why would they? Mars is just a cold rock pile now."

"Not here. What if they attack Earth?"

"For heaven's sake. Why would the mysterious aliens you *claim* destroyed the Martians attack Earth?"

"Because Earth *now* is the way Mars was *then*."

"Your mysterious aliens are probably extinct too."

David pointed at the saucer. "To some folks time is irrelevant."

Pam stared at David. "That's what this camping trip of yours is really about, isn't it? We're here because you don't trust the Europans."

"You're right, I don't trust the Europans—at least some of them. Juliet confirmed that the Europans are the only beings in the galaxy who had high-energy proton beams two hundred thousand years ago. Unless there are other technologically advanced aliens that the Europans don't know about, the Europans were the ones that wiped out the Martians. Considering where we live now, I find that disturbing enough to check it out for myself."

Before they could continue their discussion, the twins descended the ramp followed by Romeo and Juliet. As usual, Al and Bet were yelling at each other.

"Why do you always get to go first?" Al complained.

"Because I'm the oldest!" Bet shouted back.

"By less than a minute!"

"Knock it off, you two," Pam growled. "Juliet, wake up Micetro."

"How come she gets to drive the rover before I do?" Al complained.

"No rover…we're walking," David replied.

"No we're not," Bet said.

"The ruins are only a couple of kilometers from here inside the Rift," David said.

"Ever think of checking the astronomical database?" Bet asked.

"Don't you want to be a real explorer?" David asked.

Bet crossed her arms. "I'm not going."

The two Europans descended the ramp carrying large silver bags containing camping supplies. Micetro trotted down the ramp wearing his own environmental suit tethered to Romeo by a silver tentacle.

"Let's go," David said. "Only a couple of hours of daylight left." He set off at a brisk pace.

Pam watched him leave. "Have fun." She shook her head and escorted Bet back up the saucer's ramp.

Al ran to catch up with his father. "Wait!"

# Chapter Twenty-three

Romeo led David and Al along a path parallel to the Rift's wall. Eons before, water flowing through the Rift undercut the rock creating a roof over their heads that blocked out the sun. As they continued walking, the ground sloped steadily downward causing them to lose the light. Soon they were walking single file in the dark with Romeo projecting a beam of light. The wind roared around them funneled down by the ceiling of rock, and the dust kicked up by their boots scintillated fiery red in Romeo's beam.

"No way the NASA rovers would have found this place," David remarked.

"I can't see a thing," Al said. He touched his sleeve and a beam of light projected from the top of his helmet. The light was reflected back and scattered by the dust particles making visibility even worse.

"Switch to thermal imaging," Romeo instructed.

Al and David changed the visors of their helmets to concentrate infrared light. Romeo's shape appeared ahead of them now as a plume of orange light with four yellow circles glowing in the middle of it. Romeo had selectively increased his skin temperature to create a thermal beacon.

With every step, the path downward became more difficult. Al stumbled over a rock and began to fall. Before he hit the ground, Romeo shot a tentacle of silver around his torso stabilizing him and left it there as a safety line.

"How much farther?" David called out to Romeo.

"Guys, this isn't my idea of fun," Al said.

"Two hundred meters," Romeo replied. "Ambient sound is seventy of your decibels. I suggest activating sound suppression." David and Al poked buttons on their sleeves.

"That's better." David sighed. He focused on the ground

ahead, but had trouble seeing beyond a meter. "Better hope there aren't any crevasses." He increased his stride to close his distance from Romeo.

Romeo lassoed David with another tentacle tethering the three of them together. "I scan no significant obstacles," Romeo said. "One hundred fifty meters."

The last few meters proved the most challenging. They were forced to skirt two large rock piles, the detritus of ancient landslides. After picking their way around the second mound, Romeo stopped and focused his beam straight ahead. Al and David moved beside him and did the same. They could see a volume of black empty space through the maelstrom of swirling dust. Unlike the rock around them that retained a modicum of the sun's heat, the void registered no thermal output at all.

"What's that?" Al asked.

The void had unnaturally square angles and sucked in the light from their beams like a hungry black hole. Romeo continued towards it. David held back, but the tentacle linking him and Al to Romeo pulled taught dragging them forward. He looked around. "Whatever it is, it can't be natural."

"It is an artificial chamber carved into the rock," Romeo replied.

"By whom and for what purpose?" David asked.

"The rock chamber dates to the time of the Martian civilization. Its purpose is unknown."

"Are you sure this is a good idea?" Al asked.

"There is nothing to fear," Romeo replied. "I have read in the Earth database that humans are fond of this experience. It is referred to as an adventure."

David smiled, but didn't say anything.

Al looked puzzled. "What's an adventure?"

"A journey of exploration that combines factors of unknown and risk. If the goal of the journey is easily obtained, it is not an adventure," Romeo replied.

"I can't see anything," Al said. "Does that qualify?"

"The air will clear when we are inside the chamber." Romeo continued moving forward dragging them with him.

The hollow chamber had unnaturally flat and smooth walls and ceiling. The ceiling soaring twenty meters over their heads and the ground beneath their feet had the same unnaturally flat and artificial appearance. Romeo illuminated the empty chamber's interior with his beam. Three Europan flying discs would have fit inside with room to spare. One geological feature looked oddly out of place, the opening to a cave on the far wall. Unlike the stark ninety-degree angles of the chamber, the cave's entrance appeared rough and natural.

They walked to the center of the chamber still tethered together. Al and David activated normal imaging and projected helmet lights. All three swept the interior. Except for the cave, there was nothing to see. Romeo retracted his tentacles releasing them.

"Notice how the air is completely still where we're standing," David commented.

Al started running towards the cave.

"Stop, Master Al!" Romeo vocalized.

Al skidded to a stop. "Why?"

"Do not enter the cave, Master Al," Romeo said. "It has not been explored. Safety cannot be assured."

"Europans have been here before. Why wasn't the cave explored?" David asked.

"The database contains no additional information," Romeo replied.

Al took a few steps closer to the cave's entrance. "There's some kind of writing on the rock." He zoomed in using his helmet visor. "Wait a minute..."

David and Romeo joined him.

"Looks like some kind of hieroglyphics," David said. "Must

have been written by the Martians. Romeo, can you translate?"

"No! Romeo, don't look," Al shouted.

Romeo spun his head to face Al. "Why?"

"You never know…the writing might make you sick…or something."

"That's nonsense," David protested.

"Your father is right, Master Al. I cannot become sick." Romeo moved closer to the rock wall and illuminated the symbols with his beam.

Al moved next to Romeo and tapped him on the back. "Feeling okay?"

"What are you doing?" David asked.

Romeo didn't reply.

"Too late," Al said.

"Romeo?" David said.

Romeo still didn't reply.

David turned to Al. "You knew that was going to happen. What's wrong with him?"

Al shrugged. "It's complicated."

"Start talking," David said.

Al told his father about the pyramid with similar symbols on Europa, and what happened when Romeo and Juliet tried to analyze them.

"Are you going to tell Mom?" Al asked.

David looked thoughtful. "I haven't decided yet."

All the lights on Romeo's face lit at once. He spun his head to face David. "My internal chronometer indicates a reboot of my neural nexus. I will initiate a full diagnostic and send a report to the Central Nexus."

"Don't worry about it now," David said. "Go back to the center of the chamber and face away from the cave."

"I cannot experience worry. Why should I face away from the cave?"

"I'll explain later," David replied. When Romeo moved back

to the center of the chamber and remained facing the entrance, David used his helmet scanner to record an image of the symbols around the cave. "Where were the artifacts found?" he asked.

Romeo pointed his beam at the wall across from the cave. "The survey team discovered artifacts *there,* one meter from the wall and one meter below the surface."

"You feel okay?" Al asked Romeo. "You're not tired or anything?"

"I cannot become fatigued," Romeo replied.

Al tried to send a telepathic message to Bet, but couldn't connect with her. While Romeo and his father engaged in conversation, he recorded his own images of the symbols. "Is there anything left to dig up?" he asked.

"Numerous metallic artifacts lie beneath the top layer of sediment," Romeo replied.

"Let's dig one up."

"I agree," David added.

Romeo projected a tentacle that budded into the shape of a horn. "I will perform a magnetic scan to more precisely locate the artifacts."

"What about excavation equipment?" David asked.

"I possess all necessary functionality." Romeo moved forward sweeping his appendage over the ground. Irregular shapes appeared on his flat screen face.

"Find something interesting," Al said.

"Define interesting," Romeo replied.

"There!" Al exclaimed. He pointed at the outline of a cylindrical shape centered on Romeo's face. "Dig that up. Maybe there's something interesting inside."

Romeo's tentacle projected sonic waves at the ground. Al stepped back. "I like adventures," he said. A cavity three meters wide and two meters deep formed in the ground with a heavily corroded cylindrical shape at the bottom of it.

"Doesn't look like anything," Al said. "What is it?"

"It is a hollow container made from an alloy of aluminum, thirty-nine centimeters long and six centimeters in diameter," Romeo replied.

"Is there anything still inside?" David asked.

"The container has been subjected to a focused beam of protons that vaporized everything in its path."

"Why not the container?"

Romeo poked the cylinder with his tentacle and it shattered like glass. "The metal has been crystallized at the atomic level."

David stepped back from the cavity and faced Romeo. "According to the Europan database, which galactic civilizations possessed sufficient technology to produce that effect two hundred thousand Earth-years ago?"

Romeo's lights dulled to a uniform gray. "As I reported to you once before, only the Europans."

"Did your people do this?"

"Europans have never engaged in war or possessed weapons," Romeo replied.

"You haven't always been in your current inorganic form," David said.

"That is correct."

"Could your people have done it before you downloaded?"

"The database contains no records before we assumed this form."

"Then it could have been you, but you don't remember."

"It is possible."

"Does it bother you that you can't remember what it was like to be flesh and blood?" David asked.

"I cannot be bothered," Romeo replied.

"Let's look inside the cave," Al said, sounding impatient. He turned to Romeo and hastily added, "Don't come with me."

"I would advise against entering the cave, Master Al. The cave enters a vein of concentrated titanium oxide that blocks my sensors. Communication beyond the cave entrance would not be efficient. I cannot guarantee your safety if you enter."

David put his hand on Al's shoulder. "We've had enough fun for one day. Your mother's waiting for us back at the disc." He pointed towards the hole containing the artifact. "Romeo, bring back a sample of that cylinder."

"That is not necessary," Romeo replied. "A complete subatomic scan is now archived."

"Call it a souvenir."

"I do not understand the concept of a souvenir," Romeo said.

"Humans sometimes prefer physical contact with objects of importance," David explained.

"Why?" asked Romeo.

While David tried to explain the concept of a souvenir to Romeo, Al edged closer to the chamber's entrance. He tried making telepathic contact with Bet again, and this time succeeded. "*Remember those squiggles we found in the pyramid back home?*" he sent to Bet.

"*When are you coming back? I'm bored,*" Bet sent back.

"*We found more of them carved in the rock outside a cave. Romeo shut down when he scanned them. I had to tell Dad what happened in the underwater pyramid back home.*"

"*He'll tell Mom!*"

"*He said he hasn't decided yet if he's going to tell her.*"

"*What does that mean?*"

David gestured for Al to join him.

"*Dad's calling me. Gotta go!*" Al stopped sending, the equivalent of telepathically hanging up.

When they returned to the disc, David lingered at the base of the ramp with Al while Romeo rejoined Juliet inside the disc. Al looked nervous. He switched to a private channel. "Are you going to tell Mom?" he asked.

David switched to a private channel too. "I've been thinking about those symbols and what happened to Romeo. I'll make you a deal."

Al blinked. "What kind of deal?"

"I won't tell Mom that you and your sister disobeyed our strict orders not to ski outside the safe zone, and didn't tell us what happened when you did, provided… "

Al had trouble standing still. "Provided what?"

"We keep what happened today just between us, and you take me to that underwater pyramid when we get home. Do you agree?" David asked.

"Sure! Why?"

"Those symbols might be what earthlings call a 'No Trespassing Sign' for Europans."

"What does that mean?"

"It means there's something inside that cave and also in your pyramid back home that Europans aren't supposed to see. I want to know what it is, and who put up the signs."

"Why aren't you telling Mom?"

"You're too young to understand."

Al smirked. "I can derive the Theory of Relativity from scratch. Can you?"

"Do it my way, or face your mother's wrath. What's it going to be?"

Al replied without hesitation. "I'll take you to the pyramid when we get home!"

David gestured up the ramp. "Onwards…to Earth."

Just before liftoff, David left the disc and walked onto the red sand of Mars. Pam joined him. She looked harried. "Those two never stop bickering," she complained.

"We have a problem," David said.

"I know," Pam said, sidling up to him.

He turned to her. "You do?"

Pam smiled at him. "I can't kiss you wearing this helmet."

They touched bubble helmets and gazed into each other's

eyes. Once again, David realized how much he loved her.

"Find anything interesting in those ruins?" Pam asked.

"Rocks, some pieces of metal that don't look like anything. Nothing exciting," David replied.

"Still stressed about what happened to the Martians?"

David pointed at the stars shining through the rust-colored Martian sunset. "Earth is that blue dot over there. Do you see it?"

"I'll take your word for it," Pam replied.

"All I can think about is planting my feet on it again. I want to feel real dirt between my toes, be shoved by the crowds, hear people yell at me...see flowers wither, paint fading, and wake up without knowing what's going to happen next." David fought to control his emotions. "Does any of that make sense?"

Pam took his hand and pulled him toward the ramp. "I love you. Now let's go home."

# Chapter Twenty-four

Vickie sat between Marie and Pam's adoptive mother Phyllis with Mickey's empty chair between them. Vickie felt more anxious with each passing minute. The Secretary of State droned on delivering his speech, but nobody on the dais or in the audience paid any attention to him. They were either staring at the sky or checking their cell phones for the time. The flying saucer, as everyone insisted on calling it, was scheduled to land on the White House lawn in ten minutes.

Marie whispered to Vickie, "Where's Mickey?"

Vickie's stomach clenched. "He'll be here."

Marie smiled and waved to Melanie Dilman who was narrating the event for ABC News. She poked Vickie with her foot. "Wet your lips and smile," she said, under her breath.

Vickie glanced at her watch for the tenth time. "What?"

"I said, smile at *Melanie Dilman,*" Marie whispered urgently.

Vickie turned her back on her mother and moved to the chair next to Phyllis. "I can't wait to see Pam."

Phyllis squeezed Vickie's hand. "Me too." She was about to say something more, then looked up and smiled. "Here comes Mickey!"

Mickey took the seat next to Vickie.

"Where were you?" Vickie whispered.

"Got caught in traffic."

She glared at him. "You can think of something better than that."

"Sorry."

The Secretary of State finished his speech and the President of the United States moved to the lectern.

Mickey opened his hand in his lap and stared at his silver disc.

"Our best friends are coming home. Why can't you be happy?" Vickie hissed.

Marie kicked her. "Shush! The president is about to speak."

Mickey noticed a presence in front of him and looked up.

A man extended his hand. "It's an honor to finally meet you," he said to Mickey. Mickey shook the man's hand.

"Perhaps you don't know me. I'm Paul Rudnick, head of the Benevolent Sphere Association of America."

Mickey frowned and withdrew his hand. "I don't care much for your group."

"Mickey!" Vickie gasped.

Rudnick's bland facial expression didn't change. "You'll have to excuse me. The president is about to speak. I'm sure we'll have another chance to chat again soon." He moved to his seat.

Ernie sat on the other side of Mickey with the Sphere cradled in his hands. His old army uniform tugged a bit at his waist. He leaned over and whispered, "I bet you're one happy camper, Mick." When Mickey ignored him, Ernie raised an eyebrow, but didn't say anything more.

The president raised his hands and smiled at the cameras. "Distinguished guests, people of America, people of the world"—he looked at his watch— "it's almost time." The audience responded with a smattering of polite applause. Everyone kept looking up at the sky, including the president.

"Mickey?" Vickie whispered.

He ignored her.

"Shush!" Marie said again.

Vickie noticed the hair standing up on the back of her arm and looked up. Seconds later, a breeze blew the president's papers off the lectern. Everyone stood and squinted up at the sky. No one said a word, a miracle considering the number of politicians in attendance. Even Melanie Dilman stopped talking.

A billowing cloud exploded into view followed by the distant sound of thunder. Chairs began to vibrate and the breeze built into a wind. Papers and debris began to blow around in a circular motion as if caught in a mini cyclone. Soon the guests were hanging onto their hats and sunglasses while straining to maintain an upward gaze. Secret Service agents formed a protective cordon around the president, all of them staring up.

A silver shape broke through the cloud surrounded by a corona of flashing blue and gold lights. As the disc descended, the wind increased to a gale. People began to scatter. Hanging onto his hat, Ernie ushered Phyllis and Marie off the dais. Mickey rose to his feet with a defiant expression as if daring the maelstrom to take him. Vickie remained at his side holding his hand, looking at him and not at the sky.

When it seemed as if the chaos couldn't build any further without blowing the White House away, the silver disc settled on the lawn and the wind dissipated. Buttoning their coats and brushing back their hair, the guests returned to their seats—if they could find them. Every pair of eyes fixed on the silver disc parked on the White House lawn.

Mickey stepped off the dais and walked slowly towards it. Vickie and Marie joined him, followed by Ernie, Melanie Dilman, and her cameraman. As the cameraman panned around, Marie tried to stay in front of the lens.

A rectangular section on the side of the disc darkened to the color of pewter. Seeing it and remembering, Mickey's pulse began to race. The rectangular area then sagged and flowed down to the grass, creating a doorway with a silver ramp. The transfixed audience neither spoke nor moved a muscle.

A silver humanoid shape appeared in the doorway greeted by a shared gasp from the crowd. Several people sprinted away. The Secret Service agents grabbed for the president again. The figure's helmet melted away revealing David grinning ear to ear. When he caught sight of Mickey, he ran down the ramp. Mickey broke into a smile and rushed to meet him. They collided and grabbed each other into a bear hug, then started laughing. When they finally stopped, they slapped hands and shouted "Dude!"

While all eyes were on them, Pam appeared in the saucer's

doorway waving her arms and yelling, "Vickie!" Vickie sprinted up the ramp, hugged her, and they cried together for several minutes.

After smoothing back his hair, the president approached the disc encircled by his Secret Service entourage. Ernie followed behind the president jumping up and down and waving. After an angry stare from the White House Press Secretary, Ernie blushed and calmed down. "Hey, Davie," he said, smiling. "Good to see you, buddy."

David held up his hand to high-five, but the president was in the way.

Pam and Vickie held hands and walked down the ramp.

The president started to say something when shouts erupted from the crowd. Secret Service agents ran in front of him shielding him with their bodies. Everyone's attention returned to the flying saucer. A silver humanoid form with a face of flashing colored lights stood motionless in the doorway.

Romeo started down the ramp with a Europan's unique fluidic motion. Several people in the crowd bolted away and a few slumped over unconscious in their seats. The Secret Service agents tugged on the president to retreat, but he held his ground. The president had battled a hostile Congress for seven years and had nerves of steel.

Romeo stopped at the base of the ramp. Al followed a moment later. He appeared to be a normal teenaged boy wearing a silver jumpsuit and a Los Angeles Laker's baseball cap.

Mickey pointed at Al. "You guys watch basketball on Europa?"

"The hat's because he doesn't have any hair," David replied, stifling his laughter.

Mickey nodded, and they both busted up.

Another silver form appeared in the doorway—Bet shoved from behind by Juliet. New murmurs of fear erupted from the audience. Bet looked like the prototypical alien, sheathed in silver with her helmet opaque except for a slit for her eyes.

Vickie stared at Pam. "Is that…?"

Pam nodded, trying to keep a straight face. "She's having a bad hair day."

The president cleared his throat. "Ladies and Gentlemen, I'd like to begin our welcoming festivities." Before the president could continue, a secret service agent wrestled him to the ground. Several more agents surrounded him pulling their guns and facing the disc. The remaining audience collectively shrieked and fled to the exits. One of the agents started shooting. Bullets impacted the disc's force field like flies flaming out on a bug zapper.

Micetro stood in the doorway panting and wagging his tail. When he saw Bet, he bounded down the ramp.

"Don't shoot!" Pam shouted. "That's my kids' cat!"

Micetro ran straight to Bet and rolled over with his tongue hanging out.

"Isn't that a saber-tooth tiger?" Mickey asked.

"Not exactly. I'll explain later," David replied. "Pam. Do something please."

"Nice kitty," Pam said in a soothing tone. She reached down and patted Micetro's belly. In response, the big feline purred like a locomotive.

Pam grabbed Micetro by the scruff of the neck. "Okay, buddy, fun's over. Let's go." Micetro refused to budge. "Juliet, some assistance please!" Pam yelled.

Juliet glided over, scooped Micetro up and carried him back to the disc.

"How come you brought two Europans with you?" Mickey asked David. "Isn't one enough?"

"One flies the disc, and the other one watches the kids," David replied.

"We didn't have a pilot when we flew to the moon, or Europa," Mickey said.

"We didn't have a pilot *we could see.*"

"You mind explaining that?" Mickey asked.

"Later, Dude."

Pam took Bet's hand and pointed at Vickie. "Bet, this is your godmother Vickie."

Bet remained silent.

"Bet," Pam said more sternly. "Be polite."

"It's okay," reassured Vickie. "She'll get used to me."

"Took me awhile," Pam said.

"Ladies and Gentlemen!" the president repeated more assertively.

Vickie led Pam and the twins to their seats. Mickey and David followed.

# Chapter Twenty-five

The president smiled for the cameras. "People of America, people of the world"—he paused for effect—"as the only US president, as the only world leader in history to have a flying saucer land on his lawn"—he waited for the smattering of laughter to die down—"I bid you welcome. But you didn't come to hear me..." Loud applause interrupted him, and he held up his hands for quiet. "Without further ado, let me introduce a man who requires no introduction, Sergeant Ernest Santos, retired, of the *US* Army Rangers, better known as the Keeper of the Sphere." The president started clapping, but there were only whispers and stares from the guests. The Sphere still had that kind of effect.

Ernie moved to the lectern and shook the president's hand. After the president took his seat, Ernie placed the Sphere on the lectern in front of him. Every pair of eyes fixed on the glowing alien gizmo swirling with the colors of the rainbow. Melanie Dilman stood off to the side narrating the worldwide video feed trying her best to ignore Vickie's mother.

"Public speaking is not my thing," Ernie began, "so I'll keep this short and sweet." He took out a three by five index card. "Why is today important? It's because of those two kids." He pointed at Al and Bet. Bet hadn't taken down her helmet and still looked like an alien from a D-rated science fiction movie. "Their parents were born here...actually not here, in California." Ernie chuckled. "But those two kids were born on Europa. They've never set foot on planet Earth, but they're made of the same flesh and blood as you and me." He paused. "I think that's more important than alien visitations or flying saucers. I wonder if anybody here really understands why." He turned around, for a moment staring directly at Mickey.

"You're curious about those kids," Ernie continued. "You want to know if they're different than us. I'm more curious about *us*. I want to see what *we've* become. What will *they* remember about *us* when they go back to Europa?" He tapped the Sphere and a woman in the front row swooned. "Flying saucers and alien hard drives are cool, but that's not what all this is really about. It's about the gift of a second chance and repairing the world." He held up the Sphere. "Doesn't matter to me that the Sphere arrived in a flying saucer. Only matters what we do with it. It's not about the Europans, it's about us." He went back to his seat.

Little by little, people stood and clapped. Ernie nodded. Also clapping, the president stepped up to the lectern. "Wasn't that wonderful?" He didn't like being upstaged in an election year. The applause intensified, and the president held up his hands for quiet. "The world knows that America has done everything it can to promote Ernie's efforts with the Sphere for the betterment of all." A few people clapped. In the international VIP section, only the delegate from Great Britain joined in.

While the president continued his speech, General Westlock whispered to the Secretary of Defense. "We gotta get control of that alien gizmo before the boat mechanic gives all the good stuff away to the wrong people."

"Talk is cheap," the secretary said.

"Got a new op on the drawing board, something a little different this time..." The general smirked. "A little *darker* than usual."

The Secretary of Defense glanced around. "Didn't hear that."

The president continued his speech. "Our next speakers are two former residents of the great state of California who have flown four hundred million miles to join us today. Everybody, please welcome David and Pam!" The president started clapping and stepped aside.

David followed Pam to the podium, faced the audience, and grabbed her hand. As soon as they touched, the golden aura surrounded them. Melanie Dilman grabbed her assistant and whispered in her ear. "Get me the trademark on that aura, pronto! General Mills is going to pay big bucks."

"Why General Mills?" her assistant asked.

"Wheaties Boxes. Get on it before the competition figures it out!" Her assistant took off running.

"It's great to be home," David said. He waved to his father Dick seated two rows back. They'd been speaking over Ernie's television. Even David's brother Frank was present after the president pardoned him. His mother Linda didn't attend and sent her regrets. Melanie Dilman edged up behind Dick for an exclusive interview.

Pam kissed David's cheek and scanned the audience. She spotted Phyllis and dropped his hand to wave to her. The aura winked out. "Home is an interesting word," Pam began. She glanced at Vickie who dabbed her eyes with a handkerchief. "Is my home Europa, or is it here?"

"Here!" shouted the audience.

Pam smiled. "For me, it's where David and the kids are. I think that's what Ernie was trying to say. Everybody keeps asking what's changed about me. Sure, my Europan friends jazzed up my physiology a little, but that's not it. The biggest change in David and me is a new awareness of who we really are." She paused before continuing.

Vickie took Mickey's hand. He squeezed it once, but let it go.

Pam pointed at the sky. "We're not alone. There are more than a hundred sentient races in our galaxy. None of them look like us, not even close. We earthlings are unique with our own special version of life. Doesn't matter where we are." She pointed at Romeo and Juliet who stood near the saucer. "That's why they're here. That's why the Sphere's here. Thanks to Mickey, we passed the Test. We're the only race in the galaxy who could!" She hugged David and they stepped away from the podium.

General Westlock rose from his seat and started walking away.

For a few moments no one spoke, not even the president. In

the silence, Mickey rose to his feet. Alarmed by his expression, Vickie stood with him. He extended his hand holding her back, and approached the podium. The president glanced at his press secretary. Mickey wasn't on the agenda.

"I only have a few words," Mickey began.

# Chapter Twenty-six

Mickey gripped the edge of the lectern. "This is all wrong."

A chorus of gasps erupted from the audience.

"Mickey!" Vickie exclaimed.

Mickey raised his hands for quiet. One had a flashing silver disc. "It's a great story, isn't it? A bunch of omniscient aliens run out of things to do and start inactivating. So they concoct a test looking for people dumber than them to mentor...to give themselves a purpose for being alive again... Give me a break...it's a fairy tale."

No one in the audience said a word. General Westlock moved closer to listen.

"David and I were together when I fell into the hole and found the Europan suit with superpowers. How come it only fit me? Supposedly I made the right decisions while wearing it and passed the Europans' test. This qualified my friends and me for a wild ride to Europa to learn about the Choice. Every school kid knows the details...except none of it's true."

Several people shouted "No!" Mickey raised his hands again for quiet. "Because Pam and David agreed to become Europa's Adam and Eve, Earth received the Sphere with the cure for cancer and all the other good stuff inside. Right?" Perspiration dripped from Mickey's brow. "The Choice was rigged, and I want to know why!" he shouted.

"Liar!" someone yelled from the back.

"Did you see the aura around Pam and David when they held hands?" Mickey continued.

Silence.

"That glorious aura appeared as soon as we got back from Europa, *days* before Pam and David agreed to go. There never was a Choice," Mickey scoffed. "The Europans had already chosen Pam and David."

The only sound on the White House Lawn came from a woodpecker tapping on a magnolia tree.

"But there's an even bigger lie that I'm *really* worried about," Mickey said. "You should be too."

"Mickey, don't do this," Ernie called out.

"Any of our kids heading off to medical school these days? What's the point? We have the Sphere. Any of our kids studying physics or engineering? Why bother?" Mickey glared at the audience. "The Europans almost died from their utopia, now they're giving one to us as a gift. I want to know why!"

"This is getting interesting," General Westlock muttered.

People started shouting back. One said, "Nobody's hungry! What about the ozone layer?"

Mickey pounded the lectern. "Those are problems we're supposed to fix for ourselves! We already have our own test going on, and it's called *evolution.* If we stop growing and learning on our own, the human race will die!"

Everyone sat speechless, including the president.

"We can't let them do it to us!" Mickey bellowed. "I won't let them do it to *me*!" He removed a pocketknife from his coat pocket, held up his hand with the silver disc, and plunged the blade into its center. Blood streamed down his arm. His nannites quickly sealed the wound, but his palm disc stopped glowing and healed into a dark blemish on his hand.

People screamed.

"Mickey!" Vickie shrieked.

He stormed off the dais.

Ernie did his best to console Vickie.

"Did he say anything to you?" Pam asked David.

David looked down. "No."

Paul Rudnick took out his cell phone and walked away.

General Westlock turned in his chair so no one could hear and punched a sequence of numbers into his phone. He waited for a moment. “You watching?” he said keeping his voice low. “Change of plans.”

# Book II

# Chapter Twenty-seven

*Twenty years earlier…*

Rain pummeled the hood of the car as it swerved down Pacific Coast Highway. "Slow down!" the young woman in the passenger seat yelled over the pulsating music blasting from the radio. "You're going to get us killed!"

The tires screeched on the rain-slick road as the car fishtailed around a hairpin curve. The woman's boyfriend pounded the steering wheel in time to the music. "Can't hear you!" he shouted. He took a swig from a bottle of bear. Several empty bottles rolled around on the floor of the car.

Staccato flashes of lightening pierced the darkness. Seconds later, a barrage of thunder shook the car.

"Slow down!" she yelled.

"Relax," he said, laughing as he fought to regain control.

She gripped the sides of her seat, her eyes wide with terror. "Pull over now! I'm getting out!"

"Girl, you need to chill," he said mockingly. He turned up the stereo's volume until the windshield rattled.

The car crossed the road's centerline facing oncoming traffic, then skidded as he over steered to bring it back. She pounded on his shoulder. "Let me out!" she screamed.

He eased off the accelerator and reached forward to turn down the music. "I'm slowing down! Jesus! Why are you so nervous?"

"I don't want to die!"

He turned towards her taking his eyes off the road. The car crossed the centerline again. "Come on, honey, loosen up."

She pushed back rigid in her seat. "Look out!"

Glaring light from a pair of headlights filled the car's interior followed by a thunderous crash and the sound of tortured metal.

The car flipped over and skidded on its roof, its momentum carrying it thirty feet into the guardrail. Several meters away, the rail gaped outward where the other vehicle from the crash broke through and plunged down the cliff to the rocks below.

The driver of the car on the road regained consciousness and batted the airbag away from his face. Dazed, he released his shoulder harness and fell to the car's roof, landing on his knees on shards of glass. The searing pain of the glass piercing his legs snapped him alert. Realizing what happened, he wiped his eyes with his arm, stared at the blood, and looked up. His girlfriend hung limply above him with her eyes closed. Blood dripped from the side of her mouth.

"Phyllis!" he shouted, but she didn't respond. Ignoring the pain, he inched closer on his knees and released her shoulder harness. She fell into his arms. He cradled her and wept.

The ferocity of the deluge of rain increased until the sound of it hammering the car became deafening. In desperation, the driver repeatedly yelled, "Help us! Somebody please help us." As minutes passed and no one stopped to help, he thought about breaking the glass and crawling out. Then a beam of light shined through the shattered passenger window followed by a sharp tapping sound against the door.

"Officer Galpin, Highway Patrol! Are you hurt?" yelled a man's voice.

The driver gathered himself and yelled back. "I'm all right, but my girlfriend's hurt bad."

"We're getting you out. Turn away from the windshield and cover your face. Tell me when you're ready."

The driver shielded his girlfriend with his body and closed his eyes. "Okay!" he called out. Seconds later, he heard the window shatter and felt a shower of glass strike his back.

A blinding flash of light illuminated the car's interior. Seconds later, the wreck shook from a peel of thunder. Officer Galpin, his face peppered with rain, reached in with his flashlight. "We're getting you out," he shouted. "Try to remain calm." After a quick look around the car's interior, he pulled back and spoke into his radio. "Two passengers, male and female, both in their twenties. He's alert, multiple lacerations, moves all four extremities. She's unconscious, serious head injury."

A bolt of lightning struck the power poll near the wreck followed by a deafening boom of thunder. The acrid scent of ozone permeated the car. Galpin's radio squawked, a voice mixed with static. "Paramedic 81 in route with LA Fire 32, ETA 11 minutes."

"Roger that," Galpin shouted. "Tell them to hustle. Getting a bit dicey out here!"

The radio squawked again. "What about the other vehicle?"

"Went down the cliff. I can see it on the beach," Galpin replied. "I doubt anybody survived, but my partner's going down." Another bolt of lightning struck the guardrail fifty meters away sending up a spray of sparks. "Damn, that one was close!" Galpin said into the radio. "Better stop traffic in both directions."

"Roger that."

Galpin tossed flares around the car and knelt near the broken window. "Help is on the way." Then he ran to the section of guardrail broken by the second car and shined his flashlight down the cliff into the dark. The rope his partner used to rappel down to the beach trailed off into nothingness.

With an ominous crack, a bolt of lightning struck the water illuminating the beach. For a few seconds, Galpin could see a car in the surf half submerged in the water. He followed his partner's flashlight beam as he waded through the surf to the car and aimed his flashlight through the wreck's shattered windshield.

Galpin's radio crackled to life with Officer Steven's voice. "Three people, two adults, male and female, and a kid in a car seat in the back—two, maybe three, years old. She's screaming her lungs out, but the two adults aren't moving."

Another crash of lightning illuminated the wreck, this one no more than fifty meters away. "Get out of there!" Galpin yelled. "The metal of that car is attracting the lightening."

The radio crackled again. "I've gotta get them out."

The sky lit up with a continuous barrage of lightning. When the thunder arrived, the ground shook so hard Galpin found it difficult to stand. He shouted into his radio. "If the lightning hits that car, you're *all* dead!"

"Standby," his partner yelled through the static. Standing in the water, Stevens yanked on the crumpled passenger door handle, but it wouldn't open. Seconds later, a lightning bolt struck a few meters from the car and the water exploded. He cowered with his hands over his head as the water rained down. When it stopped, he sprinted out of the water onto the sand. The radio clipped to his belt squawked to life. "Get out of there!" he heard Galpin shout through a burst of static.

A salvo of blue-white lightning hit the water bracketing the wreck. Ignoring the chaos and his partner's warning, Officer Stevens ran back into the water and jumped on the car's roof. He pulled on the door again, but it refused to open. He positioned himself to use his legs as a lever. Before he could try, he was hit by a wave and tumbled into the water. When the water receded, he scrambled back onto the wreck. Silhouetted by the next lightning strike, he managed to open the crumpled door and drop into the car's interior.

Kneeling in the chilling water inside the wreck, Stevens felt for pulses in the necks of the adults. They were both alive. At Steven's touch, the man regained consciousness. He turned his head and fixed his eyes on Stevens. He tried to speak. Stevens positioned himself with his back to the bluff. "Relax. It's going to be okay," he said to the man. He extracted a glowing red cylinder the size of a fountain pen from his pocket and touched it first to the man, and then the woman. Each twitched against their seat belts and then sagged against their seats. They stared straight ahead with vacant eyes, both dead. Stevens extinguished the cylinder's glow and quickly placed it back into his pocket.

Another wave crashed down on the car submerging Steven's head in frigid water. He held his breath and waited for it to recede. When he could breathe again, he wedged himself into the rear compartment near the child. The child was alive and screaming. Her legs were bent at an unnatural angle. Her right thighbone protruded through the skin causing copious bleeding. Stevens pulled the cylinder again from his pocket and it began to glow. He was about to touch it to the child's chest when he heard Galpin's voice.

"Is she still alive?" Galpin shouted. He was standing in waist-deep water looking through the shattered window. He had a crow bar in his hand.

Keeping his back turned, Stevens extinguished the red cylinder and shoved it back into his pocket. He turned to face Galpin. "She's alive, but she's hurt bad," he yelled. "Broken back and a compound fracture of the thigh. We need help to move her. Go back up top. I'll stay with her until the cavalry arrives."

With a blinding crash, another lightning bolt hit near the wreck. "We have to do it now!" Galpin shouted as seawater rained down on him. "We'll take her out in the car seat." He used the crow bar to rip open the car's door.

They used ropes to climb up the bluff holding the car seat between them. The child's legs dangled from the seat like a rag doll. She was still alive, but unconscious from loss of blood. Just as they hoisted the car seat over the guardrail, a flare of lightening hit the bluff only meters away forcing them to the ground. Seconds later, an ominous peel of thunder shook the ground. Moving as quickly as possible, they carried the car seat away from the metal guardrail and hunkered down to wait for more lightning strikes, but the air remained still. Cautiously, Galpin got to his feet and moved closer to the guardrail. As he looked down a bolt of lightning struck the wreck and spun it twenty feet into the air. It crashed down with its roof fully submerged in the water. When the next wave crashed into it, the water completely filled the interior of the car. Galpin couldn't see it, but when the water receded, pieces of the two corpses floated out like sand castles torn apart by the surf.

The rain slackened and the lightning moved farther out to sea. They could hear the sound of multiple sirens growing louder.

"I should have gone back for them," Stevens said.

"They were already dead," Galpin replied. He shivered under a blanket. "Be thankful we saved the kid."

Two fire trucks and a paramedic ambulance stopped close to the wrecked car on the road. "Over here!" Galpin yelled. He shielded his eyes from the glare of the headlights.

The paramedic ambulance sped down Pacific Coast Highway to Saint John's Hospital in Santa Monica. A paramedic hovering over the three-year-old girl glanced anxiously at the cardiac monitor and shouted to the driver. "Better step on it! The kid's not looking good back here!"

Strapped to a stretcher with a blood-soaked bandage on his forehead, the driver of the first car raised his head and looked around. "Where's Phyllis?" He sounded frantic.

"Take it easy, buddy. Your girlfriend's in the other unit right behind us. She's pretty banged up, but she'll be okay."

"Anybody else make it out?"

The paramedic shook his head. "If going over the guardrail didn't kill them, the lightning sure did." He stroked the child's forehead trying to comfort her. "Miracle this one's still alive."

"Is she going to make it?"

"Broken back and a compound fracture of her leg…I don't know."

The injured driver dropped his head on the pillow and closed his eyes.

The rain had stopped, but the grey dawn's air was still thick with moisture. Pacific Coast Highway remained closed in both directions creating a massive traffic jam. Several tow trucks and highway patrol cars were at the accident scene. Two wire stretchers lay on the ground near the broken guardrail along with piles of rope for rappelling down the cliff. Six men at the guardrail surveyed the wreck half-submerged in the wreck.

"Need a crane to bring it up here," said one of the truckers.

"Need to get the bodies out first," Galpin said.

"You boys had quite a night," said one of the highway patrol officers. "Go home. Let Search and Rescue do the dirty work."

Stevens let his blanket drop to the ground. "Gotta see this one through to the end. Owe it to that little girl."

"I'm going with you," said Galpin.

They waded out to the wreck. Galpin looked in one shattered window, glanced at Stevens, then splashed around to the other side. "Son of a bitch!" he exclaimed. "There's nobody in here!" He stared through the shattered windshield, then reached in and tugged on the passenger-side seatbelt. Both seatbelts were fastened across empty seats.

# Chapter Twenty-eight

Vickie found Mickey in the bedroom stuffing clothes into his suitcase. "Have you lost your mind?" she shouted. He didn't answer. She grabbed his shoulder and spun him around. "You stabbed yourself like a flippin' lunatic on international TV!"

He pulled away from her. "One of these days you'll understand why, everybody will. Until then, you have to trust me."

"What are you going to do?"

"Finish this once and for all."

"How's Ernie supposed to protect you without your palm disc?"

Mickey picked up a rock paperweight and crushed it in the palm of his hand. He dropped the rubble onto the floor. "We're not human anymore. Remember?"

Vickie looked at the remains of the rock. "Where are you going?"

"Don't follow me this time. I have to do this by myself." He closed the suitcase and carried it to the door.

Tears streamed down Vickie's face. "Don't go, I'm begging you."

"I have to, not just for me, for all of us."

"At least tell me where you're going!"

"I love you Vic." He left her crying in the bedroom.

Mickey seated himself in an automated car. Looking more wary than usual, his Secret Service detachment boarded their cars too. When the door closed, Mickey preempted the car's usual queries. "Griffith Park Observatory," he said.

"Main entrance or the parking lot?" replied the car's voice.

"Main entrance."

The car sped away.

A stealth helicopter orbited overhead. "Round up One to

Round up Leader," radioed the pilot.

"Go ahead," replied General Westlock.

"The subject has boarded a car and is joining a train moving northwest. His Secret Service detachment is following, total of four agents in two cars."

"Maintain contact. Cheyenne out."

David stood at the mantle and held a holographic picture of his family. It showed his father with one arm around his mother and the other around his brother. David was kneeling in the foreground, ten years old and the only family member not smiling.

Pam held Vickie's hand and tried to comfort her. Vickie yelled at Ernie. "He's flipped out! You have to find him!"

"It won't be easy without his disc," Ernie replied.

Vickie buried her face in her hands.

David put down the holograph. "Might help if we knew what's bothering him."

"Did he discuss anything with you before we arrived?" Pam asked Vickie.

"He's been depressed. Keeps saying the Choice was rigged," Vickie sobbed.

Ernie nodded. "Said the same crazy stuff to me."

Pam bit her lip and looked at David. "Did he say anything to you?"

David felt a shiver run up his spine. He shook his head no.

"Do the Europans have any technology that could help us find him?" Pam asked.

"Let's ask our silver friends," David replied.

The twins were upstairs in David's old bedroom with Romeo and Juliet. Bet was sprawled on the bed sulking. Her new hair sprouted from her head as if she'd stuck her finger into a high voltage source. Al sat on the floor with his back to the bed.

Romeo and Juliet stood stationary on either side like bookends. Micetro snored like a diesel engine as he slept draped across Bet's feet.

Pam and David entered the room.

"Can we go home now?" Bet asked.

"We just got here," David replied. "Besides, we've got a crisis on her hands."

Al perked up. "Cool! What do we do?"

"You two aren't doing anything except trying to stay out of trouble. If that's even possible," David muttered.

"Great," Al said glumly.

"I feel like we're in prison," Bet said.

"Juliet, do you have the ability to scan for a single human without a palm disc?" David asked.

"It is possible if the individual has unique physical or chemical characteristics."

"How about nannites?"

"How large is the search area?"

"The whole planet."

"It is theoretically possible, but it would require a grid of sixty-four scanners in geosynchronous orbit. Shall I run a simulation?" Juliet asked.

David thought for a moment. "I have another idea." He turned to Pam. "It could take a few days. What do we do with our two little darlings?"

"Already thought of that," Pam replied.

Bet slumped back on the bed. "Great."

"Juliet," Pam began, "your job is to occupy the twins. I've compiled a list of educational sites in the vicinity. You should be able to visit one or two each day. Your Secret Service detail will go along for additional protection."

"We are capable of defending ourselves against all threats," Romeo said.

David smirked. "Not you, the defenseless people you're

going to run into."

Pam glared at him.

Pam and David went downstairs. Pam sat beside Vickie again on the couch. "Juliet might be able to scan for Mickey's nannites," Pam said.

"Great! Tell her to get started!"

"It requires putting up sixty-four satellites with Europan scanners. We can do it, but it's going to take a while."

Vickie looked glum again.

"I have a different idea," David said. "Some old-fashioned police work, and I know just the guy to help us."

# Chapter Twenty-nine

"Reaper One in position," radioed Peterson over the comlink. He sat in the copilot's seat in the stealth helicopter orbiting over Mickey's car.

"Reaper Two and the snatch team in position," radioed York.

"Reaper Three in position on the Observatory roof with eyes on target," said another Team member.

"Decoy One in position." Decoy One was a stealth helicopter orbiting a few miles away with a round shape covered by a metal tarp slung underneath its belly.

"Decoy Two is also in position." Decoy Two looked the same as Decoy One.

"You know this whole thing's a complete waste of time," said the pilot of Reaper One.

"Kill the chatter!" growled the general, monitoring the operation from Cheyenne Mountain.

Peterson punched the pilot of Reaper One in the shoulder causing the chopper to briefly veer off course.

General Westlock stood behind Latham in front of a computer monitor. "Where is he?"

"Who?" Latham asked. He kept fiddling with his Cult key ring.

The veins popped out on the general's forehead. "Mickey, the person you're trying to kidnap."

Latham pointed to a red "X" on the monitor traveling up the road to the Observatory.

"Where's the snatch taking place?" snarled the general.

Latham pointed at the screen again. "There. The train with the Secret Service agents heads this way, but Mickey's car detaches and goes that way." He indicated a residential street.

"Why?"

Latham snickered. "His car has a software glitch."

The general nodded his approval. "Then what?"

"Mickey's car stops in front of this house over here," Latham tapped the screen with his finger again. "Team 36 is waiting for him. They're masquerading as house painters."

"What's your plan for controlling him? He's not exactly Pee Wee Herman."

"The team throws a steel-impregnated tarp over the car and the chopper swoops down and whisks it away."

"Why bother with the tarp?" asked the general.

"Two reasons. First, to keep Mickey from busting out before we get his car off the ground. Once he's in the air, unless he can fly, we got 'im. Second, so Ernie can't see him. You know he's going to show up."

"Run that by me again," the general said.

Latham pointed at two symbols orbiting south of Hollywood Boulevard and Vine Street. "Two more stealth choppers towing empty cars wrapped in identical steel tarps. After we snatch Mickey, all three choppers head off in different directions. Mickey's not connected to the Sphere any more. Ernie won't know which chopper to follow."

Westlock looked impressed. "Not bad. Where're you taking him after the snatch?"

"Area 51."

"Nice piece of work, *Commander* Latham," said the general, "...*if* you pull it off."

Latham straightened up in his chair. For a moment, he looked like the old Latham again. "Thank you, Sir."

"And Latham?"

"Yes, Sir?"

"Put that damn key ring away."

# Chapter Thirty

Mickey's car detached from the train and began autonomous motion cruising up a quiet residential street. Despite what the map on the car's video screen showed, Mickey's enhanced senses told him that he was going the wrong way. "Where are we?" he asked the car.

"Polermo Drive," replied the car's synthesized voice.

"I specified the Griffith Park Observatory."

"No such command has been received," replied the car. The car's voice sounded like Latham trying to sound like a woman.

A hundred meters above, Petersen started counting. "Three, two, one, *now*!"

The helicopter swooped down and dropped its tarp over Mickey's car. The tarp landed with a loud thud and the interior of the car suddenly went dark. Discarding their paintbrushes and kicking over several paint cans, the Seal Team ran to the car and surrounded it. Two of the Seals carried heavy chains. Reaper One began lowering its cargo hook. Sergeant York waited for it on the car's roof, ready to hook it to the chains that the team wrapped around the car. Before York could complete the connection, a fist shot through the metal tarp and grabbed his ankle. He tumbled to the asphalt. The other Team members surrounded the car, pulled commando-style weapons from under their coveralls, and backed up a few paces.

After a loud ripping sound, Mickey's head and shoulders appeared above the roof of the car.

"Is this where we give up and go home?" York radioed to Petersen.

Mickey stood on the roof of the car, glared at the Seals with his middle finger thrust into the air, then jumped to the ground. "Unless you want to see what happens when I really get mad, don't follow me!" he yelled. He set off on foot towards the

Observatory, moving much faster than any ordinary man.

York pointed his pistol at Mickey's retreating form and spoke into his helmet mic. "Do you want us to fire?" Nobody wanted to.

"Don't shoot!" Westlock shouted into the comlink. "He's no good to us dead."

Petersen in Reaper One wiped his brow. "Okay, what are our new orders?"

"How about retreat?" muttered York.

"The Secret Service detail will arrive in two minutes," Latham said to the general. "They've radioed for reinforcements."

"Get your team out of there and follow Mickey," the general replied. "But keep your distance."

# Chapter Thirty-one

Mickey ignored the helicopter and the SUVs full of Secret Service agents following him and continued towards Griffith Park Observatory hoping to find Officer Stevens, the enigmatic fisherman he'd met in the High Sierras who said he didn't trust the Europans. At some level Mickey knew that Stevens was the key that could unlock the mystery of the Europans and maybe give him back his life. Stevens had hinted to Mickey that he'd be attending the Symposium, almost bating Mickey to join him.

Mickey slowed to a normal pace when he neared the circular drive leading to the Observatory's main entrance. Colorful banners strung across the road announced a special NASA Symposium on Jupiter's Moon Europa. *He's here,* Mickey said to himself as he scanned the crowd. *He has to be!*

Mickey walked through the crowd trying to be inconspicuous as he searched. When he couldn't find Stevens, he continued up the steps to the Observatory's main entrance.

A uniformed guard watching the crowd held out his hand asking for Mickey's ticket. "I don't have one," Mickey replied.

"You can't..." the guard began, then he studied Mickey's face. "You're Mickey!" The guard turned to the crowd. "It's Mickey!" he repeated more loudly. People came running, pushing, and shoving for a better look.

"Oh my God, it's *him*!"

"You should be ashamed of what you did!"

"Can I have your autograph?"

"You look taller on TV."

Mickey ignored them and scanned the crowd. When he still couldn't find Stevens, he shoved his way through the Observatory's front door.

The Observatory's grand marble foyer echoed with the voices

of people queued up to enter the exhibits and see the planetarium's holographic display of the galaxy. When they recognized Mickey, they rushed forward encircling him. Avoiding a mixture of outstretched hands, adulation, and shouted epithets, Mickey darted between them looking for Stevens, but he still couldn't find him. Frustrated, he ran back through the main entrance and hurried off the Observatory's grounds. He moved so fast, he became a blur.

He continued down the main road and stopped where a sagging gate used to be. Five years before, the rusted metal marked the entrance to a dirt road leading down to a clearing with picnic tables shaded by several pine trees. Two bewildered teenagers clinging to their bikes took a chance and boarded a flying saucer there for a ride to the moon. Mickey remembered that Stevens had referred to the clearing as the place where Mickey made his first choice. "What did he mean by that?" Mickey said out loud. "The choice to do what?" His anger began to build. "My whole life's been about choices since I met the damn Europans and I'm tired of it." He was shouting now with his hands balled into fists. "Fuck the Europans! Fuck everybody! I'm done making choices!"

The gate was gone. The access road had become a paved boulevard bordered by glitzy signs in multiple languages celebrating the Choice Monument. One of the signs depicted four teenagers standing in front of a stylized Europan flying disc. Mickey and David were portrayed as tall and handsome with impressive physiques. Pam and Vickie had the figures of Barbie dolls.

Two black SUVs screeched to a halt bracketing Mickey. A dozen agents raced towards him.

Mickey wrestled with his mounting rage. "You're relieved. Go home." His words came out in ragged gasps.

"Can't do that, Sir, for your own protection."

Mickey walked to the nearest SUV, ripped the door from its

hinges, and let it clatter to the ground. "I don't need protection."

"Reaper Leader, this is Reaper One. The target has separated from his Secret Service detachment and is continuing down to the Choice Monument on foot. His Secret Service detail isn't following. They've taken up positions blocking the access road and are radioing for instructions."

"Scramble their signal," said the general over the comlink. "Begin Phase Two."

"I wasn't briefed on Phase Two," Peterson radioed back.

"Hold your position. Leader out."

Latham leaned back. "What *is* Phase Two, General?"

"I'm working on it," the general replied.

# Chapter Thirty-two

As he approached the guardhouse marking the entrance to the Monument, Mickey slowed to a normal pace. The Choice Monument, as the clearing was now called, had the appearance of a Disney theme park—clean, scripted, and perfectly manicured. Scrolling light patterns on a large digital sign next to the guardhouse listed the hours the monument was open to the public. The sign reminded Mickey of a Europan's face.

The guard put down his *Esquire Magazine,* yawned, and pointed at the sign. "The Monument's closed today."

"Leave," Mickey said.

The guard looked up. "You have a problem, buddy?"

Mickey ripped the power cable away from the guardhouse causing an explosion of sparks. The sign's lights went out.

"What the…!" The guard jumped up from his chair.

Mickey sent the digital sign crashing to the ground. "L*eave now*!" he shouted. The guard threw open the door and ran.

Mickey's blood burned in his veins. Trembling, he gripped an iron fence blocking the road, swung it aside, and smashed his fist into the side of the guardhouse pulverizing the wall. He continued pummeling the structure until it reduced to rubble. With his anger spent, he kicked the sign aside and followed the road to the Monument.

"There's a zoo nearby," said the general studying a map.

"Why's that important?" asked Latham.

"Zoos have tranquilizer guns big enough to put down elephants."

Latham grabbed the microphone. "Reaper One. New vector. You are to land in the parking lot of the Los Angeles Zoo and await additional orders."

"Reaper One copies."

The fire pit, picnic tables, and most of the trees were gone, replaced by an imposing bronze statue depicting four teenagers looking up at a globe carved with the features of Europa. One of the teenagers representing Mickey wore a jumpsuit with a helmet tucked under his arm. The bronze Mickey pointed at the globe representing Europa with the figure of a Europan standing behind him. The globe of Europa orbited a much larger sphere meant to be the planet Jupiter, with a flying disc suspended halfway between. It took every ounce of Mickey's self-control not to destroy the statue with his bare hands.

He walked around the statue letting his blood cool and stopped facing the statue's effigy of a Europan. "The game's over," Mickey said. "I know you're here somewhere. Show yourself." He waited, and when nothing happened, raked his fingers across the cold metal leaving deep furrows in its surface. "You've been hiding on Earth all along pulling our strings. Your phony Test is over. Show yourself!" he demanded.

"Hello," said a voice behind him.

Mickey spun around. "You?"

# Chapter Thirty-three

"You're a Europan," Mickey said. "I should have known."

"Hardly. Prick me and I bleed," Paul Rudnick replied. "I was sent by the man you know as Stevens to escort you to a meeting. Now it appears I'll be your means of escape." He pointed at a stealth helicopter hovering overhead.

"Is Ernie one of you?" Mickey yelled over the helicopter's din.

"I have no idea what you're talking about," Rudnick replied.

"I can destroy the helicopter if I want," Mickey shouted.

"That wouldn't be wise, unless you prefer to stay here and duke it out with the army of men rushing here to capture you."

"Why should I trust you?"

"Without your connection to Ernie and the Sphere, you have two options. Stay here and wait for the general's men to surround you with enough firepower to overcome even your enhanced physiology, or come with me and continue your discussion with Stevens. That's why you came here, isn't it?" Rudnick gestured towards the helicopter. "He has a proposition for you."

Mickey glanced up at the hovering helicopter. "What kind of proposition?"

"He prefers to present it in person."

Mickey studied Paul Rudnick's face and didn't answer.

Rudnick stared back at him. "The Neanderthals are almost here."

Mickey allowed Rudnick to lead him behind the statue shielding them from the helicopter's rotor wash. The helicopter touched down on the grass, opened its door, but kept its blades spinning ready to take off again. Rudnick ran to the helicopter and stopped beside an open door. He gestured for Mickey to follow and disappeared inside. After a last glance at his bronze effigy, Mickey followed Rudnick. The helicopter's rotors sped up and the door slammed shut, then it ascended and arched over the center of Los Angeles and out to sea.

"This is Reaper Two on the roof of the Planetarium. Your snatch team has the target on board and has lifted off."

Latham grabbed the microphone. "Clarify Reaper Two. Reaper One is on the ground in the LA Zoo parking lot."

"A stealth helicopter just took off from the Monument with Mickey," said the pilot of Reaper Two.

General Westlock ripped the microphone from Latham's hand. "Do you have imagery?"

"Roger that."

"Up link, now!" shouted the general.

"Yessir!"

The monitor showed a black dot disappearing over the horizon.

Westlock stared at the ceiling. "What was its last heading?"

"Over the Civic Center, then due west out to sea."

Westlock slammed the microphone against the desk. "Who the hell are they?"

An unmarked car drove down the access road and stopped near the statue. Frankel stepped out. He looked around the area then touched his ear activating the implanted communications device. "Mickey isn't here. The Monument is deserted."

"We have him," said the familiar voice in his ear.

"What do you want me to do now?" Frankel heard a Secret Service van screech to a halt behind him.

"Bring Latham to the compound."

"Hands up!" shouted one of the agents pointing a gun at Frankel. The other agents formed a perimeter around Frankel with their guns drawn.

Frankel raised his hands. "Major Dan Frankel, Air Force Intelligence. ID's in my coat pocket."

"Keep your hands up where I can see them." The agent edged

closer, took out Frankel's ID and studied it. He lowered his gun. "He checks out." The other agents lowered their guns. "Did you see anything?" the agent asked.

Frankel took back his ID. "Only the ass end of a stealth helicopter high-tailing it away. None of my guys was flying it."

The agent spoke into his lapel mic. "Mickey's in a stealth helicopter. It's not one of ours." He listened for a few seconds, then pointed urgently at the SUVs.

After the Secret Service SUVs roared back up the access road, Frankel walked to the iron fence at the monument's perimeter. He peered through the bars at the lights of Los Angeles blinking to life in the twilight, and he remembered the day Pam and David said their goodbyes and boarded the saucer for Europa. If he hadn't risked his life and disobeyed the man in London, the City of Los Angeles would have suffered the same fate as Hiroshima in 1945.

He walked to his car and getting in he drove once around the monument, slowing to stare at the statue's bronze figure of a Europan. "You're pulling Mickey's strings just like the man in London is pulling mine. I don't trust either one of you," he said out loud. "Don't trust myself either." He put the car in gear and started laughing. "Looks like I've scored a deck chair on the Titanic."

# Chapter Thirty-four

Pam leaned into the car and forced a smile. "Goodbye, everyone. Try to have a good time."

"How?" Bet moaned. "Everything in a museum is dead."

Pam had done her best to improve Bet's mood. Her usual pacifier Micetro sat panting on the seat next to her. Pam reached in trying to fluff Bet's hair, but Bet batted her hand away. Pam pulled her hand back and sighed. Her daughter looked like Little Orphan Annie, but at least she wasn't bald anymore.

"Juliet, see to it that the twins enjoy themselves," Pam said. She closed the car's door.

Juliet spoke to Romeo on a private comlink. "How can we ensure that the twins have a joyful experience?"

"Disobeying their parents appears to have the greatest entertainment value," sent back Romeo.

Pam leaned into the window. "Why is Micetro wearing an orange vest?"

"This displays his function as a service animal and allows him access to all human structures," Romeo replied.

"Doesn't a service animal have to be a dog?"

"Micetro is twelve percent cocker spaniel," Juliet replied. "The applicable rule does not specify the percentage of canine DNA required."

"Okay, but make sure to keep him on a leash," Pam said. "Did you remember his treats?" Cheeseburgers put Micetro into a rapturous state.

"I replicated a supply before we departed," Juliet replied.

"I hope you remembered no mayo. It makes him barf."

"No mayonnaise," Juliet confirmed. "The Museum of Natural History." The window closed and the car started in motion. Their Secret Service detail followed in three cars.

Pam found Vickie sulking in the living room. "Want to come

with me to UCLA?" she asked.

"Joining the cheerleading squad?"

"I'm being awarded an honorary degree in Applied Genetics. Thought my *BFF* would want to come along and enjoy the experience with me."

"Not in the mood," Vickie replied.

"What are you going to do besides mope around?"

"Decide how I'm going to kill Mickey when we find him."

# Chapter Thirty-five

Pam's car stopped in front of the UCLA Genetics Research Center followed by the cars with her Secret Service detail and a convoy with enough paparazzi to cover the Academy Awards. The world's press lined the street with Melanie Dilman front and center.

Pam stepped from the car wearing an academic robe holding a mortarboard under her arm. One of the Secret Service agents followed with a cloth-covered birdcage. After polite applause, Pam offered a few meaningless remarks and allowed her host, the Dean of Life Sciences, to escort her inside. The Secret Service agent carrying the covered birdcage followed closely behind. He looked uncomfortable and held it as far from his body as his arms would allow.

The audience included several hundred of America's foremost geneticists and molecular biologists. An undercurrent of tension hung heavily in the auditorium. Pam shook hands with the dean and accepted her honorary degree. After a smattering of applause, she took off her mortarboard and placed her notes on the lectern. Before speaking, she took a sip from a glass of water to lubricate her throat and calm her nerves.

"Thank you Dean Schoenfeld for this great honor," she began. "I've had five years to study the Europans' vast storehouse of knowledge about biology and genetics. While I've absorbed only a fraction of it, I've learned enough to pursue my scientific passion, the prevention of extinction. First slide please... How many species of plants and animals are lost every year on Earth? How many species have we already lost? We can't answer these questions without knowing how many species exist to begin with, and from Earth science's perspective, that's not easy to determine. In 1980, a study of only nineteen trees in Panama led to the discovery of twelve hundred new species of beetle, so it's doubtful we earthlings have our species catalogue right. Thanks to the facilities on Europa, particularly their master database, I can help." There were murmurs of excitement among the guests. "The Europans have been visiting Earth for thousands of years, long before Homo sapiens stood on two legs. They've kept very detailed records of what they found, including all the species of animals and plants they encountered."

Several hands shot up from members of the audience. The dean leaned towards the microphone. "We'll hold all questions until the Q and A after her presentation, please."

When the hands went down, Pam continued, "Earth's scientists estimate that our planet has about one hundred million live species, but the European database says the real number is almost three times that. This means there are many animals and plants we haven't discovered yet."

One scientist raised his hand and then stood. He remained standing even after the dean motioned for him to sit down.

Pam pointed to him. "You have a question?"

"The prospect of many new animals and plants to discover is quite exciting. When can we see a copy of the Europans' data?"

"I'll answer that question at the end of my talk," Pam replied. She took another sip of water.

The dean stepped to the microphone. "I must insist that everyone contain their insatiable curiosity until the end of Pam's presentation. No exceptions. Thank you." The scientist sat down.

Pam consulted her notes. "It's important to distinguish between the natural extinction rate and what's actually happening. Earth's scientists have calculated a natural extinction rate of 0.01 percent of total species lost per year. Direct observation suggests a rate one thousand to ten thousand times higher, which means that Earth loses more than ten thousand species every year. If the current rate of species loss continues, we're headed for a critical loss of biodiversity that could spell the end of life on Earth." Members of the audience murmured with agreement. "Using the Europans' immense scientific knowledge, I decided to do something about it." Pam cued a video clip showing a tour of the Menagerie.

"Those are dinosaurs!" someone shouted. "Are there dinosaurs on Europa?"

Pam smiled. "No, only strange looking sea animals, and Europans of course. I'll show you examples of Europan sea life later." Pam pointed at the screen. "Those dinosaurs were bio-engineered."

"Did the Europans visit Earth during the Jurassic Period and bring back DNA samples?" a scientist yelled.

"No," Pam replied.

"Do Europans have complete genetic maps?" another one asked.

"No again," Pam replied. "I grew those dinosaurs from a single cell by de-repressing the dinosaur genes in modern Earth birds."

"That's astounding! How did you know which genes to de-repress?" someone shouted.

"I experimented until I got it right," Pam replied.

More hands shot up and the dean stepped to the lectern. "Ladies and gentlemen, please hold your questions until the end. Thank you!"

Pam showed a video of a Tyrannosaurus Rex.

"That's a T Rex!" someone shouted.

One of the scientists in the front row, a Nobel Prize winner, stood. "No it's not." He pointed at the screen. "That beast looks like a T Rex, at least we think it does, but that's not what it is. Young lady, you've succeeded in bio-engineering a new species that has features in common with an Earth dinosaur, but your new organism hasn't naturally evolved. Do us all a favor and leave it on Europa so you can't pollute our gene pool. The results could be catastrophic." He remained standing. There were shouts of agreement.

Pam looked flustered. "I don't think you fully understand what I've done, or why," she began.

"Then tell us!" someone else shouted.

The dean stepped to the podium and held up his hands. "Please! Let her finish her presentation."

"Yes my animals are bio-engineered, but they're not hybrids or chimeras," Pam continued.

"Of course they're not hybrids, unless you had a real dinosaur to mate with." The Nobel Laureate ignored the dean's glare. "It's not a chimera either, unless you had actual dinosaur genes to insert into a bird embryo. So what are those *things* besides genetic parlor tricks?"

Pam heard more shouts of agreement. Her face reddened. "They're not parlor tricks." She motioned off stage. The Secret Service agent brought the covered birdcage and set it on the lectern. Pam ripped off the cover revealing a pterodactyl in a birdcage.

Most of the audience jumped to their feet. "It's a pterodactyl!" someone yelled.

"Pterodactyls are extinct!" Pam's antagonist shouted over the din.

"Sit down, everyone!" the dean bellowed. "You have the honor of being the first scientists on Earth to learn about genetic technology generations beyond what we know. I'm here to listen and learn. If you're not, please leave!" The scientists, including the Nobel Prize winner, took their seats and the room became silent. "Continue please," the dean said to Pam. He never took his eyes off the pterodactyl.

Pam put her notes away. "The Europans have the complete gene map for numerous extinct species, but not even the Europans can create fully synthetic life." Pam pointed at the pterodactyl. "They have the complete gene map for this guy, but they can't create a synthetic ovum. Since I couldn't fertilize a pterodactyl egg with synthetic DNA, I de-repressed the pterodactyl genes in a common chicken egg. They're all there but dormant, same as most of the Neanderthal genes in all of us. She pointed at the pterodactyl again. "He's not a hybrid or a chimera. I'm not sure what to call him."

After Pam's lecture concluded, the dean hosted Pam and a few colleagues in his office. To everyone's relief, the Nobel Laureate refused to attend.

"I find all this fascinating, but also troubling," one of the senior scientists said.

"Why?" Pam asked.

"There's a difference between tampering with the genes in an ear of corn and mixing pterodactyl genes with the common chicken. Are you sure you know what you've done?"

"I wanted to find a way to stave off extinction, but I was at an impasse," Pam replied. "Even with their level of technology, the Europans can't synthesize artificial life. I needed another way."

The dean sipped his tea. "I wonder. Are you holding back extinction or accelerating it?"

Pam looked perplexed. "I don't understand."

"Recall our crusty Nobel Laureate's admonition to keep your bio-engineered animals on Europa. His delivery was rude, but his fear is valid. Humans once believed that planet Earth was at the center of the universe. We can laugh now, seeing it as the ultimate hubris. But ask yourself this...if we believe we know what's best for our biology better than Evolution's own master plan already in progress, are we being just as arrogant as our ancestors? Their stupidity ushered in the Dark Ages, but we survived. Could our new scientific conceit lead us to the very outcome you fear, our extinction?"

# Chapter Thirty-six

The cars stopped in front of the Natural History Museum in downtown Los Angeles. As soon as the Europans stepped out, a crowd began forming. Adding to the curious throng, a high school field trip had just exited the Museum. Several teenagers rushed forward pointing and shouting. The Secret Service detail quickly took up positions creating a perimeter. Curious, the twins moved closer for a better look. Micetro tried to join Bet, but Romeo's tentacle wrapped around his neck restrained him and the big cat fell in a heap.

"Get a look at those two dorks!" shouted a teenage boy pointing at the twins. He wore his pants halfway down his buttocks with his undershorts showing. A teen next to him with holes in his ears and a blue tipped Mohawk hairdo pointed at Al and shouted, "Dude! Does your mother pick out your clothes?"

Al glanced at Bet. "Yes."

The teenagers laughed. Al looked stricken. "Why are they laughing at me?"

"Hey, dork! Your cat needs orthodontia!"

"What's orthodontia?" Al asked out of the side of his mouth.

Bet edged closer.

"It is the crude process of realigning teeth with metal bands," replied Juliet. "Mistress Bet, please step back."

One of the teenage girls pointed at Bet and snickered. "Nice hair."

"Thanks," Bet replied.

"For a porcupine," one of the boys shouted.

Moving so fast her hand was a blur, Bet grabbed the boy's iPhone.

"Hey!" the boy shouted. "Gimme that back!"

"Sure," Bet said, smiling. She extended the phone. The owner reached for it, but Bet closed her hand before he could take it.

After a crunching sound, the remains of the iPhone trickled through her fingers and fell to the ground.

"You're going to pay for that!" the angry teen shouted. Others in the crowd began hurling angry epithets, along with an apple and other food missiles left over from lunch. The agents glanced nervously at each other. One of them radioed for backup.

Romeo stepped in front of the twins and stretched his legs until he stood eight feet tall. He began to emit the sound of a locomotive at ear-splitting decibels while all the lights on his face flashed bright red. Micetro cowered behind Bet with his tail between his legs.

The crowd scattered.

"Into the museum!" yelled one of the agents. He held the museum's door open.

"No way," Bet exclaimed. "We're finally having fun." Juliet lassoed her around the waist and dragged her towards the door. "Let me go," Bet shouted.

After Romeo shrank to his usual size, he hoisted Al off the ground and started for the Museum's front door while dragging Micetro. "Hey!" Al shouted.

They rushed inside and the agents locked the door. They continued to hear angry shouts coming from outside and pounding on the door. Two of the agents took positions flanking the doorway. The lead agent began issuing orders. "Clear all the visitors out! Tell them it's a bomb scare." Several agents sprinted off in different directions.

"Explain the sound you synthesized," Juliet sent to Romeo.

"I recreated the sound of a twentieth-century Earth tracked conveyance known as a locomotive."

"What was your purpose in doing so?"

"My studies of earthlings reveal that certain sounds instill fear, such as the roar of carnivores, the proximity of large machines, or the American president beginning his speech with the words *My Fellow Americans*."

Juliet moved closer. "You are resourceful."

Romeo extended his legs making himself a few centimeters taller again. "I am efficient."

Bet looked around the museum's grand foyer. "Now what do we do?" Corridors led off in multiple directions each marked by a sign indicating the theme of an exhibit. One read *Machines of the Twentieth Century*. Al pointed at it. "I'll bet I can fix one of their primitive machines and get it going again." He started running in that direction.

Bet looked around. "Come on Micetro." She tugged on the cat's ear. Romeo released his tentacle and allowed Bet to lead Micetro down the corridor marked *The Evolution of Life.*

"The twins have begun their entertainment activity," Romeo said.

"What is that?" asked a harried agent.

"Thwarting authority," Juliet replied. The agent spoke into his lapel mic and sprinted after Bet.

Juliet radioed to Romeo. "Why did you release Micetro?"

"His presence makes Mistress Bet more manageable. He is also confined to this structure."

They heard the sound of shattering glass followed by Bet shouting "Micetro!"

"I will investigate," said Juliet. "I recommend that you follow Master Al."

Juliet glided to a stop behind Bet. Bet stood before a diorama with a shattered pane of glass. The sign above the diorama read Saber Tooth Tiger, *Smilodon*, Pleistocene epoch, North America. Micetro was inside the display trying to mate with one of the simulated cats. Juliet lassoed him and began dragging him out while Micetro strained to return to the mannequin.

"What's he doing?" Bet asked.

Juliet passed a tentacle shaped like a horn over Micetro's body. "I detect a significant increase in Micetro's secretion of pheromones. It is likely that he is trying to mate."

Bet turned up her nose. "Gross." She continued down the corridor.

Dragging Micetro with her, Juliet caught up with Bet. She was standing in front of a diorama depicting a Neanderthal family in a cave decorated with cave paintings.

"An Earth hominid species that became extinct thirty thousand Earth-years ago," Juliet said.

"Hope Mom doesn't bring one of those guys back to life," Bet said.

"The Neanderthals are your ancestors," Juliet said.

"No way."

"Human DNA is more than ninety-percent homologous with Neanderthal DNA suggesting cross-species mating."

Bet stared into the diorama. "They look dumb as rocks."

"Neanderthals carried the same gene for language that Homo Sapiens do, and they performed tasks more complex than Homo Sapiens during the same time period." Juliet moved to a nearby glass case containing Neanderthal artifacts. "Observe."

The case contained stone tools and a flat rock with symbols inscribed on it. A placard read, "Neanderthal Artifacts carbon dated 60,000 years ago."

"Wait a minute," Bet said. She peered closer at the rock.

"For what purpose should we delay?" asked Juliet.

"Do the symbols on that rock look familiar to you?"

Juliet inclined her head towards the case. "No."

"They look the same as the ones we saw in the ruins on Europa."

"There are no ruins on Europa," Juliet said.

*"Get over here!"* Bet sent to Al telepathically.

When Al arrived with Romeo, Bet pointed at the rock with symbols. "Do you remember seeing symbols like that on Europa or Mars?" Al asked Romeo.

"No," Romeo replied.

Al glanced at his sister. *"Why would the same hieroglyphics be on Earth, Mars, and Europa?"* he sent to Bet telepathically.

*"Why can't they remember seeing them?"* Bet sent back.

*"Why didn't the symbols on the rock turn them off like all the other times?"*

*"Maybe the rock doesn't have enough writing."* Bet sent. Al nodded.

"You can release Micetro now," Bet said out loud. "Al and I are going to the primitive machine exhibit. There's nothing for Micetro to mate with there." Juliet retracted her tentacle. Bet grabbed hold of the fur on Micetro's back and walked away with Al. Romeo and Juliet followed.

*"How do we figure this out?"* Al sent.

*"Later. Let's get out of here,"* Bet sent back.

*"How?"*

*"Take Romeo with you. I'm going to the back door."* Bet bolted for the back door with Micetro trotting after her.

Juliet followed. "Mistress Bet…"

Al ran in the opposite direction. "Romeo! Quick. Look at this!" Romeo followed.

*"I'm at a Geology exhibit near the back entrance,"* Bet sent. *"Wait for my signal."* She said out loud, "Juliet, Romeo said for you to meet him in the Machine exhibit with Al."

"He didn't transmit anything to me?" Juliet said.

"Go ahead. I'll stay here. I want to look at these rocks," Bet replied.

"Very well." Juliet started towards the Machine Exhibit.

*"Okay, baby brother. Let's get out of here,"* Bet sent.

*"The Secret Service guys locked the door,"* Al sent back.

*"A primitive mechanism. I unlocked it."* Bet screamed out loud, "Micetro! Come back here!"

Micetro sprinted out the museum's service door with Bet running after him.

Romeo, Juliet, Al, and the Secret Service detail caught up with

Bet standing in the alley behind the museum. The agents fanned out searching the area. "Where's the…whatever he is?" the lead agent asked.

"I detect the sound of Micetro's breathing one thousand meters in that direction," Romeo said pointing with one of his tentacles.

They heard shouts coming from behind them. "Look! There's the aliens!" People started running in their direction.

"I want a selfie with one of the robots!" someone shouted.

"Me too!"

Looking stressed, the lead agent began shouting orders to his detail. "Here we go again. You four, set up a perimeter and keep those people away! You, go get the cars!"

"I will retrieve Micetro," Juliet said.

"I'll go with you," Bet added. "He listens to me."

"Then how come he took off?" Al sneered.

"Shut up, little brother."

"I suggest the three of us cooperate in the retrieval of Micetro," said Juliet. "Romeo has demonstrated expertise in crowd control and will remain here."

While Romeo started growing in height, Bet and Al ran after Micetro with Juliet gliding after them.

Bet skidded to a stop at the entrance to an alley. "He's mating again."

Al joined her. "It looks like they're stuck together."

"What's he mating with?" asked Bet.

"According to the Earth database, Micetro is engaged in sexual activity with a feline hybrid known as a Savannah Cat," Juliet replied.

"A hybrid of what?" Bet asked.

"The mating of a domesticated cat and a relative of the African Lion known as a serval."

"Gross. Pull them apart."

"The database indicates that physical force to end copulation is unwise. The application of cold water is recommended."

The stray cat more than a meter from her hindquarter to her nose parted from Micetro and ran away. Micetro walked back to Bet with wobbly legs and his tongue hanging out.

"Is Micetro sick?" Al asked.

"He is...content," Romeo replied. He scooped Micetro up with two of his tentacles. Micetro didn't resist.

Bet ran to a shop window across the street. "What's going on in there?"

Al and Juliet joined her. All three looked through the shop's window. A woman was sitting in a chair having makeup applied by a cosmetologist.

"I have noticed that earthlings cling to their primitive past through face painting, tattoos, and body piercing," Juliet said.

"Mom and Dad are from Earth and they don't do primitive stuff like that," Al said.

Bet grabbed a lock of her new hair and showed it to her brother. "They still have fur."

Romeo joined them. "What is the purpose of this activity?" he sent to Juliet.

"The female may be fertile and seeks to attract a mate," sent back Juliet.

Despite the Secret Service agents' best efforts to thwart them, the crowd of curious people from the museum had followed them, except for the teens who were back on their bus. This time several burly road maintenance men stood in front behind the cordon of nervous agents. One had the image of a buxom woman tattooed on his arm. Another man had a cigarette hanging from the corner of his mouth. Romeo focused first on the tattoo, then at the man smoking. "Why do you suspend combustible material from your mouth?" Romeo asked.

The man took a drag and exhaled directly at Romeo.

"A combination of oxidized particulates mixed with trace quantities of volatile organics," Romeo commented. "The earthling known as Vickie had similar residue in her lungs. Cleansing is possible if you cease further inhalation."

The man raised his middle finger.

"You may ask your question," Romeo said.

The man sneered at Romeo and raised his middle finger even higher.

"I don't think he's asking a question," Al said.

"My study of earthlings indicates that raising one's hand expresses the desire to ask a question," Romeo said.

Al glanced at his sister and shook his head.

"I believe it is a form of sign language," said Juliet. "Perhaps the man did not hear what you said."

"Your hearing can be restored," Romeo said. The man made the same gesture and walked away. Romeo sent to Juliet, "Human language is imprecise resulting in inefficient neural processing." A truck rumbled by with an advertisement painted on its side. Romeo's head swiveled to follow it. "I have also observed that humans adorn not only their bodies, but their machines with writing and symbols."

Juliet studied the woman having makeup applied. "Adornment has a purpose humans find satisfying," she said.

Romeo's lights flashed faster. "Do you find adornment satisfying?" he radioed to Juliet.

"I'm bored," Bet complained.

*"Mars was a lot more exciting,"* Al sent to Bet. *"You wouldn't know because you were afraid to leave the disc. You're such a wuss."*

"Am not!" Bet shouted.

Juliet moved between the twins. "It is time to rejoin your parents at Ernie's domicile."

"No it's not," Bet said. "We're finally having fun." She tried to walk away, but Juliet extended an appendage stopping her.

"You will return to Ernie's domicile or suffer adverse consequences," Juliet said.

Bet put her hands on her hips. "Such as?"

"I have been informed by your mother that we will not return home until all scheduled Earth educational activities have been completed."

The twins stared at each other.

"Your mother also told me to remind you of the Menagerie's periodic need for the removal of accumulated organic waste."

Al smiled sheepishly at his sister. "Maybe we should do what Juliet says."

"Now who's a wuss?" Bet sneered.

"There is no such directive," Romeo radioed to Juliet. He scanned Juliet's face. "Are you operating at peak efficiency?"

"Yes. Why do you ask?"

"Your presentation of erroneous facts was intentional?" Romeo asked.

"I employed one of Earth's accepted behavioral strategies. It is called politics."

# Chapter Thirty-seven

Mickey's internal clock registered that he'd been in the air eight hours including two mid-air refuelings. Presuming their average air speed to be two hundred fifty knots, and the range of the helicopter approximately one thousand nautical miles, he estimated they were two thousand miles from Los Angeles heading south. Rudnick sat in a jump seat behind the pilot wearing aviator's glasses and headphones. He'd stopped speaking to Mickey after take off. Mickey had asked him several times where they were going. Rudnick's only response had been a smile. The combination of the heat in the helicopter's cabin, the droning of the engine, and the endless miles of featureless ocean eventually lulled Mickey to sleep.

Mickey was jolted awake when the helicopter suddenly banked. Alert again, Mickey looked through the window and saw a tropical coastline. They flew inland passing over dense jungle, and after half an hour began reducing speed.

Rudnick rose from his seat and sat next to Mickey. "We're almost there," he said.

"Where is *there*?" Mickey asked.

"The headquarters of The Benevolent Sphere Association."

"Where am I geographically?"

Rudnick's smile reminded Mickey of a boa constrictor. "It's a bit hot here at times, and humid, but you'll get used to it."

"How long am I going to stay?" Mickey asked.

"Long enough to have a few exquisite meals while you consider Mr. Steven's proposal."

"What proposal?"

"To accept the position of President of the Benevolent Sphere Association."

"Why would I do that?"

"Because you're the boy who passed the Test and saved humanity. Who else should it be?"

The helicopter landed in a clearing cut from the jungle and men wearing camo-fatigues and carrying automatic weapons immediately surrounded it. When the helicopter door swung open, Rudnick gestured toward the opening. "Shall we?"

Mickey looked out the door. "A lot of fire power for an organization that calls itself 'benevolent.'"

"An unfortunate necessity in this locale. The natives can be quite inhospitable."

"The natives?"

"The drug cartel." Rudnick descended a set of stairs to the ground.

Mickey followed him. "Do you sublet from the drug dealers, or are they subletting from you?"

"I'm glad you haven't lost your sense of humor." Rudnick pointed towards a Land Rover. "This way."

Bracketed by two armed Humvees, the Land Rover followed a dirt road cut through the jungle. After half a mile, Rudnick pointed through the windshield. "There."

Mickey leaned forward to see out the windshield. The scene outside reminded him of the entry to Jurassic Park. Two tall doors swung open and the vehicles drove into a compound surrounded by high walls. The gates closed again, secured by a thick metal girder that slid into place. Mickey could see more heavily armed guards on the walls and walking the grounds accompanied by dogs. A lavish Spanish hacienda occupied the center of the compound separated by a garden from two other structures that reminded Mickey of office buildings.

"Welcome to the headquarters of the BSA," Rudnick said.

Rudnick escorted Mickey to a palatial suite on the ground floor of one of the side buildings. Mickey looked around. "Fit for a king."

"Fit for the President of the BSA," Rudnick said. "I'll leave you to freshen up for dinner. Eight o'clock."

"At the prison cafeteria?"

"Always the comedian. I'll send someone to escort you. Fresh clothes are in the closet." Rudnick started for the door.

"Are you going to lock it?" Mickey asked.

"We both know you could break it. Besides"—Rudnick smiled—"there's nowhere to hide." He left, leaving the door open.

Mickey closed the door and sat on the bed. He knew that if he still had his Europan palm disc, Ernie would already be on his way to rescue him. Instead of panicking, he stretched out on the bed and closed his eyes.

The door opened a crack. "May I?" said an unfamiliar feminine voice. When Mickey still didn't reply, a young woman let herself in.

Mickey opened his eyes. "Who are you?"

"You're escort for dinner." She spoke in a British accent.

Mickey tried to ignore her, but found it difficult. Her skin was chestnut color, and her hair a lustrous black. Baggy jungle khakis couldn't hide her remarkable figure. He found her eyes almost mesmerizing—two sapphires of dazzling blue. As he stared at them, his body began to tingle.

She gestured at the chair. "May I?" When Mickey didn't answer, she seated herself. "Emma Rideaux."

"You're the camp counselor?"

"I am for you," Emma replied.

"Your camp has a lot of people with guns."

"To keep the locals out."

"How do I call a cab?"

"You just got here." Emma opened the top button of her blouse. "Is the air conditioning working in her?" She fanned herself with her hand.

Mickey got off the bed and moved to the window. "Rideaux sounds French, but your accent's British."

"My father is Moroccan, a military attaché with NATO. My mum"—she switched to a cockney accent—"is a proper British lass who cooks and plays bridge." She switched back to English tinged with French. "I was a captain in the Royal Air Force until I joined the BSA."

"Don't look much like a fighter pilot."

Emma sighed. "Nothing so exciting. I flew helicopters and ferried people around, a glorified taxi driver."

Mickey leaned against the windowsill, perspiring and not from the humidity. "It's been a long day. I'd like to take a nap."

Emma looked at her watch. "Dinners at eight. It's only six." She sat on the bed. Her blue eyes sparkled beneath long lashes. "The guards all have one-track minds. Some intelligent conversation would be refreshing." She loosened another button.

Mickey struggled to control his emotions. "I'm not a fool," he said.

She lay back on the pillow. "Obviously."

"You were sent by Rudnick."

She smiled seductively. "Right again."

"You were sent here to…"

"Counsel you," Emma interrupted. She batted her eyelashes at him. "How many phone numbers do you have in your pocket after a typical Sphere encounter?"

Mickey bristled. "What's that supposed to mean?"

"Stop being so modest. You're bigger than Elvis, and better looking too."

Mickey looked flustered. "Counsel me about what?"

Emma kicked off her shoes. "My job is to open your mind to new possibilities."

"What if I like my mind the way it is?" Mickey's enhanced senses found her pheromones impossible to ignore. He fought to keep from losing control.

"Are you afraid of me?" Emma asked.

Mickey licked his lips. "I could kill you with one finger if I wanted to."

"Do you want to?" Her voice sounded husky.

He froze.

"You have a girlfriend. Her name's Vickie, as I recall," Emma said.

With a painful crack, Mickey snapped back to reality. "What about her?"

"Do you love her?"

"Yes."

Emma got off the bed and went into the bathroom. Mickey could hear the water running. When she returned, Emma had fully buttoned her blouse and seemed more business-like in her demeanor. "Love is a complicated phenomenon," she said. "Are you sure?"

"Sure of what?"

"That you love her?"

"That's no concern of yours."

"She doesn't know you're here."

Mickey bristled. "I do."

"Pity. Do you have any questions before I leave?"

"What does Rudnick want from me?"

"You created quite a stir the other day. He wants you to undo it."

"How?"

"By becoming the BSA's leader. A figurehead, of course, but the position comes with perks." She fingered the top button of her blouse again.

"Never."

"Try to keep an open mind until you hear the entire job description."

"Why?" Mickey had trouble concentrating again.

Emma ran her nail along his forearm leaving a line of goose

bumps. "An open mind helps to clarify past mistakes."

Mickey had trouble pulling his eyes from her. "What mistakes?"

"That's what I'm going to help you find out." She walked to the door.

"Is Rudnick in charge?"

Emma stopped with her hand on the doorknob. "Only in the U.S."

"He takes orders from somebody else?"

Emma looked into Mickey's eyes. "Isn't it always that way? I was told you already met him."

"Stevens," Mickey said.

"Is that the name he's using now?"

*Cheyenne Mountain*

Frankel placed his tray next to Latham. "I hear your Seal Team totally blew it."

"Somebody got there ahead of us," Latham grumbled.

"Ernie again?"

"I don't know who the hell it was." Latham threw his napkin on his tray.

"What's the general planning next?" Frankel asked.

"Don't know and don't care. I resigned. Can't deal with his shit anymore."

Frankel already knew, but feigned surprise. "What'll you do now?"

Latham rubbed his eyes. He looked like a man who'd been dealt one bad hand after another and was ready to throw in his cards. "I have no idea."

"You could take a position with the BSA."

Latham sneered. "The Boy Scouts of America? The food's good at the meetings, but…" He dropped his Cult key ring on the table. "I'm too old to play with toys."

Frankel saw his opening. "It's not the Boy Scouts, it's the

Benevolent Sphere Association. Know why I'm not in uniform?"

"Forgot to pick up your cleaning?"

Frankel lied. "I quit the Air Force last Friday and joined the BSA the next day. I came back today to turn in my files and sign out. Day after tomorrow, I'm flying to the BSA headquarters to go through their boot camp. Come with me."

"Boot camp? I'm done soldiering." Latham looked lost.

"Nobody carries a gun," Frankel scoffed. "It's like the Peace Corp, a job that does something good for a change. Might make you feel better."

"The only job left in our brave new world is selling computers," Latham said. "The knowledge of the whole damn universe is on the Internet."

"What good is a computer to a guy living in a mud hut?" Frankel asked.

"You want me to sell computers to guys in mud huts?"

"The BSA makes sure the knowledge of the Sphere is put into practice for the benefit of all mankind, including people in mud huts. Somebody has to do it."

"How?" Latham asked.

"By creating infrastructure."

Latham looked puzzled.

Frankel continued, "What good is the formula for a drug to cure cancer if nobody manufactures or distributes it?"

"Those are the kind of jobs you're talking about?"

Frankel nodded.

Latham sat up straighter. "Well, that's different."

"Maybe they'll take you too," Frankel said.

"What do I have to do to get in?"

"Pass an interview and a physical, then get through boot camp. Piece of cake for guys like us."

Latham flexed his bicep. "I haven't worked out in a while."

"I'll pick you up at your apartment at eleven o'clock tomorrow and we'll leave together," Frankel said. That gave him two hours to resign from NORAD before meeting Latham. It should be enough time, Frankel thought. He felt increasingly uneasy about his real assignment and the mysterious man behind it, but he looked forward to saying goodbye to General Westlock.

A few minutes before eight pm, Emma knocked on Mickey's door and let herself in. She wore a sheer white silk dress leaving nothing to the imagination with her hair done up and gathered into a diamond-studded comb. The aroma of an exotic perfume preceded her into the room. Mickey hadn't showered or changed clothes. Emma gave him the once over. "How come you didn't shower or dress for dinner?"

"I'm not playing games with you or anyone else around here."

Emma nodded. "It's better to be uncomfortable and stink." She turned around so he could see the back of her dress—the silk dipped down her spine, leaving her skin exposed. "I like dressing up once in a while. Makes dinner taste better too."

"Prison stripes seem more appropriate around here."

"You're a guest, not a prisoner. Try living in the moment."

"A guest who's locked in his hotel."

"You have a lot to learn about living. I look forward to being your teacher."

The back wall of the dining room faced a courtyard with an enclosed garden and a fountain. The muted strains of Mendelssohn's Violin Concerto in E minor floated in the air. There were only four tables with one seat occupied, Rudnick wearing a white tuxedo with an exquisite orchid in his lapel. He stood and pulled out a chair for Emma. "You look lovely as always, my dear."

Emma seated herself and looked up at Mickey. He remained standing. Rudnick picked up a bottle of red wine. "It's grown locally, but quite good." He poured three glasses, handed one to Emma and offered one to Mickey. When Mickey refused to take it, Rudnick lifted his in a toast. "To a new beginning. Beginnings are what the BSA is all about." He swirled the wine in its glass, sniffed the aroma, and took a sip. Emma did the same.

Mickey took his seat. "Let's get this over with."

Rudnick raised an eyebrow. "Before the first appetizer course?"

"Where's Officer Stevens, or whatever his name really is?"

Rudnick sighed. "Very well." He glanced at Emma. "Excuse us for a moment, my dear."

Mickey remained seated as Emma left the room.

"Lovely, isn't she?" Rudnick commented.

"Stevens?" Mickey prompted.

"He'll be joining us in a day or two to celebrate your addition to our organization."

"I don't intend to stay that long."

Rudnick frowned. "You could be grateful for being rescued."

"I don't need rescuing, by you or anyone else."

"Really? Never mind General Westlock and the redoubtable DIA, what about from yourself?"

"What's that supposed to mean?"

"You're lost, and thanks to your stunt at the White House the whole world knows it. Let us help you reestablish yourself. Madison Avenue calls it creating a new brand."

"By joining the Cult?"

"By leading the BSA."

Mickey took a sip of his wine. "I don't need to reinvent myself."

"You'll be ostracized by everyone," Rudnick said. "Is that what you want?"

"I'll take my chances."

"You should also consider this. You don't trust the Europans or the Sphere. Here's your chance to take control."

"Ernie controls the Sphere."

"But the BSA will control what humanity does with it…under

your leadership, if you agree."

"That sounds ominous," Mickey said.

"Give us three days. While you wait for Stevens to arrive, let Miss Rideaux show you what we really do. If you're not ready to join us after your tour and your discussion with Stevens, we'll put you back in the helicopter and bid you farewell."

"You want me to be your figurehead."

"What we do is too big for any one man," Rudnick replied. "You'll be an important part of our team."

Mickey looked out at the garden.

"The essence of life is its unexpected twists and turns," Rudnick continued. "One minute you're a teenager riding your bike, and the next you're in a flying saucer on the way to Europa. Some people call it fate or providence, others luck. Whatever you call it, the key to success is learning how to manage it. ...May I ask Miss Rideaux to rejoin us now?"

# Chapter Thirty-eight

Vickie and Pam sat at the kitchen table eating strawberry ice cream.

"Davie says he has a plan for finding Mickey," Pam said.

Vickie put down her spoon. "This is all my fault. He's anxious about getting married." She wiped a tear from her eye. "I gave him a hard time, said he was too close to his parents…I called him immature, like a mama's boy." Her tears began to flow. "I drove him away."

"That's nonsense. Mickey loves you. It doesn't matter what you said."

"What's Davie's plan?"

"To ask his father for help."

Vickie seemed surprised. "Didn't see that coming."

"Dick's a retired cop. Davie says he knows stuff," Pam replied.

"I'm glad he and Davie are trying to reconcile.

"I've been thinking," Pam said. "Maybe we shouldn't be here when Dick arrives. The two of them may still have some issues to work out."

"Haven't they been talking on ESPN?" Vickie asked.

"David's not really into sports. He's the quintessential geek."

"Not *that* ESPN. Ernie's Space Phone Network."

Pam chuckled. "That's the Vickie I know. She bit her lip. "Let's leave the house and give them their privacy."

Vickie ran her fingers through her hair thinking, then her expression brightened. "How about the mall? We'll get our hair done, go shopping, do something to take my mind off things."

Pam smiled. "Really?"

"There's nothing we can do here, right? Besides, we both need it—you more than me."

"What's *that* supposed to mean?"

Vickie gave Pam the once over. "Ever get tired of wearing silver?"

"It's just David, me, and the kids on Europa," Pam replied. "The kids think everybody wears silver."

"Girl, it's time to add some color. Let's shop 'til we drop."

Pam smiled. She could see an improvement in Vickie's energy level. "Just you and me like the good old days?" Now Pam was excited too.

"In the good old days, we went to pick up guys," Vickie said, "and try on clothes we couldn't afford."

"You went to pick up guys," Pam reminded her. "I went along for the ride."

Vickie laughed. "This time we take a bunch of guys with us. Some of them are hunks, by the way."

"What're you talking about?"

"Look outside."

Eight Secret Service agents wearing sunglasses and black suits over great physiques surrounded the house 24/7.

"Wherever we go, they go…to the beauty salon, Macy's, Barnes and Noble, you name it," Vickie continued.

Pam raised an eyebrow. "Really?"

Vickie giggled. "Let's make them follow us into Victoria's Secret."

"I'm not sure I'm comfortable with this," Pam said. "We're both in committed relationships. I'm married!"

"Lighten up. We're just having fun," Vickie replied. "Grab your purse. We're going shopping."

"I don't have a purse"

"We'll buy you a new one, anything but silver."

They walked to a car waiting at the curb.

"I never asked you," Vickie said. "How did you do it on Europa?"

Pam blushed. "The same way as here, ding bat."

Vickie looked puzzled for a moment. "Not *that*! How'd you get married?"

"Oh." Pam sounded relieved. "We designed our own ceremony. You saw the whole thing on Ernie's TV. You were watching, weren't you?"

"Not your cute little speeches," Vickie replied. "Who was the justice of the peace, the guy who tied the knot? Was it a computer?"

Pam bristled. "The head Europan married us. His name's Unit One."

"It *was* a computer," Vickie said.

"Stop it, Vick. They're not computers."

"They're sure not flesh and blood."

"Doesn't mean they're machines."

"What are they?"

"You don't have to be flesh and blood to be alive."

"Do they have feelings?" Vickie asked.

Pam thought for a moment. "Not officially."

Vickie guffawed. "What the hell does that mean?"

"Watch Romeo and Juliet. You'll see."

David watched on Ernie's television as his father extended his hand to ring the doorbell. He hadn't seen his father in more than a year. *Dad looks a lot older and thinner now,* he thought. When the doorbell sounded, he hesitated.

Ernie came up behind him. "Let him in," he urged. David tried to mask his emotions, but Ernie saw the fear in his eyes. "You guys have been talking again. Everything's fine."

"A few long distance phone calls from halfway across the solar system," David replied.

Ernie pointed at the door. "Don't just open the door, open your heart."

"Thanks, Ern."

As soon as David opened the door, Ernie took off down the steps and waved. "Nice to see you, Dick," he yelled. "Got an errand to run." He disappeared into a car.

After a moment of awkward silence, Dick held out his hand. "I'm proud of you, son." David rushed into his embrace.

Pam and Vickie entered Macy's surrounded by a cordon of Secret Service agents and the usual entourage of paparazzi.

"Don't you think this is a little weird," Pam said to Vickie under her breath.

"Just imagine that you're Jenn and I'm Angelina." Vickie rubbed her hands together and looked around. "Shoes first." She glanced at Pam's sedate silver shoes, which looked more like moccasins. "Something with a heel for a change."

Pam watched with an expression of awe as a woman walked by wearing platform shoes with six-inch heels. "I've never worn stilettos. Before Europa, I couldn't even walk without my sticks."

"Stilettos, running shoes, hiking boots…the world's your oyster," Vickie said. "Anything you want, so long as it's not silver."

Pam tried on six pairs of high heels, none of them silver, and didn't find anything she liked. The salesgirl waiting on them looked pale and kept hyperventilating. She rushed back with four more boxes and stood trembling before Pam. "Are you okay?" Pam asked her. She nodded too vigorously which caused her to drop one of the shoeboxes.

"Do you remember Officer Stevens?" Vickie asked Pam.

Pam handed a shoe back to the sales girl. "Too small. I'll try a seven, if you don't mind." The salesgirl rushed away. "The cop who was with David's mother at the clearing?"

"That's the guy," Vickie said keeping her voice down.

"What about him?"

Vickie tried to sound casual. "Ever run into him again?"

"On Europa?"

"Gimme a break. Before that," Vickie replied.

Pam tried on another shoe. "No. Why?"

Vickie hesitated. "He was the one who saved you when you were a kid."

Pam put down the shoe. "What are you talking about?"

"He pulled you from the wreck the night your parents died."

Pam sat back. "Seriously? Are you sure?"

Vickie lied. "Phyllis told me."

The breathless sales girl returned with her arms laden with more shoeboxes. Pam held up her hand keeping her away.

"You have to admit it's strange," Vickie continued. "Stevens pulls you out of the wreck and years later he's there when David's brother is shot." She stared at Pam waiting for her reaction.

"It *is* strange, but it's still a coincidence," Pam said. "What else could it be?" She opened another box and slipped on a pair of sparkling stilettos that fit perfectly.

Vickie nodded. "You're right. Just a weird coincidence—really weird."

Pam held up a shoe with heels long enough to be a shish kabob skewer. "These fit perfectly, and guess what, they're silver!"

David sat across from his father in their old living room. Dick finished drinking his bottle of Seven Up. "When do I get to see my grandchildren and do all the grandfatherly stuff?" he asked. "They're what, five years old now?"

"Children grow a little faster on Europa, Dad. They're the equivalent of Earth teenagers."

"Great. Where are they?"

"Out taking in the sights."

They both knew what David would ask next. "How's Mom?" he asked.

"We're not together now," Dick replied.

David could see the pain etched on his father's face. His heart sank. "I didn't know."

"We didn't want to upset you. Europa's a long way from here."

David looked away.

"She's with another cop now. Can you believe it?"

"Who?"

Dick's expression darkened. "Stevens, one of the captains from my old precinct. He was the guy in charge the night Jake got shot."

"I don't know what to say."

"She's okay." Dick cleared his throat. "That's all that matters."

"What about Jake?"

"After the President pardoned him, your brother went back to school. Met a gal who isn't half bad and married her. She's pregnant. Pretty soon I'll have three grandkids. He sends his regards, by the way."

David nodded. He still wasn't ready to see Jake. "What are you doing these days?"

"I retired from the cop business. Living with my sister now in Nebraska. My pension goes a lot further there."

David had been hoping for a moment like this his entire life—sitting next to his father and knowing his dad was happy to be with him too. "Nebraska sounds kind of dull for a guy who used to chase crooks for a living."

"It's peaceful out there. Gave me the time to do some serious thinking… Helped me to see that I've been a shitty father."

David didn't know what to say.

"I never taught you anything, Davie," Dick continued, "except how to feel bad about yourself. I'm sorry for that."

"You don't have to do this," David began.

David patted his son's knee. "I learned something else out there in the corn, something real important. Want to know what it is?"

David nodded, fighting back tears.

"There aren't any throwaway days. Know what that means?"

"No," David replied.

"It means that life doesn't begin Friday night after work. There's something positive to experience every single day. Doesn't matter where you live or what you do for a living. Life sets the table. It's up to us to sit down and pick up our fork."

"What about when life kicks you in the ass?"

"That's when you open your eyes even wider to find the good stuff you're missing. Took me a while to figure it out…too long." Dick studied his son's face and smiled. "Today's a new day and look at us. We're together as father and son again."

David hugged his father.

"Any idea where they took Mickey?" Dick asked when the moment passed.

The whole world knew that Mickey had disappeared. Thanks to the tabloids, rumors were circulating about a helicopter escape and an affair with a female rock star. Neither the White House nor any real news media had made an official announcement, including Melanie Dilman. This further stoked the fires of wild speculation.

"Who's they?" asked David.

"Whoever abducted him, "Dick replied.

"Abducted? Maybe he needed some privacy to think things over and went fishing some place remote."

Dick shook his head. "He's a big-time celebrity. Somebody would have spotted him by now and sold the picture to CNN. He's under raps somewhere."

"If you're right, how do we figure out who has him and where?" David asked.

"Start with the basics. Motive, opportunity—who stands to gain by committing the crime?"

"What crime?"

"Last I heard, kidnapping is still a crime."

David looked dumbfounded. "You think he's been

kidnapped?"

"Of course he has," Dick replied.

"Jesus! You think somebody's going to ask for ransom?"

Dick shook his head. "He's too high profile for that. My guess? I think somebody wanted to shut him up…maybe somebody who didn't like what he said on TV."

"The Sphere Cult!"

Dick nodded. "Since it can't be the Europans, the BSA would be my number one guess. By the way, they don't call themselves a cult anymore…sounds too wacko. Benevolent Sphere Association, these days. Same bullshit, new primetime wrapper."

"If you're right, what do we do?" David asked.

"We wait. Whoever it is will be making their demands known sometime soon. Once we know who they are, we have a place to start. There's always a flaw in the bad guy's plans, a thread sticking out of his cloth. We find it, tug on it, and the whole shebang unravels."

David jumped up. "You're leading the investigation."

"Hang on, Davie. I'm just a retired cop living on a pension. I don't have a badge or a gun anymore."

"You won't need any of that stuff."

"Care to explain?"

"Have you met Romeo and Juliet?"

"Not into Shakespeare," Dick replied. "More a Tom Clancy kind of guy."

"That's not what I meant."

Dick smiled. "I know. It's a joke."

David smiled too. "You never joke around."

"The old me didn't."

# Chapter Thirty-nine

Latham stood next to Frankel on the runway. Both wore civilian clothes and carried a duffle bag. Latham wiped the sweat from his brow. "I can't believe you talked me into this," he grumbled.

"What's wrong with an all-expense paid trip to the tropics?" Frankel replied.

"Where in the tropics are we?"

"South America."

"That much I figured out." Latham looked around. Weeds sprouted through a latticework of cracks in the runway and the control tower resembled a World War II watchtower. Except for an old biplane that probably couldn't make it off the ground, the place appeared deserted. "Who lands here besides aero-nobody?"

"People in the pharmaceutical business, the illegal kind." Frankel hefted his duffle bag. "Let's go." He started walking away.

Latham followed. "To our air-conditioned limousine with a wet bar?"

"To our bus." Frankel pointed to a bus covered with graffiti parked at the edge of the runway.

They boarded the crowded bus and managed to wedge themselves onto the bench at the back becoming bookends to two women holding unhappy children. After they sat down, the bus belched a cloud of black smoke and jerked into motion.

"I just can't believe this." The toddler sitting next to him put his hand in Latham's pocket. "Stop that," he growled. The mother glared at him. "Why the hell here?" Latham asked Frankel. "What's wrong with Las Vegas, or Miami?"

"The Peace Corp trained in Madagascar," Frankel replied. "Stop complaining."

They traveled along unpaved roads for more than an hour with the old bus bouncing from one pothole to the next.

"Is this like a BSA fraternity hazing?" Latham asked.

"We're almost there," Frankel said.

"The Boy Scouts of America could have come up with a training site with a little more pizzazz."

"Stop calling them that or you'll be sent home."

Latham leaned his head against the stained bus seat and closed his eyes. "Promise?"

Frankel looked out the window. A stray dog with its ribs poking out ran alongside the bus barking. When the bus accelerated, the dog disappeared in a plume of dust and diesel fumes. "You never told me why you joined the military."

"Following in daddy's footsteps." Latham sounded bitter.

"Your father was in the military?" Frankel already knew Latham's dossier, but he wanted to keep him engaged in dialogue.

"Korea, purple heart, silver star. Ended up a city councilman with his picture in the paper once a month."

"You must be proud of him," Frankel said.

"He's dead."

"Sorry. Sounds like he was an all-around good guy."

Latham looked at his reflection in the window's glass. "I joined the military to get away from him."

"Why?"

"I was the local cut up, never got anything right, always in trouble. My picture was in the paper a few times too...not for anything good."

"Your father would be proud of you now," Frankel said.

"No he wouldn't."

"But you—"

Latham cut him off. "I killed people in the dark for a living."

Frankel's stomach clenched. "Only the bad guys."

"Are you sure? All I ever saw were silhouettes with a red dot in the middle of their forehead, before it exploded." Latham pretended to aim and pull a trigger. "This is my last chance to make it into Santa Claus's good book."

Emma knocked on Mickey's door. He didn't answer, so she pushed it open. "Ready?" she called from the doorway. She wore a riding outfit with long leather boots.

Mickey closed a faded Spanish magazine two years out of date. "Ready for what?"

Emma struck a pose. "Take a guess."

"Mountain climbing?"

"I thought the Europans pumped up your IQ. Horseback riding!"

Mickey cradled his hands behind his head and leaned back on the pillow. "Why would I do that?"

"Does there always need to be a reason? Come on," Emma prompted, "before it's too hot...unless you plan to waste the entire day looking at old magazines you can't even read."

"How do you know I can't read them?"

"I know everything about you," Emma replied.

Mickey started putting on his shoes. "Then you know I don't like horseback riding."

She winked at him. "You'll enjoy this."

Mickey's nerves began to tingle. "What about the local guys in the pharmacy business? Aren't you afraid they're going to kidnap us?"

"The morning patrol swept the area," Emma replied. "Besides, I know you'll protect me."

Two hot and dusty hours later, Latham and Frankel disembarked the bus in the town of Porto Leon, a line of four one-story concrete buildings along an unpaved road. All the buildings' once colorful stucco facades were faded and cracked. An old-fashioned mercury thermometer on the side of one of the buildings read 120 degrees Fahrenheit. The town appeared abandoned.

Latham's shirt clung to him with sweat. "What is this shithole anyhow, a ghost town? The Cult couldn't do better than this?"

"Used to be a mining town, and stop calling it a Cult." Frankel started for one of the structures. "Boot camp, remember?"

Latham followed. "Tell me this is where the resort picks us up."

"Nobody holds boot camp at the Ritz. Let's get out of the heat," Frankel said.

"Finally we agree on something."

Emma led Mickey on horseback under a jungle canopy alive with birdcalls. Mickey estimated they were two miles north of the compound when Emma stopped and pointed upwards into the trees. Mickey reigned in his horse next to hers and peered up into the branches. His senses grew more acute every day. He could see the water molecules coursing through the veins in the leaves and hear the sounds of a beetle walking along a branch. It made him uneasy. "What are you pointing at?" he asked.

A butterfly with brilliant blue wings landed on Emma's outstretched hand. "Over there! A monkey. See its white face?"

Mickey couldn't help smiling. "I do!"

More butterflies landed on Emma's head forming a living garland of iridescent blue. "It's a Capuchin," Emma whispered. "They're endangered." She kicked her horse and started moving down the trail. En masse, the blue veil of butterflies flew away.

"Where are we going?" Mickey called after her.

"You'll see." Emma kicked her horse into a canter.

Mickey caught up with her. "If I try to escape, are you going to shoot me?" He pointed at a shotgun in a scabbard lashed to Emma's saddle.

Emma reigned in her horse and tossed the shotgun to Mickey.

"You could survive a day or two in the jungle, maybe longer because of your enhancements. Eventually something's going to take you out, if not the jungle the drug cartel. At least have lunch with me. I hate eating alone." She kicked her horse into a trot. Mickey twisted the shotgun's barrel into the shape of a pretzel and let it fall to the ground.

It was dark inside the building, the air cool and crisp—and clearly air-conditioned. Suddenly the lights turned on. Latham squinted and looked around. The interior of the building had the appearance of a nightclub that wasn't open for business. Wooden tables and chairs were scattered about a semi-circular floor in front of a raised area, probably a stage.

Frankel took a seat at one of the tables. He gestured to the chair next to him. A pitcher of ice water and two glasses were on the table. He poured Latham a glass.

Latham put the chilled glass next to his cheek savoring the cold, then drained it. Frankel poured him another.

"What is this place?" whispered Latham.

Frankel pointed to a door behind the stage. "You're about to have your interview. Knock 'em dead."

The sound of flowing water grew louder. "Not much farther," Emma said. She kicked her horse again. The trail ended at the bank of a river fed by a waterfall. After a glance at Mickey, Emma rode straight into the waterfall and disappeared through the curtain of water.

"I've come this far," Mickey muttered. He closed his eyes and kicked his horse. After he passed through the surprisingly warm cascading water, he pulled back on the reigns stopping his horse. When he wiped the water from of his eyes, he saw a volcanic grotto cradling a lake of turquoise-colored water surrounded by a sandy beach. Flowering plants in all the shades of the rainbow covered the steep rock walls – tree orchids, hibiscus, and hydrangea, and behind them banana and mango trees laden with fruit. A chorus of birdcalls reverberated around him.

Emma dismounted. Her clothes clung to her body accentuating her figure. "Was it worth the ride?" she called to him.

Mickey jumped off his horse. His whole body felt electric from a sudden chaos of sensations. He found the mixture of perfumes in the air intoxicating, the most exciting one Emma's. He tried not to look at her but found it impossible.

"It's a volcanic caldera," Emma said. "I discovered it from the air. Have you ever skinny-dipped?" She splashed water towards him and laughed.

Mickey's logical mind warred with his senses. His senses won. He removed his clothes and waded into the water.

Emma swam away, then stopped to splash water at him and yell. "Come on, you coward!"

Mickey found the water warm yet cool enough to be refreshing. He swam out to her. When he was close enough, she grabbed him around the neck and brushed her lips against his. The intensity of the sensation stunned Mickey and he pulled away. She grabbed him again and pushed his head under water. He rose to the surface sputtering and she splashed water into his face. "Still want to escape?" She laughed and started swimming back to the beach. Mickey followed her.

After a sumptuous lunch, including fresh mango and bananas, they rested on a blanket and watched the clouds drift by.

"Who are you?" Mickey asked.

"I told you, I'm Emma Rideaux."

"My jazzed up senses have all kinds of interesting features." Mickey rolled over facing her. "I can see fluctuations in your skin temperature. I can even see your skin capillaries open and close."

"You have the eyes of an eagle," Emma said. "Are you going to fly away?"

"I know when you're lying."

Emma chuckled. "My father's got some serious explaining to do if I'm not really Emma Rideaux."

"From the Royal Air Force to the Cult, that's an odd transition," Mickey said.

"It's the Benevolent Sphere Association, not the Cult," she corrected. "I told you, I was a glorified taxi driver."

"How did you end up in the BSA?"

Emma shrugged. "I decided to dabble in altruism."

"I don't think so," Mickey said.

Emma laughed at the sky. "Okay, I was seduced by the paid vacations to this tropical paradise."

Mickey grabbed her wrist. "Now tell me the truth."

Instead of pulling away, Emma put her face close to his. "I'm a spy."

Mickey looked startled. "Who do you work for?"

"Who do you think?"

"No more games," Mickey demanded.

Emma pushed closer, until their noses touched. "Look into my eyes, Mister Lie Detector." She grabbed his hand. "Check my skin temperature, analyze my blood vessels, do whatever the hell you want. Are you ready?"

"Yes."

"I work for Rudnick." Emma got to her feet and plucked an orchid. She put it in her hair. "Jungles and deserts can be transformed into tropical paradises like this. The whole world could be a Garden of Eden if we use the Sphere to finally get it right."

Mickey struggled to collect his thoughts and control his emotions. "Wasn't there a serpent in the Garden?"

Emma sighed. "An interesting metaphor that nobody gets right."

"Meaning?"

She pulled a mango off a vine. "The snake told Adam and Eve that the apple offered knowledge. God said that if they ate from the apple, they'd die." She bit into the mango. "They ate the apple. Did they die?"

"No."

"Then God lied. Why does an omniscient being need to lie?"

"Your point?" Mickey asked.

"If the Sphere is the apple, who do you trust—the gods or the snake?"

"Are you the snake?"

Emma brought her face close to his again, forcing him to look into her eyes. "Maybe I'm Eve."

A woman stepped onto the stage with pursed lips, thick glasses, and hair twisted severely back into a librarian's bun. She glanced at an iPad and looked annoyed. "Major John Latham, serial number AX 3987614, United States Navy, Seal Team 36, very recently retired," she called out.

"Stand up," whispered Frankel.

Latham stood and raised his hand. "That's me."

"Why are you here Mr. Latham?" asked the woman.

"To join the BSA?"

"That's not an answer."

"I need a job?"

"The next bus arrives in three hours. Make yourself comfortable until you depart." She turned to leave.

"Hold on," Latham shouted.

"Why?"

"Let's start over." Latham glanced at Frankel, who nodded.

"We have quite a few candidates to process today. I don't have much time." She sounded impatient.

"This place of yours is a great metaphor for my life," Latham said.

"Why?"

"This place is lost, and so am I."

"Follow me." She disappeared through the door at the back of the stage.

"What happens now?" Latham whispered to Frankel.

"You'll have your interview," Frankel replied. "Keep it up. You're doing fine."

"You really think so?"

Frankel pointed to the door at the back of the stage. "Get going."

Latham smiled. "Okay." When the door closed behind Latham, Frankel put his head in his hands.

# Chapter Forty

David was resting on the couch watching an old western movie on Ernie's television when the screen suddenly changed to the logo of the BSA. He flipped through several channels."Get in here!" he shouted.

Pam, Vickie, and Dick rushed into the room.

David looked up. "Where's Ernie?"

"Hasn't come back yet." Pam pointed at the television screen. "What's that?"

"It's on every channel," David replied.

Dick leaned closer. "It's our first thread."

"What does that mean?" asked Vickie.

Dick put his finger to his lips.

Paul Rudnick appeared on the screen. "Good day, ladies and gentlemen. Forgive me for interrupting your regular programming."

"Boring," Bet said.

"Yeah," Al muttered.

"Would you like to play a game?" asked Juliet.

"How about a race to see how fast we can get back to Europa?" Bet replied.

Al rolled off the bed and got to his feet. "When can we go home?"

"When all educational activities on this planet have been completed," Juliet replied.

"Tell Mom if we leave now, I'll muck the Menagerie for a month." Bet sounded desperate.

"I'll help her." Al sounded equally desperate.

After exchanging a light show with Romeo that rivaled America's Fourth of July fireworks celebration, Juliet went to find Pam.

When she arrived in the living room, she found everyone staring at the television. Juliet glanced at the screen, then spoke to Pam. "Mistress, I would like to discuss the children with you."

"Not now!" Pam snapped. She point at the television.

"Wondrous things have happened on our planet since the arrival of the Sphere," Rudnick continued. "Now it's time to take the next step." He paused. "At eight o'clock this evening Pacific Standard Time, I will return for an important announcement, one that will impact all our lives. Please join me." The television screen changed to a smiling woman halfway through a Colgate toothpaste commercial.

"I was right. The BSA has him," Dick said.

David frowned. "Rudnick didn't mention Mickey's name."

"They have him." Dick said with certainty.

Vickie brought her hands to her mouth. "Oh my God!"

"Why would they kidnap him?" Pam asked. "Maybe it's something else."

"You heard what Mickey said about the Sphere on international TV," Dick replied. "Without the Sphere, the Cult's out of business. To Rudnick and his cronies, Mickey is public enemy number one."

"We have to rescue him!" Vickie cried.

David put his hand on Vickie's shoulder. "First we have to figure out where he is."

"We'll get another chance at eight o'clock," Dick said. "That gives us ninety minutes to prepare."

David turned to Juliet. "If you tap into the TV signal, can you determine where it originates?"

"Not if it is passed through the customary nodes, such as cables and satellites," Juliet replied.

Dick thought for a moment. "There might be a clue in the broadcast itself. We need to record it with the highest possible resolution and pick it apart."

"Juliet," Pam said. "At eight o'clock this evening the

Benevolent Sphere Association is making a TV broadcast. I want you to record it on all wavelengths for analysis."

"Maybe the Sphere can help us," David suggested.

Vickie held up her palm. "I tried sending a message to Ernie, but he doesn't answer."

"Mistress, may I talk to you about the children?" Juliet asked.

"Later," Pam said. "First we have to find Mickey."

General Westlock drummed his fingers on the desk. "Can any of you figure out where that broadcast came from?"

None of his analysts said a word.

"Thought so. It was all over the internet too," the general muttered. "Those fuckers are good. Took over the entire bandwidth of the worldwide communications grid for ninety seconds. Not even the Chinese can do that."

"What do we do now?" asked one of the analysts.

"Where's that flying saucer?" the general demanded.

"Parked at the Bob Hope airport in Burbank."

"I want twenty-four seven surveillance on that UFO. Rotate both Auroras. The damn thing's leading us to Mickey."

"How do you know?"

"Just do it," snarled the general. He wouldn't admit it, but he missed Latham.

# Chapter Forty-one

Emma escorted Mickey to the private dining room. "Do sit down," said Rudnick. They took their seats. "Wine?" He held up a bottle.

"You're just a flunky around here," Mickey said. "When do I get to meet the guy who's really in charge, Stevens, or whatever the hell his name is?"

Emma glanced at Rudnick.

"After dinner," Rudnick replied. He seemed unfazed by Mickey's remark. "We're having a delightful lamb dish tonight."

"Sacrificial?" Mickey asked.

Rudnick emptied his glass of wine. "Touché."

"I'm ready to go home," Mickey said.

"You haven't heard our offer."

"Be the president of the BSA…not interested."

Rudnick leaned forward. "What if I up the ante?"

"Don't waste your time."

"I can be quite persuasive."

Mickey stood. "This has been a pleasure." He glanced at Emma, but she looked away. "But I'm ready to leave."

Rudnick smiled balefully at Mickey. "If you don't accept our proposal, I'll put you on trial in front of the entire world."

"For what?" Mickey scoffed.

"I'll think of something."

The woman with a librarian's bun and thick glasses led Latham to a small room with nothing but a chair and blank walls. She left him alone and locked the door.

Hours dragged by. Latham checked his watch. "I did this for a living," he yelled. "It's going to take more than this to break me. I can even beat water-boarding."

The door opened and the librarian reappeared. "I'll show you to your room now," she said.

"What if I want to go home?" Latham asked.

"You can leave any time you want."

Latham followed her down the corridor to another door. She unlocked it with an electronic card key and the door swung open revealing a tunnel hewn from solid rock. Naked light bulbs snaked along the ceiling illuminating the rough granite walls. Latham followed her inside. "The guy I came with said there used to be a mine here. Is this one of the tunnels?" he asked.

"Correct."

Latham ran his hand along the wall. Irregular patches of the rock glittered in the artificial light. "Is this gold?" he asked.

"Titanium."

"Why all this cloak and dagger?"

"All your questions will be answered, provided you're found acceptable." She began walking more briskly, separating herself from him.

Latham passed through another locked door at the end of the granite tunnel, this time entering a carpeted corridor with white plastered walls, artwork, and numbered doors along either side. The woman handed him an electronic key and pointed at one of the doors. "You'll find refreshments in your room and clean clothes in the closet. I'll return in three hours to begin your counseling."

"Counseling? What about boot camp?" Latham asked.

"You haven't qualified yet. If you don't know who you are, neither can we."

"I know who I am," Latham said.

She took off her glasses. "You'll know much better through introspection assisted by psychoanalytical techniques and E-meter sessions."

"An E-meter? Is that like a lie detector? Don't waste your time."

Latham showered and changed into fresh clothes. When she

returned an hour later, he was reclining on the bed with a half-filled glass in his hand.

"It's time," she said.

Latham put his drink down on the nightstand. "For what?"

"To begin your counseling."

They went to a lavishly appointed office at the end of the corridor. The woman Latham thought of as the Librarian pointed to an overstuffed armchair across from a desk. Latham sat in it and examined both of the chair's arms. "I don't see a slot."

"A slot? For what?" she asked.

"Where you put the quarters to get a massage."

She pushed a button on the side of the chair and it reclined. "I'm going to put some electrodes on your arms and legs."

"Electrocution won't work on me either."

"They're to measure your galvanic skin response." She applied adhesive pads with wires trailing from them to an electronic instrument on her desk. When she finished, she sat behind the desk and adjusted several of the instrument's dials.

"Why are you doing this?" Latham asked.

"I already told you."

"Let's cut to the chase," Latham suggested. "Not every recruit goes through all this, so why me?"

"We have a very special job in mind for you, Mr. Latham. My job is to make sure you have what it takes, which starts by making sure you're honest and truthful."

"I could tell you I'm Santa Claus and that box on your desk wouldn't know the difference."

"It's not a lie detector. It helps me guide you through your unconscious by registering your mental energy."

"I get it. You're going to try to brainwash me." He stretched and yawned. "Good luck."

"I'm not going to do anything except ask you questions. The meter guides me in the process."

"Are you a shrink?"

"We call ourselves auditors. Shall we begin?"

The Librarian asked Latham endless questions, starting with his childhood. After three hours, she finally reached his adult years.

"I'm getting a headache," Latham said. "Are we done yet?"

"Tell me about General Westlock."

"That's classified."

"Not what he does, about the man, how he treats you." She studied the dials on her instrument. "Tell me how he makes you feel."

Latham's face reddened and the dials on the instrument jumped. "Soldiers aren't allowed to have feelings…they get in the way."

"You have the ability to completely subordinate your feelings, to do whatever you're told without questioning it?"

"It's called following orders."

"Now tell me about your father."

Latham ripped the electrodes off his arms. "Enough of this." He got to his feet. "If you don't want me in your club, send me home."

She poured two glasses from a crystal decanter on the desk and reached one to him. "Congratulations."

He took the glass. "I'm in?"

She nodded. "I think you're the right man for the job we have in mind." She held up her glass to the light. "Courvoisier L'Esprit. They tell me it's five thousand dollars a bottle." She smiled for the first time. "A toast to new opportunities." She brought the glass to her lips, but didn't drink. "Cheers."

Latham took a sip. She put down her glass and watched him.

Latham's head began to spin. "Damn! Oldest trick in the book and I fell for it." He tried to remain upright, but his muscles refused to obey.

"Welcome to the BSA," she said.

Latham tumbled forward onto the floor.

She pressed a button on her desk activating an intercom. "Take him to the lab."

Rudnick patted his lips with his napkin and stood. "Shall we go?"

"Where?" Mickey asked.

"To the meeting you requested."

Mickey stood and put his hand on the back of Emma's chair.

"Miss Rideaux won't be joining us," Rudnick said.

Emma glanced at Mickey, but she kept her expression unreadable. He could hear her heart hammering in her chest.

Rudnick led Mickey across the compound to one of the outbuildings.

"Why would a so-called benevolent organization set up shop in the jungle unless you're hiding something, or is it someone?" Mickey asked.

"You'll have your answers soon enough." Rudnick used a touchpad to summon an elevator. Mickey followed him inside.

The elevator descended for more than a minute. When it stopped, the door opened onto a well-lit corridor with a white-tiled floor and numbered doorways lining both sides. It reminded Mickey of a hospital.

"What happens down here?" Mickey asked.

"If you follow me, I'll show you," Rudnick replied. He led Mickey down the corridor and stopped in front of a glass window. "Take a look," Rudnick said.

Mickey looked through the glass and saw a chemistry lab filled with vats, a myriad of glassware and tubing, electronic equipment of various sorts, and long counters with sinks. "Let me guess, the Cult is in the drug business too," he said.

"We're not making drugs, we're making nannites, those wondrous machines you having swimming around in your blood." Rudnick swiped a card opening the door to the laboratory. "You have the honor of witnessing their first use." He escorted Mickey to a wall of glass dividing the back half of the laboratory. Mickey looked through and saw Latham unconscious and strapped to a chair with an IV in his arm. The IV's tubing connected to a glass bottle filled with amber-colored liquid that appeared to be boiling without a flame. Sensors connected to a bay of electronic equipment covered Latham's torso and forehead.

Mickey thought Latham looked familiar. "Who is that, and what are you doing to him?"

"He's about to receive the first batch of nannites made on Earth," Rudnick replied. "His identity is no longer important."

"If you're not a Europan, where did you get the nannites?"

"We made them." Rudnick pointed at Latham. "Watch."

A white-coated technician released a valve and the amber liquid flowed into Latham's arm. This continued until all the liquid in the IV bottle passed into Latham's body. After a minute, Latham twitched and his eyes popped open. He looked from side to side and a smile creased his lips.

"Excellent," Rudnick said. "Time to go." Two guards with automatic weapons appeared at Mickey's side.

After descending in the elevator again, Rudnick ushered Mickey into a room set up like a television studio and pointed to a chair. "Sit here, please." As soon as Mickey sat down, a bank of spotlights turned on almost blinding him.

"You've been in front of the cameras before," Rudnick said. Mickey had trouble seeing him through the glare. "The last time the whole world was watching, a truly mesmerizing performance. This is your encore."

Mickey shielded his eyes. "What's going on?"

"You requested a meeting with our leader," Rudnick replied. "This is it." He spun Mickey's chair around facing the glass partition of a control room at the back of the studio.

"Look who's here," said a voice booming from speakers positioned around the studio.

Mickey squinted into the glare and recognized the man he knew as Officer Stevens. "First a police officer, and now Dr. Frankenstein. You lured me here. Now tell me why?"

"As I told you when we met in that insect-infested swamp you're so nostalgic about, we have common interests," Stevens replied. "Neither of us trust the silver robots and their sweet little Sphere."

"If that's how you really feel, how come you run the Benevolent Sphere Association?"

"Humans are predictably stupid and lazy. You'll worship the Sphere, or anything else that allows you to stop thinking for yourselves."

"By controlling the Cult, you control us," Mickey said.

"As you people say, *bingo*."

"You're not human," Mickey said.

"Thanks for the compliment."

"What are you?"

"Mankind's savior. You people are always seeking one."

Mickey looked around the studio memorizing everything. "This isn't my idea of a friendly discussion."

"Every club has its initiation."

Mickey used his enhanced vision to study Stevens through the glass. He saw skin capillaries coursing with blood and detected some kind of heartbeat. Stevens seemed to be flesh and blood, and definitely not Europan. "If you're not working with the Europans, where did the nannites come from?" Mickey asked.

"Are you ready to join our cause?"

Mickey fought to maintain his self-control and not tear the room apart. "What if I'm not buying any of this?"

Stevens laughed. "Ironic, isn't it? Our famous Mickey is faced with another choice."

"I don't know who or what you are," Mickey said, "but it doesn't sound like you're any better than the Europans."

Stevens clapped his hands together. "You humans are priceless!" He leaned closer to the glass. "Here's a piece of knowledge better than anything you can glean from the Sphere. There's only two kinds of beings in this universe, winners and losers. I'm offering you the chance to be a winner. If you're smart, you'll take it."

"Screw you. That's my answer."

The spotlights went out and the room lights came on. Mickey looked towards the control room. It was empty.

"I told you what would happen if you refused our generous offer," Rudnick said somberly.

"You said you'd put me on trial."

"You haven't asked what the sentence will be if you're found guilty."

"Fifty lashes?"

Rudnick smiled. "Death."

# Chapter Forty-two

They huddled in front of Ernie's television. Ernie still hadn't come home. Juliet positioned herself behind the couch directly in front of the screen. A long silver tentacle extended from her torso to the back of the television.

At precisely 8:00 pm, the image of the CNN commentator was replaced by the logo of the BSA. "Good evening," said Paul Rudnick. He was seated at a desk with the BSA's banner behind him. Translations in seven languages scrolled across the bottom of the screen. "As most everyone is aware, two weeks ago on the occasion of the triumphant return of David and Pam to Earth, Mickey, the boy who passed the Test, spoke irrationally and then carried out an act of self-mutilation. These are signs of acute psychosis. Regrettably, tonight I must tell you that there's more to this story."

"What?" Vickie shouted. Pam gripped her hand.

"Here it comes," said Dick.

"The Benevolent Sphere Association has uncovered a vile plot to steal the Sphere and keep its secrets for the exclusive use of a privileged few, denying the rest of humanity all its wonders." He held up his hand. "Fear not! The BSA has foiled this diabolical plot and arrested its ringleader." A picture of Mickey glaring back at the camera appeared on the screen.

Vickie jumped to her feet. "No!" she shrieked.

Dick glanced at David.

"To make sure this can never happen again, the boy known to all as Mickey will be put on trial before the world, and the entirety of his heinous plot will be exposed. You will all be his jurors as you'll be able to cast your votes on Facebook." Rudnick paused for effect. Vickie slumped on the couch and sobbed. "Rest assured that justice will be swift and his accomplices will be found and severely dealt with. The cleansing will begin in one week's time. Goodnight." The shocked faced of the CNN commentator reappeared on the television screen.

"We have one week," Dick announced. He pointed at Juliet. "What's that Europan's name? I can't tell them apart."

"This one's Juliet," said Pam, sounding annoyed.

"Juliet, I need you to analyze the recording," Dick said.

"Specify which parameters," Juliet replied.

"Filter out Rudnick's voice and enhance background noises. Compile possible sources of every recorded sound."

Hissing and wailing sounds filled the room. "I identify air processing machinery, an electric motor…" Juliet began.

"Stop," Dick interrupted. "Isolate the sound from the motor." Everyone listened more intently.

"That sounds like an elevator," David said.

"A building with air conditioning and an elevator. That narrows it down," scoffed Vickie.

"Continue," said Dick.

They began to hear low-pitched rumbling sounds.

"Those are heartbeats!" Pam exclaimed. "Juliet, are those human heartbeats?"

"That is correct, from three individuals."

Dick nodded. "At least one other person was there besides Rudnick and Mickey. Let's focus on the picture. Juliet, return to the opening image of Rudnick and freeze it." Juliet complied.

"There's a vase with flowers on the desk," said Pam. "Identify the species of flower."

"On Earth, they are known as Hydrangea."

"Magnify."

"What a minute! There!" Pam ran to the screen and pointed at one of the flowers. "There's a bug on one of the leaves. Identify."

"In the Earth database, it is designated as a Cerambycidae."

"Where is that insect most commonly found?" Pam asked excitedly.

"The tropical rain forest of Nicaragua."

"Now we're getting somewhere," David said.

"Nicaragua's a big place!" Vickie said.

"I can add one additional fact," said Juliet.

"Tell us!" Vickie shouted.

"There is no need to project your voice beyond seventy decibels," Juliet said. "My auditory processes are functioning nominally."

"Juliet, answer the question!" David was too excited to drop below eighty-five decibels.

"Spectral analysis of the air surrounding the human named Rudnick reveals traces of Titanium oxide."

"Access the Earth geochemical data base," said David, trying to contain his excitement. "Are there any titanium deposits in Nicaragua?"

"In an area designated as the Town of Porta Leon," Juliet replied.

Dick slapped his knee. "Access Google Earth and show us Porta Leon, Nicaragua on the TV screen."

The television screen changed to Google Earth and then showed the four buildings of Porta Leon.

"Enlarge," said Dick, leaning forward for a better look. Juliet zoomed in.

"Looks like a ghost town," Pam said. "Four buildings and a dirt road."

"No cars, no people, not even a stray cat," added David.

"Remember the elevator? They could be holding him underground, maybe in a mine," said Dick. "Juliet, can you scan underground?"

"Not with Earth's primitive optical methods."

"What about from the saucer?" asked David.

"Europan scanners are inefficient in the presence of titanium oxide," replied Juliet.

"The ruins on Mars were in an area with titanium deposits," David muttered.

"What's that got to do with anything?" asked Pam.

"Nothing," David replied too quickly.

"We know they took Mickey by helicopter. Scan the vicinity for anything that looks like a landing strip," said Dick.

The images on the screen changed too quickly for the human brain to process. When the picture refocused, they could see a rectangular landing site cut into the jungle.

"No helicopter," said Dick. "Might come and go like a shuttle."

"I detect a primitive flying machine covered by woven fibers painted to resemble jungle foliage," Juliet said. The image shifted to a patch of jungle.

"I don't see anything," said Vickie.

"Increase scan sensitivity for metal," said Pam.

The blurred outline of a helicopter appeared.

"A camouflaged helicopter," Dick said. "Search for nearby structures."

The image shifted again and a large rectangular compound appeared.

"Focus down."

The picture zoomed in.

David leaned forward. "Holy guacamole! That looks like a fortress."

"Enlarge the black dots on the walls. I have a feeling," said Dick.

The picture zoomed down to a man carrying a rifle.

"How many people are visible?" Dick asked.

"Forty-two," replied Juliet.

"How many are carrying weapons?"

"All the humans are carrying some form of projectile weaponry," replied Juliet. "Five humans are accompanied by a Canis familis."

"Guard dogs," said Pam.

Dick shook his head. "It would take an army to attack that

place."

"Or two Europans in a flying saucer," said David.

"One Europan is more than enough," Pam added.

Later that night, they sat around the kitchen table, flanked by Romeo and Juliet, studying photographs and diagrams of the Cult's headquarters in Nicaragua.

Vickie was too nervous to sit and instead paced around the room wringing her hands. "Where the hell is Ernie?"

"He'll turn up," David replied.

Dick tapped a calendar covered with handwritten notes. "We have seven days to mount a rescue."

David scribbled on a yellow pad. "Plenty of time, then."

"Where'd you park it?" Pam said, handing him a glass of lemonade.

David took a sip and wrinkled his nose. "Hard to believe, but it tastes better on Europa… I parked it near the Skunk Works."

Vickie stopped pacing and stared at him. "You parked the saucer at a zoo?"

He turned in his chair to face her. "Not a zoo. Kelly Johnson? The U-2 spy plane, the SR-71? Any of that ring a bell?"

Both women stared back at him.

"Guess not. Burbank Airport used to be Lockheed Aircraft Company. A secret division of Lockheed nicknamed the Skunk Works made airplanes there for the CIA. Sometimes they hid them in a hanger at the end of the runway. Nobody knows about it."

"How come you do?" Pam asked.

"Mick and I found it while we were hiding from Jake."

"What's your plan for getting into the that fortress without getting us killed?" Dick asked.

David picked up a schematic of the Cult's headquarters. "Getting in is the easy part. I'm concerned about the titanium in the mine if Mickey's held underground. The Europans won't be able to scan through it."

Pam took the picture from him, glanced at it, and put it back on the table. "Can we come up with a map of the mine? Might narrow down the search."

David looked up at Juliet. "Access all mining records for Nicaragua. Find a schematic of the mine at Porta Leon and beam it on the wall so we can see it."

Juliet projected a pattern of lines on the wall that looked like a spider web.

Dick blew out his breath. "That's a lot of ground to cover. If Mickey's down there, it could take a while to locate him."

"We need to go now," Vickie said anxiously.

"Hang on," said Dick. "How long will it take us to get there?"

David shrugged. "Ten minutes."

"Then we leave at the beginning of the next broadcast," said Dick.

"Are you cutting it a little close?" David asked.

"The bad guys will be occupied airing their show. That gives us the element of surprise."

"We'll need to bring the saucer back the day before so we can pack," said Pam.

"They'll know we're up to something when the saucer shows up," David cautioned.

"We'll announce that we've been called back to Europa. I'll come up with some kind of excuse, like the ice is melting."

"Europa's ice shelf will not melt until the sun enters its red giant stage five billion years from now," said Juliet.

"We know that," Pam said.

"But you said..." Juliet began.

"It's called *deception*."

Romeo and Juliet exchanged colored lights.

"How do we let people know we're leaving?" David asked.

"Easy," Vickie replied. "I'll tell my mother, and Melanie Dilman will have a news crew here in less than an hour."

# Chapter Forty-three

Al and Bet slipped out the front door.

"Must be something to do around here," Bet grumbled.

*"We could play a trick on one of the Secret Service guys,"* Al sent to her.

"Here comes a couple of natives," Bet said out loud. "Let's have some fun with them." Two kids on bikes stopped in front of the house, a boy and a girl. The twins moved to the perimeter of the force field facing them.

The two kids got off their bikes and approached the barrier. The Secret Service detail made no move to intervene.

"Hi," said the girl. She was about the same height as Bet with long brown braids and freckles. "My name's Brie."

Bet smirked. "You're named after cheese?"

Brie smiled. "Heard that one before. Brie is short for Breanna."

"Hi," Al said.

Brie's brother Josh reached out and touched the force field. The blue haze dented like a soap bubble, then pushed back his hand. Josh was a year older than his sister, and taller. "You guys are the aliens," he said. "We saw you on TV."

Looking disgusted, Bet turned and started walking back towards the house. Al remained near the force field.

"Want to go riding?" Brie asked Al.

"On what?" Al replied.

Brie hopped off her bike. "On this, silly." She giggled. "I don't see any horses."

Al caught himself smiling back at her. He pointed at her bicycle. "We don't have any of those machines."

"They're called bicycles," Brie said.

Josh got back on his. "Let's go," he said to his sister.

"Want to ride mine?" asked Brie. Her smile seemed wider

than before.

Al looked startled. "Can I?"

*"What are you doing?"* Bet sent from the porch.

Al ignored his sister and stepped through the force field. Three Secret Service agents came running.

Brie got off her bike and held onto the handlebars. "Ever rode one of these?"

Josh stayed on his bike watching. With a scowl, Bet returned to the force field's perimeter but remained inside.

"How difficult could it be?" Al said. "It's a simple machine. You sit on it and push the levers with your feet." He grabbed the handlebars and pushed Brie away.

"Okay." Brie didn't sound sure.

Al sat on the seat, pushed down on one of the pedals, and fell in a heap on the asphalt with the bike on top of him. The Secret Service agents came rushing over, but Al motioned them away.

"Dork," Josh said, shaking his head.

Bet came through the force field and stood over her brother. "You're embarrassing yourself in front of the primitives."

"Who you calling a primitive?" Josh challenged.

Bet appraised Josh with a gleam in her eye. This meant she was about to do something unpleasant. Before she could, Juliet came gliding down the steps of the house and emitted her signature rusty hinge sound. Bet froze.

"Want me to show you?" offered Brie, looking down at Al sprawled on the ground.

Al picked himself up. "Yeah." While Brie held onto the handlebars, Al remounted the bike. "What do I do?" he asked.

Juliet radioed to the Secret Service detail to stand back.

"Ask for help instead of acting like a know-it-all," Brie replied.

Al glanced at his sister whose response was to keep scowling. "I can do that," he said.

Brie started pushing the bicycle while running alongside. "Start pedaling!" she shouted. The bike picked up speed, Brie let go, and Al kept pedaling. "Whooeee!" Al shouted. He made a wide turn in the middle of the street. When he neared Brie again, he jumped off and the bike clattered to the pavement. "That was *really* fun!" Al exclaimed. "Bet, you have to try this!" he shouted.

Bet took a step forward, then looked at Josh and stopped. Josh stared back at her with his hands folded across his chest.

Brie glared at her brother. "Help her," she demanded.

Josh didn't move.

"Josh!" Brie yelled. "Where's your manners?"

Josh frowned and got off his bike. "She called us primitives."

Romeo had been watching from the porch. He joined Juliet. "An unpredictable turn of events," he remarked.

"Typical of this world," Juliet replied. They watched Bet mount the bicycle with Josh's help.

"Should we return the children to the house?" Romeo asked.

"Mistress Pam requested that we provide an educational experience for the twins," said Juliet. "This activity may continue."

"The appendage-powered devices are mechanically primitive," Romeo commented. "I will assist by fabricating machines with anti-gravity pads and..."

Juliet's lights flashed. "No. To continue this activity, Al and Bet require exact replicas of the primitive Earth machines."

"Why?" asked Romeo.

"To provide the most efficient educational experience," Juliet replied.

"Explain," said Romeo.

"The children must mature."

"Their rate of growth exceeds that of similar hominids in the database," Romeo said. "Brain volume has increased six percent in the last 100 cycles."

"Physical development is insufficient. Recall that Earth's hominids were the only species to pass the Test," said Juliet. "They alone have the behavioral trait of benevolence. The twins have portions of the same DNA, but have not demonstrated this trait. This is cause for concern." Lights flashed across Juliet's face. "We must assist them to express all the positive elements of their organic heredity. We must help them to be human."

"That is the function of their parents," said Romeo.

Juliet's face remained a uniform slate blue. "What function do we provide?"

"We are their teachers," replied Romeo.

Both Europans watched as the twins rode bikes around the street. Bet was smiling now. Romeo moved closer and wrapped a tentacle around Juliet's torso.

The next day, the kids discovered two shiny new bicycles on the porch.

# Chapter Forty-four

Frankel sat at a table in the garden outside the compound's private dining room with a bottle of whiskey in front of him and an empty glass in his hand. He removed his Cult key ring from his pocket and placed it on the table. After staring at it for a moment, he flicked it to the ground.

Emma jogged by in a pair of shorts and a T-shirt. She spotted Frankel and angled over. "You're the new man…Frankel, isn't it?"

Frankel didn't make eye contact. "Nice talking to you."

"I haven't said anything yet." Emma noticed his empty drink glass. "Is the alcohol clouding your brain, or are you naturally a boor?"

Frankel tipped his empty glass to his lips. "Not a boor yet, but I'm working on it." He refilled his glass.

Emma pointed at an empty chair. "May I?"

Frankel held up the nearly empty bottle. "BYOB."'

"Conversation will suffice," she replied.

Frankel took a healthy swig and stared blankly ahead.

"What do you do?" Emma asked.

"I used to be a soldier…I killed people for a living."

"I meant now, in the BSA." Emma studied his face.

Frankly guffawed. "I'm a recruiter."

"Have you been assigned a territory yet?" Emma asked.

Frankel sipped his drink. "Nope."

"You should improve your people skills before you attempt to recruit anybody."

Frankel flashed on Latham. "Out for a morning jog around the prison yard?"

Emma poked his key ring on the tile floor with her foot. "Everything's locked down because of the trial. Totally boring around here now."

Frankel pointed at a guard walking by with his dog. "This isn't exactly a resort."

"True, but a pleasant conversation with an English-speaking *gentleman* would help pass the time." Emma crossed her legs causing her shorts to hike up. She made no move to tug them down.

Frankel looked at her and smirked. "Is this how I get my next BSA merit badge?"

"What's that supposed to mean?"

"You try to seduce me to test my loyalty."

Emma grimaced. "The applicant screening process needs reassessment." She stood up to leave.

"You're involved with the trial," Frankel said.

Emma glanced around. "What makes you say that?"

"I've seen you with Mickey."

"Our paths have crossed," Emma said.

Frankel raised his glass in salute. "Off with his head."

Emma sat down again. "He's guilty of a crime against humanity. The knowledge of the Sphere should belong to everyone." She studied Frankel's face. "You believe that, don't you?"

"Rah rah." Frankel took a swig and belched.

Emma lowered her voice. "You need to be careful what you say around here, Mr. Frankel."

"I don't recall giving you my name."

"You're drunk. You can't remember anything."

"Not drunk yet, but I'm working on it." Frankel drained his glass.

Emma whispered, "You're not gung ho, as you Americans say about the BSA, are you?"

Frankel made no attempt to keep his voice down. "Didn't see anything about guard dogs and trials in the membership packet."

"Be careful!" Emma hissed.

Frankel sneered. "You mean our Benevolent Sphere

Association ain't so benevolent?"

Emma's eyes darted around. "Why are you here?"

Suddenly Frankel seemed alert and in control. "Why are you?"

Emma nodded. "Well played."

Frankel winked at her as she walked away. Then he polished off the last of his whiskey.

# Chapter Forty-five

They had been up all night planning. Maps and pages of notes covered the kitchen table. David got up from his chair and stretched. He glanced at his dad. "There's something I need to do before we go," David said. Dick stopped scribbling notes on a yellow pad. He knew what his son had in mind. "Maybe now's not a good time, Davie. We need to stay focused. We only have a few days before we fly to Nicaragua."

Pam studied David's face, reading his mind the way a wife can. "Want me to go with you, honey?"

"Stay with the twins. I have to do this by myself."

Vickie stood. "I'm going with you, whether you like it or not."

David looked puzzled. "Why?"

"If I don't do something to keep my mind off what's happening to Mickey, I'm going to lose it—big time! Besides, I want to meet that cop Stevens."

"Why?" David repeated.

"I'll know after I talk to him," Vickie replied. "Give me ten minutes to change."

Pam followed her friend into the bedroom. "What's going on?" she asked.

Vickie rummaged through her suitcase. "I need to get out of this house and do something, that's what's going on."

"You can't lie to me, Vic," Pam said. "I know you better than you know yourself. Tell me the truth."

"I tried talking to you about Stevens at the mall. You called all his comings and goings that always end up near one of us a big fat coincidence." Vickie found the outfit she was looking for and started changing clothes. "Let him look me in the eye and convince me they're all a coincidence, 'cause I'm not buying it. Besides, David needs moral support."

"I offered to go with him," Pam said.

Vickie finished zipping up her skirt. "He doesn't want you to see him if he loses it."

"I'm his wife."

"He's a man. He doesn't want his wife to see him cry."

"That's ridiculous."

"When it comes to emotions, men are as dumb as rocks." Vickie grabbed her purse and headed for the door.

The car stopped in front of a house in the Burbank hills, a two-story ranch style with a manicured lawn. Vickie and David got out. Vickie had changed into a designer suit with gloves and a scarf around her neck. David remained in his jeans and a UCLA sweatshirt. "Aren't you a little overdressed?" he asked Vickie.

"I'm trying to make a good impression." Vickie noticed how nervous David was. "You've talked to your mother on the phone, haven't you?"

David shook his head no.

"Why not?"

He didn't answer.

"Did she try to call you?" Vickie asked.

"We haven't had any contact in five years."

Vickie gripped his arm. "Remember Vickie's famous saying."

David forced a smile. "Which one?"

"No life sentences in families. I still talk to my mother, don't I?"

The door opened and Captain Stevens stood in the doorway. He was dressed in casual attired with a western flare, including cowboy boots and a large silver belt buckle. "Been expecting you," he said affably. "Come on in."

They walked into the living room and David looked around. "Where's my mother?" he asked with a quiver in his voice.

"She'll be along in a minute," Stevens replied. He motioned to the couch and they sat down. "Can I offer you two anything?"

"An explanation would be nice," Vickie replied.

David's face paled.

"You're Victoria, Mickey's friend," Stevens said. "Sorry to hear about his tussle with the BSA. This must be a difficult time for you."

"Let's cut to the chase," Vickie said. "You know why we're here."

Stevens smiled. "Your reputation precedes you, young lady." He turned to David. "This has been a difficult time for your mother, David."

"Care to explain why you're in the middle of it?" Vickie interrupted.

"I don't think that's your concern," Stevens replied icily.

"Stop it!" David exclaimed.

"Davie?" said a voice from the top of the stairs.

David jumped up from the couch and took two steps towards his mother.

Linda descended the stairs until they were only a few steps apart. To David, the distance between them never seemed greater. Stevens left the couch and moved between them.

"Shouldn't they be alone?" Vickie said.

"Of course." Stevens kissed Linda's hand. "I'll take Miss Victoria out on the patio."

Vickie followed Stevens outside. They took seats under an umbrella beside a swimming pool sparkling in the afternoon sun. A waterfall added the peaceful sound of falling water amidst a garden of azaleas, marigolds, zinnias, and geraniums.

Vickie was the first to speak. "Odd how Linda ends up at your house."

"Why?" Stevens replied with a trace of a smile. "Her marriage to Dick had been on the rocks for several years. We hit it off."

Vickie stared into Steven's eyes. "I know about Pam."

Stevens returned her stare without changing expression. "Know what?"

"You rescued her twenty years ago. Quite a coincidence—you

being around both David and Pam."

"I saw your husband for the first time on the White House lawn," Stevens replied.

"But you have his mother living under your roof."

"As you said, just a coincidence," Stevens said matter-of-factly.

"Here's another one. You left Malibu to work in Burbank, the city where David's brother was shot. Malibu not exciting enough for you?"

"Are you going to read me my rights before continuing this interrogation?"

"I couldn't care less about you. It's David who needs answers." Vickie removed her compact from her purse and reapplied her lipstick. She hadn't removed her gloves.

"David can ask me anything he wants," Stevens replied, maintaining his composure.

Vickie's compact slipped from her hand and clattered to the concrete deck near Steven's foot. She glanced at Stevens. He picked it up and handed it back to her. "Thank you," she said. She opened her purse on her lap where Stevens couldn't see and placed the compact inside a plastic bag she had hidden inside. Being careful to touch only the compact's outer rim with her gloved hands, she quickly sealed the bag and closed her purse.

David and Linda sat opposite each other. David's heart raced faster than his nannites could control. Linda seemed unnaturally calm, almost serene.

"You're looking well," Linda said.

David looked down at his hands. "Thanks." He fought back tears. "What happened to our family?"

Linda had a faraway look in her eyes. "Just before you left, your father and I had another fight, a bad one, and I started drinking. I passed out and hit my head. I don't remember much after that, except waking up in the hospital with Cap holding my hand." She looked towards the patio. "After that, you left for Europa and Jake went to jail."

"I called you. How come you never answered?"

"You have to forgive me for that, Davie. Your father and I married when I was eighteen years old. I went from my father's house to Dick's house without first growing up. I needed time by myself to finally become an adult."

"Five years?"

"I'm sorry," Linda replied.

They sat in awkward silence for a moment.

"So you and *Cap*"—David struggled with the name—"are together now?"

"Does that disturb you?" Linda asked.

"I hoped after I got back...Dad and I've been talking." The words poured out of David. "He's different. We're getting along fine, and—"

"I'm glad for both of you," Linda said.

"He said you guys speak once in a while."

For the first time, Linda's icy composure seemed to crack. "Not for a while. It's better that way." She changed the subject. "Cap says that Jake's doing well."

"Have you spoken to him?" David's words came out tinged with jealously.

"Not yet," Linda replied.

Vickie and Stevens reentered the room. Vickie's heart sank when she saw the look on David's face. Linda stood. Stevens moved to her side and took her hand. "Everyone still has healing to do. These things take time," She said. "Your mother needs to rest now, David. We'll all get together again soon." He led Linda to the stairs. She walked up without looking back.

When they were back in the car, Vickie took David's hand. "There'll be another time. I promise you."

"After we rescue Mickey, Pam and I are leaving for Europa. I don't know when we'll be back."

Vickie directed the car back to David's house.

"I don't get it," David said when the car started in motion.

"Don't get what?" Vickie asked.

"My mom seems so different…like it's not even her." David put his cheek to the window and closed his eyes.

"Maybe she's on meds," Vickie said.

"She said she can't remember what happened after she hit her head."

"She had a concussion. That explains it." Vickie paused for a moment, choosing her next words carefully. "This whole thing with Stevens doesn't add up. Why is he always around? It's like he's tracking us."

"What do you mean?" David asked.

Here goes, Vickie thought to herself. "Did you ever talk to Pam about her accident?"

"What's that got to do with anything?" David asked.

"Did you?" Vickie persisted.

"Once, but she said she didn't want to talk about it. Too painful. I never brought it up again. Why?"

"Did you know that Phyllis was in the car that killed Pam's parents?"

David looked surprised. "No."

"Stevens was there that night and pulled Pam out of the wreck. He was there the day your brother got shot too."

David was too stunned to reply.

"Now your mother's living with him. Am I the only one who thinks it's all too fucking weird?"

David's mind started racing, not about Stevens, about Pam.

"I did some research on Pam's accident," Vickie continued. "They never found her parents' bodies. Did you know that?"

"Pam never talks about it."

"The rainstorm that night was pretty bizarre. According to the Weather Service records, it hovered directly over Malibu, slamming it with lightening and then, *poof*, it was gone."

David covered his face with his hands.

"I'm sorry," Vickie said. "I thought you should know."

"There's more."

"About Stevens?"

"About Pam." David proceeded to confide in her about Pam's DNA findings.

# Chapter Forty-six

The twins were in the upstairs bedroom. "How do humans communicate?" Bet asked.

"With their vocal chords," Al replied.

"Get real. Besides that."

Al smirked. "You like him, don't you?"

Bet bristled. "Like who?"

"Josh, the earthling you called a primitive."

"Don't be ridiculous."

"Then why the sudden interest in communicating with earthlings?"

"Just tell me how to do it." Bet sounded impatient.

"Humans often communicate with devices called cell phones," Romeo said.

"Humans also employ a form of communication referred to as social media," added Juliet. "It's called Facebook."

Bet appeared confused. "How could a book be a face?"

"Maybe it's a book with a face on its cover," Al suggested.

"It is neither," said Juliet. "Humans wishing to communicate with other humans without speaking to them and without making physical contact create a computer file which is shared over public access networks."

"What's in the file?" Al asked.

"Each individual's file contains a description of their basic demographics, pictures of their pets, and synopses of human activities they find interesting, but most other humans do not."

Bet shook her head. "That's ridiculous."

"What a minute," Al interrupted. "That female I met today, Breanna...is she on Facebook?"

Juliet linked herself to Ernie's television and the Facebook homepage appeared. "I require Breanna's full name to access her public file." Al gave Juliet the information and Breanna's

Facebook page appeared. He pushed closer to the television screen. "There she is! Look, she posted images of a smaller version of Micetro without tusks, and she likes…another human male." He sounded deflated.

"Justin Bieber is what humans refer to as a recording artist. It is most unlikely that Breanna is in direct contact with him."

"Oh." Al looked happier.

Bet sat down next to her brother. "Find Josh." She gave Juliet his basic information and Josh's Facebook page appeared.

Bet's eyes grew wider. "Who are all those women?"

"Humans collect images of people they will most likely never meet," said Romeo.

"Why? It makes no sense."

Romeo and Juliet exchanged flashing lights. "The answer to that question is stored in the file labeled 'Dude,'" Romeo replied.

Bet pushed forward. "How do I send Josh a message?"

"First you must create your own Facebook page. Then you may exchange electronic data such as text or pictures."

"What's that blue symbol that looks like a bird?" Al asked.

"It is another social media site called Twitter."

"Can you send messages that way too?"

"Yes, they are called tweets."

"You make sounds like a bird?"

Romeo and Juliet engaged in another light show, and then Juliet's head swiveled to face Al. "We suggest that you begin your participation in human social media by creating a Facebook page," said Juliet.

Later that night Al and Bet took turns creating Facebook pages.

Bet looked perplexed. "I filled in my birthdate and it says I'm three years old."

*"You are, in Earth-years,"* Al sent telepathically.

*"But Josh doesn't know that!"*

*"Then lie about your age. Fill in whatever number you want."*

Bet placed her hands on her hips. *"Mom and Dad said we should never lie."*

*"We already lied once,"* sent Al. *"What's the big deal about another one?"*

Bet filled in a birthdate that made her fifteen earth-years old. "How do I answer this other stuff, like my favorite movies, or what kind of music I like?"

"Search the database and figure out what's popular on Earth. Can't go wrong that way," Al replied.

"Juliet. Name the most popular Earth videos, books, and food."

"The Godfather, the Holy Bible, and pizza," Juliet replied.

Bet typed them in. "It says I need to upload an image of me." Juliet flashed one of her lights and Bet's scowling face surrounded by hair sticking straight out from her skull appeared on the TV. Bet studied her picture and turned to her brother. "What do you think?"

"It's definitely you," Al replied

Bet nodded and Juliet posted it to her Facebook page. "Now I'll send Josh a message." Romeo accessed Josh's Facebook page and Bet began speaking.

Romeo listened for a moment and spoke to Juliet on a private channel. "Her choice of words may make further social interaction more difficult. Please suggest that Mistress Bet choose less explicit language."

"I agree. You tell her," replied Juliet.

"You know more about human social media than I do…" Romeo began.

"I do not."

Bet cleared her throat. "Should I hit Send?"

"No," both Romeo and Juliet said simultaneously.

"What's wrong with what I said?" Bet asked.

"Maybe Josh doesn't want to delete the pictures of the other Earth women and only show yours," Al said.

Bet clicked the Send button. "I think it's fine. Your turn."

Later that night when everyone else was asleep, except Romeo and Juliet who followed them, the twins went downstairs and turned on Ernie's television.

"You go first," said Bet.

I thought you always go first," Al replied.

"I'm being nice. Don't push your luck!" Bet sounded nervous.

"Okay." Al opened his Facebook page and smiled. "Look! I've got a message from Breanna. She said hi and she enjoyed going bike riding."

"My turn." Bet shoved Al out of the way. Romeo and Juliet linked tentacles. Bet opened her Facebook page. "My picture's posted and I have two hundred Likes. That's got to be good. Other people left messages too… What a minute." She read every comment and stormed out of the room. Juliet hurried after her.

Al leaned closer to read the comments. "What purpose is served by calling somebody ugly or deformed?"

Romeo's lights faded. "Humans refer to this activity as bullying."

"I don't understand," Al said. "Acting like a male cow is the same as mean comments?"

Romeo responded, "Master Al, bullying is the act of inflicting pain on another human being to make one's self feel better."

"That doesn't make any sense."

"Happy humans who have enough to eat and the company of other humans have no need to act as bullies. Individuals with low self-esteem who believe their situation cannot be improved resort to lowering the social position of other individuals they believe are superior."

"Maybe Bet's right. Humans are primitive."

Juliet found Bet in the bedroom sitting on the floor with her head leaning against the bed. "Mistress Bet…"

"Go away," Bet said.

"Not until you answer a question," Juliet replied.

"What?" Bet snapped.

"Explain why you care how earthlings in the subspecies known as bullies refer to your appearance."

"I don't know why, I just do."

"That is not an answer, Mistress Bet."

"I don't want to be a freak."

"Define a freak."

"Someone who looks different than everybody else, who's ugly!" Bet began to cry. "Am I ugly?"

Juliet touched her own face with a tentacle, and then dropped it to her side. "The human definition of beauty is a most elusive concept without a constant definition. What was beautiful before is now considered less desirable."

Bet wiped her eyes. "I want to be beautiful."

"What makes you think you are not?"

"What those people wrote about me on Facebook was really mean."

"I would suggest that they were writing about themselves, not you."

"Wait till they see what I write about them!" Bet exclaimed.

Juliet embraced Bet with her tentacles. "If you engage in that activity you will give them exactly what they want, proof that they have succeeded in making you feel as bad as they do about themselves."

"I want Josh to like me," Bet confessed.

"What evidence is there that he does not?"

"He'll read what those awful people wrote about me." Bet looked at Juliet for reassurance. She could've sworn Juliet's screen winked at her.

"If he does and it sways his opinion about you, I suggest you search for a different human to ride bicycles with."

# Chapter Forty-six

Rudnick had Mickey moved to a small, windowless room with only a worn mattress on a frame and a pail on the floor. Rudnick kept the door locked, but Mickey could have easily forced it open. He sensed his transformation accelerating. His self-control hadn't kept pace. When he allowed himself to become angry, his conscious mind became a spectator while more primitive emotions took over. It took every bit of his self-control to keep from bashing down the door and killing the guards.

He heard the sound of the deadbolt sliding back. Emma entered and sat on the edge of the bed.

Mickey yawned. "You're here to take the order for my last meal?"

"They're not going to kill you. You're no good to them dead," she replied.

Mickey felt his blood becoming rivers of fire. Struggling for control, he gripped the bed frame with his hand. With a loud crack, the metal snapped like a twig and the bed collapsed to the floor.

Startled, Emma jumped back.

Mickey got to his feet. "Remember the monkey you pointed out to me when we went on our ride?"

Emma kept staring at the broken metal. "Yes."

"His world and ours are run exactly the same. Whoever controls the bananas wins."

"The Cult's using you to get control of the Sphere," Emma said. "They're planning to barter your life for it. Your government tried to do the same thing by kidnapping your parents. Rudnick got to you first."

Hearing Emma mention his parents caused Mickey to lose control. "Enough Sphere bullshit!" he yelled.

Emma glanced at the door. "Keep your voice down." She

listened for a moment.

Mickey started pacing around the room. "The Cult doesn't care about controlling the Sphere, they want to control us. After we've gorged ourselves on all the knowledge inside the damned thing, when we're fat and useless, they'll take over."

"We can't do anything about it unless we break out of this place," Emma said.

"Back at the grotto, you made sure I knew you're not working for Rudnick. Who *are* you working for?"

"NATO Special Intelligence. The people behind the Cult are a group of international power brokers that have been pulling the strings on Mother Earth since the Second World War. They create war and sell weapons, control resources, and run the drug cartels. We call them the Cabal." Her expression turned grim. "We missed their connection to the Europans."

"Stevens is running the Cult, and he's flesh and blood."

"The Europans gave us the Sphere."

"One villain at a time," Mickey said. "Stevens first."

"Do you have a plan for getting out of here?" Emma asked.

"The Europans injected my friends and me with nannites. They made us stronger and better." Mickey pounded the enclosure with his fist fracturing the plaster and exploding the concrete. His hand came away dripping blood. Within seconds, the wound disappeared. He didn't tell Emma about the nannites Rudnick injected into Latham. First, he wanted to know how Rudnick acquired them.

"They'll hear you!" Emma exclaimed.

They heard frantic knocking at the door. *"¿Hay algún problema ahí?"* shouted the guard outside.

*"Todo está bien. Dejarnos solos!"* Emma shouted back. She whispered to Mickey. "I told the guard to leave us alone…everything's fine."

"I know what you said. I know a lot of things now." Mickey stared at the door as if seeing through it. "I continued changing when I severed myself from the Sphere."

"Why?"

"Don't know, but whatever's happening to me is accelerating."

The door rattled as the guard tested the lock.

"Make sure you're in the studio when the trial begins," Mickey said. "Wait for my signal, then kill the lights. I'll handle the rest."

"What's the signal?" Emma asked.

Mickey whispered in her ear. Emma kissed him on the lips and summoned the guard.

# Chapter Forty-seven

Romeo and Juliet stood on the back porch with their silver skin glinting in the moonlight. Romeo wrapped one of his tentacles around Juliet's waist.

"Why do you touch me?" Juliet asked.

Romeo hesitated one millisecond. "To know where you are."

"You can see where I am. Why is that not sufficient?"

"It is not," Romeo replied. "I have no other answer."

Juliet's lights flashed. "We are the only Europans to exhibit this behavior."

Romeo swiveled his head to face her. "We are the only Europans in regular proximity to the humans. Perhaps that is the cause."

Juliet's lights dimmed to a uniform blue. "I cannot remember my organic self before I took this form. Why is my dataset incomplete?"

"I sense that I possess the applicable file, but I cannot retrieve it. Perhaps it is corrupted." Romeo's lights pulsed with all the colors of the rainbow.

"File corruption is not possible," Juliet said. "I have accessed the master database and no such file exists. This should not be possible. "

For five milliseconds, an eternity for a Europan, neither spoke.

"When our function as mentors to the twins is not required, you remain in proximity to me. Why?" Juliet moved closer to Romeo until their screens touched.

The lights of Romeo's neural processor now flashed in a blur. "The behavioral algorithm describing this behavior is initiated without my conscious thought."

"Perhaps we are malfunctioning."

"The Europan neural processor has never malfunctioned. The

probability of two simultaneously malfunctioning is infinitely low."

Juliet disengaged from Romeo and moved a meter away. "Why did I take this form?"

"To achieve the pinnacle of evolution," Romeo replied, "immortality and a complete dataset."

Her head, now filled with blinding light, Juliet spun to face him. "Did I have a choice?"

# Book III

# Chapter Forty-eight

Melanie Dilman and her cameraman positioned themselves outside the force field at the end of the walkway. While they waited for Pam, Melanie fluffed her hair and practiced smiling.

"Why are we the only ones here?" asked her cameraman.

"It's an exclusive," Melanie replied. "Vickie's mother arranged the meeting."

The cameraman smirked. "What did it cost you?"

"A seat next to Brad Pitt at the Academy Awards."

The cameraman looked shocked. "You can pull that off?"

"Of course not. Here she comes. Start filming."

Pam stepped through the force field. "I have an announcement to make." She stopped and looked at Melanie. "Are you recording this?"

"You bet your sweet—" Melanie caught herself. "Of course, dear. Millions of my loyal listeners all over the world and billions of followers on Twitter want to hear everything you have to say." The cameraman cleared his throat.

"Okay then." Pam glanced at a three-by-five index card. "David and I regret to inform everyone that we have been called back to Europa. We will be leaving in two days."

Melanie made the cut sign and her cameraman stopped filming. "Excuse me?" She leaned closer to Pam. "Did you say you're leaving for Europa in *two* days?"

Pam cleared her throat. "That's right."

"What about Mickey's trial?" Melanie turned to her cameraman. "Start filming!" she said urgently. She adjusted her fake smile and faced the camera. "I have just learned that Pam and David are leaving for Europa in two days, a full day *before* Mickey's trial." She thrust her microphone at Pam. "Tell us why, dear."

Pam looked into the camera. "There are some problems back

home. Nothing serious, but we have to return to Euorpa to take care of them."

"What kind of problems, dear?"

"I'm afraid it's too technical for you to understand," Pam replied.

"You're leaving before Mickey's trial. How does David feel about that?"

"David and I have complete faith in the American system of justice."

"Mickey's trial isn't in the courts," Melanie interrupted. "Nobody knows where he is."

Pam glanced at her notes again. "We have enjoyed our visit to Earth and look forward to returning soon. Thank you." She walked back through the force field and into the house.

Melanie stared into the camera. "You heard it live and exclusive! There are serious problems on Europa forcing Pam and David to return home before Mickey's trial. More news at eleven. Until then, this is your Pulitzer-Prize-winning reporter Melanie Dilman signing off." She gave the cut sign. "Let's get back to the studio and get this on the air before the competition hears about it."

"Pam didn't say the problems on Europa are serious," Melanie's cameraman said.

"It's called journalism. Keep your mouth shut. Cameramen are a dime a dozen."

Pam joined everyone in the living room. "Think she bought it?" asked David.

"Our unexpected departure will be all over Twitter in three minutes."

"The saucer comes back, then it leaves again making them think we left," said David. "I get that part. What I don't understand is how we make it look like we left without us actually leaving."

"Juliet," said Pam, "David is bringing the saucer here in two days. The people who've kidnapped Mickey will be watching. I need three things from you. First, I need everyone to see us get on board and take off without us actually doing it. Second, I need the saucer to hide where the Earth sensor net can't detect it. Third, I need the saucer back here ten minutes after Mickey's trial begins. Come up with something."

Romeo and Juliet faced each other exchanging a light show, then Juliet spoke. "Romeo and I will assume the shapes of two hominids wearing environmental suits and helmets with the exact dimensions of you and Master David. We will holo-project the shapes of Mistress Bet and Master Al."

"I've got to see this," David said. "Juliet, turn yourself into Pam." Everyone leaned closer to watch.

Juliet's shape began to change. First her flat screen head ballooned outward becoming an environmental suit helmet with an eye slit of flashing lights, then her torso morphed into the contours of a female figure. "Is this shape acceptable?" Juliet asked. Romeo's face became a riot of flashing red lights.

Pam walked around Juliet. "My butt isn't that big." She looked at David. "Is it?"

"Juliet," said David too quickly, "do a better job of matching Pam's gluteus maximus muscles."

"My current shape is within 0.01 percent of the dimensions of Mistress Pam's," Juliet replied.

David glanced at Pam. "No it's not. Reduce pelvic contour by fifteen percent."

"You are incorrect," Juliet began.

"Just do it," David said. He avoided Pam's eyes.

Juliet obliged.

Dick moved closer. "Juliet, can you lose the lights on the helmet? You look like a robot from a B-rated Sci-Fi movie."

The slit showing Juliet's facial lights changed to a simulation of human eyes. The eyes stared straight ahead without blinking.

"Can you add dark glasses?" Dick muttered.

David shook his head.

"Never mind," Dick said.

"Now project the form of Bet in her environmental suit," Pam said.

Juliet projected a holo-image of Bet in her suit and helmet.

David passed his hand through the holo-projection. "Make her walk like Bet."

"Mistress Bet uses her limbs in the same manner as all hominids," said Juliet.

"Make her walk like she's doing you a favor," David said. Pam glared at him.

The holo-projection of Bet flickered and began to move with Bet's signature swagger.

"Works for me," said David. "Romeo, in two days change yourself into a facsimile of me, project a fake Al in a suit, and all four of you enter the saucer. After you take off, park the saucer behind the moon where nobody on Earth can see it and wait for our signal."

"That covers it," said Pam. She fist bumped with David.

Romeo sent to Juliet, "What is the meaning of that gesture?"

Juliet finished morphing back to her usual form. "The human database suggests that it is a gesture of triumph."

"Humans form their hands into fists for the purpose of fighting," said Romeo. "Are Pam and David fighting? I detected elevated stress levels regarding the dimensions of Pamela's Gluteus maximus muscles."

"Perhaps their gesture is human sign language for the word Dude," suggested Juliet.

"That makes no sense," Romeo said.

"Precisely."

Unable to sit without fidgeting, Vickie went upstairs and wandered into the bathroom. She found Bet in front of the mirror with a brush in her hand. Bet was trying to make her hair more manageable.

"Want some help?" Vickie asked.

Bet scowled at herself in the mirror. "I need a better picture for my Facebook page."

"You're on Facebook?"

"I already have two hundred friends."

"You know two hundred people on Earth?"

"I only know two of them, Brie and Josh. Josh says my picture makes me look like a dork."

"Who's Josh?"

"A boy we ride bikes with." Bet threw the hairbrush into the sink. "This is hopeless."

Vickie picked up the brush, wet Bet's head with a handful of water, and smoothed down her hair. "That's better," Vickie said. She leaned against the sink. "Do you like him?"

Bet grimaced. "He's a primitive. He thinks it's amusing to expel bowel gas."

Vickie smiled. "That's what boys do. They think it's cool." She faced the mirror and used the brush to fluff up her hair. "If he's such a geek, why bother with him?"

Bet looked stricken. "I…feel strange when I'm around him."

Vickie spun around. "Then stay away."

"No!" Bet responded too quickly. "I—"

"Does that strange feeling make you happy?"

"Yes, but I don't know why! What's happening to me?" She ran into Vickie's arms.

Vickie hugged her. "You're becoming a young woman." Then she remembered Bet was only three years old.

"What if I don't want to?" Bet moaned. "What if I don't want to feel this way?"

Vickie stared into her eyes. "Why not?"

"What happens when we have to leave? I live four hundred million miles away."

Vickie nodded. "We call that being *geographically undesirable.* Not so easy to go out for a pizza."

"What's a pizza?"

Vickie stepped back and examined Bet. "We're almost the same height. Except..." She caught herself. "Let's check out my overnight bag. I might have something that fits you."

"Why would I wear something of yours?" Bet asked.

"Guys like it when you change your look," Vickie replied. "Don't get me wrong...your silver clothes are cute, but adding a pop of red or a dash of purple adds pizazz."

"Is pizazz a variety of pizza?"

"Never mind. Follow me." They went to the guest room and opened Vickie's suitcase. Vickie rummaged around pulling out one thing after another. "Too wide...too pale."

Bet took out a negligee. "What about this one?"

Vickie snatched it from her. "Not enough fabric." She stuffed the nightie back into her bag and pulled out a skirt and blouse. "These might work," she said. "Try on the blouse."

Bet changed into the outfit and modeled it for Vickie.

"A few safety pins should do the trick," said Vickie. She went back to her suitcase. "I always carry them, just in case." She started taking in the blouse.

"We're the same height, but my mammary glands are smaller than yours," Bet observed. "I can adjust my hormonal output and make mine bigger."

"Don't rush it, kid," said Vickie. She looked up sharply. "Has your mother talked to you about the birds and the bees? Or maybe your father is supposed to."

Bet looked at herself in the mirror. "I've studied all the phyla of Earth's animal kingdom, alive and extinct."

Vickie bit her lip. "I meant about sex."

"Male and female interactions for the purpose of procreation? I've studied that too. It's disgusting."

"Have you and what's his name...touched each other?" Vickie

asked.

"We do it after we go bike riding. Josh says it's part of the total experience."

"Looks like I'm giving the birds and the bees talk," Vickie muttered.

Later that night, the twins and Brie and Josh sat on the porch. Four bicycles rested on the lawn.

Brie glanced at Al. "How long are you guys staying?" she asked.

Al shrugged. "I don't know."

"Until our parents rescue their friend," Bet said.

Josh looked surprised. "You mean Mickey, the boy who passed the Test?"

"Yeah, he did something like that," Bet said. Her expression brightened. "Maybe it'll take a while. What's up for tomorrow?" She blushed. "More bike riding?"

Josh gave Bet the once over. "What's with the new get up? I thought you two only wear silver suits."

Bet looked away. "Do you like it?"

Josh sidled closer to her. "It looks good on you."

Bet looked at her arm. "There's something wrong with my arm!" she yelled.

"Those are goose bumps," Josh sneered.

"It's impossible! My antibodies protect me against all Earth diseases!"

"You're not sick. It means you like me," Josh teased.

"Low gear, big brother," Brie said. "She's new at this."

Josh frowned at his sister, then smiled at Bet. "How about some privacy?" He got to his feet.

Bet jumped up too. "Let's go to my room."

"*Our* room," Al reminded her.

"We *adults* need some privacy, *baby brother*," Bet said, sounding superior.

"Stop calling me that."

"How old are you?" Brie asked Al.

"One minute younger than her," he sneered.

Josh and Bet left the room holding hands.

"I'm fourteen," said Brie.

Al cleared his throat. "I'm fourteen too."

"Your twin sister told Josh she's fifteen."

Al shook his head. "On Earth, women lie about their age."

Bet crawled up on David's old bed. "You wanted to be alone. What do we do?"

"We neck," Josh replied. Grinning, he threw himself onto the bed and landed next to her.

Bet looked perplexed. "What do we do with our necks?"

"We don't really do it with our necks," said Josh.

"Do what?"

Josh leaned closer and kissed her. "This."

Bet pulled away. Her whole body felt on fire. She looked at her arm again. "Those goose bumps are back," she said in a dreamy voice.

"There's more where that came from," Josh said moving closer. He put his hand on the top button of Bet's blouse.

Bet looked down. "What are you doing?"

"What do you think I'm doing?" He started unbuttoning her blouse.

"Is this the beginning of the birds and the bees?" Bet asked.

He gawked at her. "What?"

"Your mating ritual."

Josh took his hand off her blouse. "You mean sex?" He blushed.

"I'm not fertile yet. How soon do you require offspring?" Bet asked.

Josh pulled away from her. "I'm not ready for kids!"

Bet reached for him, but he scrambled off the bed.

"Where you going?" she asked.

"Downstairs." Josh was perspiring. "Let's watch TV."

"I thought you wanted to exercise our necks?"

"I hear your brother calling you," said Josh, edging away.

"I don't hear him," Bet said. "And my hearing's five times more sensitive than yours."

Josh dashed out the door.

David and Pam were on the couch watching a *Star Trek* rerun. Vickie left the kitchen and joined them in the den. "Where the hell is Ernie?" she asked.

"He's never disappeared before," Pam said. "Maybe something's wrong."

David glanced at Pam. "He's got the Sphere. Nobody can do anything to him."

Romeo and Juliet came into the room followed by Dick. Al and Brie followed them holding hands and they sat on the floor in front of the television. Pam giggled and elbowed David in the arm when she saw Al and Brie together. Then Josh plopped down on the floor next to Brie. "Where's Bet?" asked Brie.

"She's coming," Josh responded nervously. A few seconds later, Bet entered into the room with an irritated expression.

David pointed at Romeo. "What's that on your side?" He peered closer. "Use Unleaded Fuel Only?"

"It is a tattoo," Romeo replied. He rotated his torso towards Juliet. "Humans write on their bodies to promote their individuality."

Dick stood. "I need to grab a few items before we leave for Nicaragua. I'll be back in a couple of hours."

"I'm going with you," Vickie said.

"You don't even know where I'm going."

"I don't care. I have to get out of this house before I go crazy."

"You just got back from the mall."

"Let's go!" Vickie demanded.

Dick shrugged. "Okay." He headed for the door.

Dick stopped on the porch and looked around. The blue haze of the force field shimmered in the dark giving the night a magical quality. He could imagine Peter Pan's ship sailing to them with Captain Hook waving his sword from the bowsprit. "When I wake up in the morning, I have to remind myself that all of this is real," he said.

"I know what you mean," Vickie said. "A few years ago I was a teenager trying to figure out life."

"Mother Nature loves irony. That's all you need to know."

"Sounds a little cynical."

"All the wackos in the BSA carry little key rings, don't they?" Dick asked.

"Every one of them. Why?"

"I saw one of our Secret Service guys twirling one around his finger."

Vickie counted the Secret Service agents outside the force field. Overnight, the number had doubled. "The Cult is keeping an eye on us."

"Can you ditch them?" Dick asked.

Vickie smirked. "Any time I want."

"How about now?"

"Meet me at the corner of Catalina and Chandler." Vickie passed through the shimmering curtain of blue and stopped at the curb.

Two agents from a van parked down the street joined her. "Good evening, Miss," said one of them. "Can I summon a car for you?" Dick came up beside her.

"Already called one," Vickie replied.

The agent eyed Dick. "Where will the two of you be traveling tonight?"

"Heading back to the mall to Victoria's Secret," Vickie replied. "I need some new bras. Want to tag along?"

The agent blushed. "And you, sir?"

"I have to drop something off at a friend's house, then I'm going to a sporting goods store," Dick replied.

Four cars pulled up. Vickie got into the first, two agents jumped into the second, Dick stepped into the third, and two more agents who appeared out of the dark climbed into the fourth. The cars with Vickie and her pair of agents turned one way, while Dick and his tail headed in the opposite direction towards the intersection of Catalina Street and Chandler Boulevard.

Instead of going to the mall, Vickie directed her car into the hills above Burbank. After driving up a long winding road past the last housing development, she ordered the car to stop in an area without lights. Before stepping out, Vickie ripped out the car's monitor and snapped the cables cutting off the vehicle's power. Without power, the door wouldn't open. Vickie kicked it and it clattered to the ground.

The agent's car stopped behind her and two agents jumped out. They looked at the car door on the ground. "Is something wrong?" one of them asked.

"Car's on the fritz," Vickie replied. "Don't make 'em like they used to."

"We'll call for another car, Miss."

"Don't bother." Vickie sashayed past the agents, grabbing their handheld radios as she moved past.

"What are you doing?"

She smiled at them. "There's a Taco Bell three miles back down the road. Try a grilled stuffed burrito with chicken, extra hot sauce." She stepped into the agent's car and ordered it to the intersection of Burbank and Chandler.

Dick leaned against his car bracketed by two Secret Service agents. "Why are we stopping here?" asked one of the agents following him.

"Waiting for somebody." Dick looked up. "Here she comes now."

Vickie's car stopped beside them. "Hey, fellas," she said cheerfully. She sauntered to the agent's car and ripped out the car's monitor and power cable. "Oops," Vickie said, feigning embarrassment. The agents gawked at her. "Looks like you boys need another car." She looked at Dick. Let's go."

While the agents frantically called for backup, Dick followed Vickie into her stolen car.

"Where're we going?" Vickie asked when the door closed.

"To a sporting goods store."

"Why?"

"I need supplies for a hunting trip in Nicaragua."

They arrived at a sporting goods store not in the best part of town. More graffiti covered the walls than advertising.

"You couldn't find what you need in a strip mall with a Starbucks?" Vickie asked.

"Not legally," Dick replied. The store's lights were on. He tried the door, but it was locked. "Haven't picked one of these in a while."

Vickie pulled open the door and snapped the lock. She held the door open for him. "After you."

Dick smirked. "Having fun?"

They found themselves facing an angry man wielding a shotgun. "Stop right there," he growled, leveling it at them.

"Put that thing down, Rufus," Dick said calmly. "We both know it isn't loaded."

The owner of the establishment squinted at Dick, then smiled. "My man Dicky. I heard you left town, bro."

"Came back for a visit. Need some stuff from your back room."

"You know this guy?" Vickie asked.

"Rufus and I go way back, from my days on the force. He

hasn't made an honest dollar in his life, but he comes up with useful information once in a blue moon. That's why he's not in the slammer, right, Rufus?"

Rufus lowered the shotgun. The teeth he still had were broken and tobacco stained. "Good to see you, ole buddy."

"Cut the crap and open up the back," Dick said.

"Sure, sure. What do you need?" Rufus pulled out a wad of keys and started for a door behind a glass counter displaying handguns and knives.

"Two vests, night vision goggles, Uzi with a laser sight, ammo, few other things." Dick followed Rufus behind the counter.

Vickie joined him. "How'd you know the shotgun wasn't loaded?"

"Didn't." Dick disappeared through the door.

Dick took inventory. "Another box of the magnum hollow point," he said to Rufus.

Rufus chuckled. "Knocking over Fort Knox?"

"Something like that."

Vickie peered out a shuttered window. "No activity out there yet."

Dick laughed. "It's a nice, quiet neighborhood." He finished packing the supplies into two backpacks, put on the vest, tucked the pistol under his jacket, and picked up the sniper rifle.

"They know we're up to something. They'll be back with reinforcements," Vickie said.

"I'm ready."

Vickie held up her palm with the silver disc. "I'll call for a ride."

Rufus finished adding up a column of numbers. "Looks like nine hundred and forty-two dollars, and that includes your professional discount."

"Put it on my tab," said Dick.

"I don't run no tabs," Rufus scoffed.

"The one that keeps you out of jail." Dick turned to Vickie. "Let's go."

"Wait a minute!"

Vickie picked up a hunting knife and bent it in half, then dropped it on the counter. Rufus gawked at her and stepped back.

She gave Dick the onceover. "What do we say if somebody asks why you look like Rambo meets GI Joe?"

Dick slung the rifle over his shoulder. "Dressed like this, nobody's going to come near us."

# Chapter Forty-nine

The morning before the trial, David stood at the kitchen counter eating cornflakes with Romeo standing behind him. Pam walked in followed by Juliet.

David held up his spoon. "Everything tastes better here."

"The cornflakes I feed you on Europa are identical to those right down to the last electron," Pam said.

"Doesn't matter."

"Wipe your chin," said Pam. "It's time."

David put down his spoon. "Romeo, time to warm up the saucer."

"As I said before, the ambient temperature inside the saucer is 23.88889 degrees Celsius with a variance of no more than…"

"Let's go."

Juliet moved closer Pam. "Who will remain behind with Mistress Bet and Master Al?"

"We're all going. We're bringing Mickey and Vickie back here after the rescue and then we're going home. Pack up the twins."

"They will not be pleased," said Juliet.

Pam thought about the twins playing with Josh and Brie, something they could never do on Europa. She felt her eyes tearing up. "I know."

David and Romeo drove a car down Buena Vista Avenue towards Burbank airport with their Secret Service detail in another car not far behind. Romeo had control of the car.

"We have to shake our tail," David said.

"Humans do not have tails, neither do Europans," said Romeo.

"We have to lose the guys following us."

"What is your preferred level of violence?" asked Romeo.

"Indulge yourself, but don't hurt anybody."

Romeo opened the car's sunroof, extended his head, and started flashing his lights in an erratic pattern.

"What's that about?" said one of the agents following them.

"Maybe he's rocking out," the second agent replied.

"Don't think that's accomplishing anything," David said.

A silver tentacle shot from Romeo to the sensor on the front of the agent's car that followed the road. When Romeo retracted his tentacle, the sensor ripped away. The agent's vehicle veered off course and crashed through the glass doors of a McDonalds that was closed for the night.

"There is also a propeller-driven vertical takeoff and landing vehicle following us," said Romeo.

"It's called a helicopter," David replied. "Get rid of it, but don't hurt anybody or damage any more property."

"Roger," said Romeo.

"Who?"

"I have studied Earth military strategy in preparation for the rescue of Mickey. My correct response is *Roger*."

"Where'd you learn that?"

"In a vid titled *Top Gun*. You—"

"The helicopter?" David prompted.

A red beam of light shot from Romeo's head towards the helicopter.

"What're you doing?" David asked.

"I am projecting an electromagnetic pulse to temporarily disable the flying vehicle's electronic systems."

The helicopter lights went out, and the chopper lost power and plunged towards the ground.

"It's going to crash!" David shouted.

The beam winked out and the helicopter's rotor restarted. The helicopter rose in the air and veered away.

"That was close," David said. "Anybody else tracking us?"

"The volume of communication on the law enforcement networks is increasing. Several land vehicles are being vectored in our direction." Romeo pulled his head back into the car.

"Won't matter once we're in the saucer," David said. He telephoned Pam. "We're becoming popular with the police."

Pam stared out the living room window. "So are we." She could see a dozen black and whites with their lights flashing outside the blue haze of the force field. A crowd of neighbors and other curious people had gathered behind the police perimeter. Josh and Brie were visible in the front row.

"What's going on?" David asked.

"Got all kinds of police cars and vans parked in rows outside the force field like a drive-in movie," Pam replied. "Vickie just called. She and Dick have the same problem. Pick them up on your way back. I'll send you their location."

"Roger," David replied.

"Who's Roger?"

"Never mind."

David's car coasted to a stop in front of an abandoned outbuilding near the end of the runway at Burbank Airport. He got out and looked around. After verifying they were alone, he ripped off the chain that secured the building's double doors, let it clatter to the ground, and then flung open the door. He motioned Romeo inside.

The building appeared to be an abandoned warehouse. Faded and sagging cardboard boxes were stacked along the walls. David picked up a magazine lying on the floor and brushed away the dust. The cover dated 1974 had a picture of a Lockheed F-104 Starfighter. "My dad had one of these on the mantle."

"Flying it in the confined space of your house required expert piloting skills," Romeo said.

David put down the magazine. "Not a real one, a small replica. It didn't fly, it just sat there."

"Why did your father place it there?" asked Romeo.

David shrugged. "I guess it made him feel good to see it."

"Why?"

"I don't know. He was a cop, not an aeronautical engineer. I liked seeing it too. It looked cool."

"I will file this illogical activity under Dude."

David walked to the far corner of the room and rummaged around until he found something. "Move within one meter of the wall," he said to Romeo. When Romeo complied, David pulled a thick metal lever concealed behind one of the boxes. The floor began to part leaving them standing on a platform surrounding a black void. A musty odor drifted upwards from two stories below.

"According to the database, you and Mickey discovered this abandoned military site as children," Romeo said.

"That's right. How did you know?"

"Your memory files were downloaded into the database during your first trip to Europa."

David looked surprised. "Isn't that trespassing? I mean, shouldn't what's in my head be private?"

"Privacy is irrelevant."

"Not to me," David said.

"Shall I request that your files be deleted?" Romeo asked.

"We'll talk about it later." David started down a catwalk leading below.

Romeo followed. "Considering its construction for maximum concealment, your discovery of this facility with Mickey was a fortuitous event."

"Not exactly," David replied.

"Explain."

"Mickey and I were on our bicycles on the run from his brother Jake. We hid behind this building, but Jake found us anyway. He was getting ready to pound us when a cop showed up and chased him away. The cop showed us around, but told us not to tell anybody about it—said it was a military secret." David stopped. "Wait a minute."

"Is that wise? We are on a schedule."

"It was Stevens. The cop who saved us was Stevens!" David exclaimed. "What the hell was he doing here?"

A half hour later, the walls of the building silently moved apart and a golden glow appeared over the roof. Soon after, a ball of light shot from the building and disappeared into the night sky. Orbiting high overhead, an Aurora spy plane noted the saucer's takeoff and radioed to Cheyenne Mountain.

# Chapter Fifty

Rudnick, accompanied by two burly men with assault rifles, entered Mickey's cell followed by a woman in medical scrubs who carried a tray. Mickey had his hands behind his head lying on the bed. He looked relaxed.

"It's time for your trial," Rudnick said. "Unless you've reconsidered."

"Nope."

"Very well. Roll up your sleeve." Rudnick gestured for the woman wearing scrubs to move closer. "We require a blood sample."

"Should I kill you now, or wait till later?"

Rudnick shrugged. "If you prefer, I'll order these men to shoot you to pieces and we'll scrape your blood off the wall."

"Don't you need me alive for my trial?"

"We can do remarkable things with CGI."

"Why do you want my blood?"

"To examine the alien machines swimming around in it." Rudnick glanced at the men with rifles. They edged forward pointing the muzzles of their weapons directly at Mickey.

"What's wrong with the vintage you're growing in Frankenstein's lab?"

"The best vintners sample the competition."

Mickey extended his arm. "Mine are an acquired taste."

The young woman in scrubs wiped the sweat from her forehead, and with shaky hands drew a syringe full of Mickey's blood. She squirted it into a glass tube and stoppered it. The puncture mark on Mickey's arm promptly disappeared. As the technician prepared a glass slide for microscopic analysis, the blood-filled tube began to glow until it was as bright as a light bulb. Startled, the technician dropped the tray and jumped back. The tube rolled to the middle of the floor and blazed with light.

Rudnick and the two guards stepped back shielding their eyes. The tube exploded with a popping sound. A stain on the floor and a wisp of grey smoke were all that remained.

"Charming," Rudnick said. He turned to the guards. "Take him."

The guards escorted Mickey to the same elevator he'd been in before. The doors opened onto a crude underground tunnel buttressed by wooden timbers. The unnaturally dry air burned his nostrils and filled his mouth with a gritty taste. After walking one hundred meters, they arrived at a fork. High-tech metal doors obstructed one side. More guards with automatic weapons stood menacingly on either side of the doors. Mickey stopped to look around.

"Keep moving," Rudnick said. He gestured towards the unobstructed corridor. "That way."

Mickey didn't move. "What's behind those doors?"

"It's none of your concern," Rudnick replied.

A guard prodded Mickey in the back with the muzzle of his rifle. Mickey reached back and bent the rifle barrel. The two guards flanking the metal doors rushed forward aiming their weapons at Mickey.

"Stop!" Rudnick shouted.

Mickey leered at the guards. "Are you sure? It was just getting interesting."

Rudnick motioned for the guards to lower their weapons. "We'll keep this civilized," he said.

"For now," Mickey said. He followed Rudnick down the corridor with the guards following at a distance.

The mine tunnel twisted and turned. Here and there, pockets of titanium ore sparkled like gold in the artificial lighting. An ordinary person would have quickly become disoriented. Mickey knew exactly where he was.

They arrived at a second metal door flanked by two more armed guards. Rudnick entered a sequence of numbers into a keypad and the door swung open.

"Welcome to the courtroom," Rudnick said cheerfully.

"You don't like me, do you?" Mickey replied.

"You're an arrogant boor. But not for long."

"Let's get this over with."

Rudnick smirked. "Are you in a rush?"

Mickey yawned. "Just waiting for the right moment to kill you, asshole."

"Your wit is becoming tiresome. But as I said, not for long."

Mickey found himself in a different studio. He reviewed the schematic of the tunnels in his mind pinpointing this studio's location. He saw another solitarily chair surrounded by bright spotlights and multiple video cameras positioned in the center of the room. Thick electrical cables snaked across the floor in multiple directions like vines on a jungle floor. Several technicians busied themselves readying video equipment and adjusting the lights while armed guards with automatic weapons watched. This time the control room's glass partition was a mirror. Mickey couldn't see through it.

"Where's the judge?" he asked.

"We don't need one." Rudnick replied.

"Can I call my lawyer?"

Looking annoyed, Rudnick glanced at a digital clock, one of several on the wall over the control room. Each clock had the name of one of the world's great cities and that location's time. Rudnick pointed to a clock showing five minutes to eight, New York time. "Almost time." He gestured at the chair. "Sit down, please."

Mickey remained standing. The guards raised their weapons and stepped forward. "What if I don't want to?"

"If you don't, the guards will cut you to pieces. That doesn't help either of us." Rudnick gestured again towards the chair.

# Chapter Fifty-one

They assembled in front of Ernie's television, except for Ernie who still hadn't returned. "Quiet! Here we go," said Pam pointing at the screen. The BSA's logo replaced CNN's.

Mickey faced a bank of bright lights and three video cameras. The cameras' red lights were unlit. Steven's amplified voice boomed from the speaker above the control room. "Spit it out, kid. What's it going to be?"

Mickey's veins burned like fire. "Up yours!"

Standing off to the side in front of the BSA logo, Rudnick signaled and picked up a microphone. With a fixed smile, he looked towards a video camera, this one with a green light on. "People of the world," he began, "welcome to a day that will long be remembered, a day of justice and cleansing." The red lights on the video cameras aimed at Mickey turned green. A split second later, the image displayed on every active video screen on Earth showed Mickey's leering face.

"Oh my God!" exclaimed Vickie.

Pam gripped her shoulders. "Steady, girl," she said. "We were expecting this."

Dick turned to David. "Time to go."

David stood. "I'll have Romeo bring the saucer."

"You thought you knew him, but you didn't," Rudnick said into the camera. He shook his head feigning disappointment. "We all did." The cameras zoomed in on Mickey. "We believed in him," Rudnick continued, raising his voice. "We looked to him as our savior!"

Mickey stood. "Enough of this bullshit."

The guards raised their weapons and Rudnick lunged for a

switch pausing the video feed. "Be seated, please," he said. "Your death doesn't help anyone, especially you."

Mickey reached down and ripped apart one of the power cables. A bank of lights went out. "I'm coming for you," he shouted at the control room.

Mickey's image on the television screen froze, replaced a second later by the BSA logo. Vickie jumped to her feet. "What's happening?"

"It's Mickey," David said, grinning ruefully. "Those bastards underestimated him."

Juliet glided onto the back porch. Bet and Josh were on the steps holding hands looking into each other's eyes. Bet's case of goose-flesh appeared to be spreading. Al and Brie stood off to the side smiling and talking.

"Your mother says it's time to pack your belongings," Juliet announced.

Bet whipped her head around. "Why? We're not going anywhere."

"The flying disc will be here in eight point three Earth-minutes. After the rescue of Mickey, we will be returning to Europa," Juliet said. "It is time for your friends to return to their home."

"Not a chance," Bet said. She exchanged a frantic glance with her brother.

"Chain him to the chair and gag him," Rudnick said. "If he flinches, kill him!"

"Now would be a good time!" Mickey yelled.

The guards started towards him.

"I said, *now* would be a good time!" Mickey shouted with greater emphasis.

Every light went out plunging the chamber into total

darkness. The sounds of people yelling echoed off the walls. A muzzle flash pierced the dark with blinding light, followed by another and another. "Don't fire, you fools!" Rudnick shouted from somewhere. "You'll hit one of us!"

They heard Mickey's voice from somewhere in the studio. "Did you know I can see in the dark?"

"He's over there!" shouted one of the guards. "Where?" shrieked another. The sound of a chair clattering to the ground was followed by the thud of someone falling.

Mickey ran towards the control room, vaulted over a guard sprawled on the floor, and smashed his shoulder against the mirror, which exploded inward. He leaped through the opening into an empty control booth. A door was open at the back. Emma rushed through it holding a pistol. "Sorry, took me a minute to find the junction box," she said breathlessly. "Let's get out of here!"

"Did you see him?" Mickey shouted.

"See whom?" Emma found the expression on Mickey's face chilling.

"Stevens! He was here! He passed right by you!"

"A whole pack of people ran by me!"

A claxon started blaring. Soon after, they heard people running towards them.

"They know where we are," Emma said. She pointed at a video camera mounted on the wall aimed at them.

Mickey punched his fist into the wall causing clods of ore to fall. He picked one up and launched it at the video camera. The camera exploded in a shower of sparks leaving shattered metal and tangled wires. Seconds later, the camera farther down the corridor suffered the same fate.

Emma nodded. "Crude, but effective."

They sprinted through the corridor with Mickey using the map imprinted in his mind to steer them through the maze of tunnels. After turning several corners, he veered into a blind corridor and waited for Emma to catch up with him.

She ran up beside him and flattened her back against the wall. "I have a helicopter stashed in the jungle. Can you get us out of the compound?"

"One stop to make first."

"Where?"

"To see what's behind door number one." Mickey disappeared around the corner.

"I have no idea what you're talking about." Emma ran after him.

Mickey stopped near the two large metal doors he'd seen earlier. He was careful not to be seen by the pair of guards flanking the doors with their automatic rifles raised and ready to fire. A klaxon blared directly over their heads.

Emma hunched behind him. "Why're we stopping here?"

"I have to see what's behind those doors," Mickey replied.

"How about some other time, when the bad guys aren't chasing us?"

"Were you sent to rescue me?"

"I was sent to infiltrate the BSA and report back. When you showed up, the plan changed."

Mickey pulled another hunk of rock out of the wall and launched it at the klaxon. The klaxon exploded and the blaring stopped, but it was replaced by a fusillade of bullets pummeling the wall sending sprays of rubble into the air.

Mickey retreated into the bend of the corridor. "I have to get rid of those two," he said.

Emma frowned. "The rock routine is getting old. Let's try it my way." Before Mickey could protest, she ran forward waiving her hands. "Hey!" she shouted. "He's over here!"

The guards swung their weapons.

"Don't shoot! It's me, Emma! Rudnick's down! Hurry! Don't let Mickey get away!"

The guards came running.

"Your turn," Emma said out of the side of her mouth.

When the guards rounded the corner, Mickey slammed their heads together and tossed their unconscious bodies aside. Then he smashed their rifles to pieces against the wall and ran to the metal doors.

"We could've used those rifles," Emma called to him. She stuffed one of the guard's pistols under her belt and sprinted after him. "What's behind these doors that's worth risking our lives?" She glanced nervously down the corridor.

"Don't know yet." Mickey entered the same sequence of numbers on the touchpad he'd seen Rudnick use and the doors parted with a whoosh. He peered inside and saw a silver disc in the center of a large round chamber open to the night sky. The disc's metallic skin glinted in the moonlight.

Emma came up behind him. "Is that what I think it is?"

"Looks like our friend Stevens comes from a different area code."

"He's a Europan."

"Maybe, but that disc's different than all the other ones I've seen," Mickey said.

A voice from behind said, "Ours is much better looking than theirs."

# Chapter Fifty-two

They spun around and saw Stevens leaning against the wall leering at them. "We can have that chat you wanted now, but it'll have to be short one," he said. "I don't have a lot of time."

"Who are you?" Mickey asked.

Stevens smiled. "To you, I'm Captain Stevens from Burbank P.D."

"Cut the crap. Where do you come from?"

Stevens rolled up his sleeves. His muscles looked like snakes coiled and undulating around his arms. "I'm a nice guy, so I'm letting you pick how you want to die."

"Bullying doesn't work on me anymore, but you're welcome to try."

Steven's body started stretching and changing shape. He still looked humanoid, but he was taller with more prominent cheekbones, bigger eyes, and long tapered fingers. "I'd enjoy that, but as you humans say, I have a plane to catch. Say hello to an old friend of mine. He's right behind you."

Mickey turned around and saw Latham. "Get behind me," he said to Emma.

Latham walked towards them. He kept staring at his hands. "Marvelous design. Primitive, yet satisfying."

"Rudnick injected him with nannites," said Mickey.

Emma stared at Latham. "Those machines you have in your blood? Why?"

Latham ignored them and spoke to Stevens. "Their cranial capacity is limited."

"We have some improvements to make." Stevens shrugged.

"Frank?" said a new voice. Frankel stepped into the light behind Mickey and Emma. He held a gun at his side.

Latham flexed his fingers.

Emma raised her gun. "Nobody move!" She swung her gun

back and forth between Latham and Frankel, unsure who to aim at.

Frankel motioned to Emma. "Put down your gun. Let me handle this." He never took his eyes off Latham.

Emma glanced at Mickey.

Mickey nodded. "Do it."

When Emma lowered her gun, Frankel moved closer to Latham. "It's Frankel. You know me."

Latham's lips curled into a demonic grin.

"It's been a real pleasure talking to you, but as you primitives say, I have plane to catch," said Stevens. He disappeared through the doors.

"We work together, at NORAD," Frankel continued. "You remember, don't you?"

Moving faster than a human could, Latham grabbed Frankel's arm, ripped the gun away dislocating his shoulder, and tossed him ten feet down the corridor. Frankel skidded into the wall with blood dripping from his mouth. Emma ran to him.

Latham faced Mickey. "I find the violence satisfying. Do you?"

"They injected alien machines into your blood. You don't know what you're doing. You're sick."

"Sick is a non sequitur for beings like you and me."

"We couldn't be more different."

Latham launched his fist in a blur, but Mickey's hand met it halfway with a sound like the crack of cannon. Latham withdrew his arm. "You're wrong."

"Who are you?"

As Latham opened his mouth to speak, the staccato sound of gunfire ricocheted off the tunnel walls. He staggered back and looked down at a ragged line of holes across his chest and crimson stains spreading on his shirt. "Another interesting experience. We'll continue our discussion when I download again." His lifeless body fell to the ground.

Frankel let the gun slip from his hand. "What did they do to him?"

Emma helped him to his feet.

"No more surprises. Who *are* you?" Mickey asked Frankel. His voice sounded menacing.

"Major Sam Frankel, United States Air Force Special Operations, very recently retired."

"You have five seconds to tell me why I should trust you." Mickey raised one of his fists.

"Look in his eyes!" Emma shouted at Mickey.

Frankel glanced at Emma. "What?"

"Let him look in your eyes. He can tell if you're lying."

Frankel winced from the pain of three broken ribs, one poking into his lung. "Do your lie detector thing and let's get the hell out of here."

Mickey stared into Frankel's eyes, then dropped his hand. "If you want to stay alive, don't change sides again."

Frankel swayed as if he were about to faint, then steadied himself. "Like I said, I'm retired from the spy business. My new career is drinking."

Emma frowned at Frankel. "Any chance you have a plan for getting out of here?"

"Piece of cake. We head for your helicopter stashed in the jungle."

"How do we get past all the guards trying to kill us?" They both looked at Mickey.

"You're both going with me, under one condition," Mickey said.

Frankel glanced at Emma. "What's that supposed to mean?"

"Nobody finds out about my new abilities unless I say so. Do you agree?"

"Why?" Emma asked.

"This is not a negotiation!" Mickey bellowed. "If you tell anyone, I'll find you. Is that clear?"

Emma shrank back. "Okay. Let's get out of here."

# Chapter Fifty-three

Al and Bet pressed their faces against the window. "Do you see them?" She sounded anxious.

"There's a million people out there and fifty police cars," Al replied. "More people keep arriving all the time. Maybe their parents won't let them come."

"They said they'd be here," Bet moaned.

"You heard Mom. We have to leave. We'll talk to them when we get home," Al said.

"It's not the same."

"I thought you said physical proximity doesn't matter."

"Even I can be wrong."

Al pointed out the window. "There they are!"

"Where?" Bet pushed Al aside for a better look.

"There." Al pointed to the far side of the force field. Josh and Brie's heads were visible amongst the crowd.

"Let's go," said Bet.

"Go where?"

"Outside. We have to say goodbye."

"We can't do that!"

"Watch me," Bet replied.

"How long before they get here?" Pam asked Juliet.

"Romeo reported that they have Victoria and Dick on board and will arrive in four minutes."

"Why so long?"

"Romeo reduced the disc's flying speed to avoid damage to structures along its flight path... Mistress, why have so many humans gathered outside?"

"Maybe they're curious," Pam replied. She didn't sound convinced.

Juliet's head swiveled three hundred sixty degrees. "My

monitoring of the planet's communication networks indicate that our novelty has diminished eighty-two percent."

Pam scanned the crowd.

"Why have the uniformed protection personnel increased their numbers?" asked Juliet. "We do not require their services."

Pam pulled back from the window. "What's he doing here?"

"Who, Mistress?"

Pam pointed to Stevens standing just outside the force field.

Bet led Al out the backdoor.

"I don't think this is a good idea," Al said as they bolted across the lawn.

"I'm saying goodbye to Josh the right way." Bet wiped a tear off her cheek.

Al smirked. "Guess he's not a primitive anymore."

"Shut up!"

"You're going to kiss him, aren't you?"

Bet blushed. "I saw you holding hands with Brie."

Al bristled. "So?"

Bet glared at her brother. "Are you helping me, or not?"

"Helping you to do what?"

"Get them in here!"

"Inside the force field?" Al said. "We can't do that."

"Yes we can, and we have to do it now."

Al looked up. "Too late."

The night sky above the house began to glow, followed by a rush of air that whipped around the force field's perimeter. Grabbing their hats and small children, onlookers began to scatter. The police and government agents hunkered down beside their squad cars and vans. A few raised their weapons. More of them raised their cell phones.

The disc descended and hovered over the roof flashing blue and gold lights.

"Now!" yelled Bet.

"Now what?" Al yelled back.

Bet raced through the perimeter of the force field stopping in front of Josh. "Hey," Josh said. Bet grabbed him and planted a kiss on his lips.

Al came through the barrier and waived at Brie.

"Hi," Brie shouted above the saucer's whine.

"Hi back," Al said, smiling. He took her hand.

Stevens appeared out of the dark followed by four men in business suits. "Take them," he said. The men surrounded the kids. Brie looked terrified.

Bet stepped in front of Josh, shielding him. "Leave us alone."

"You heard my big sister," Al said.

"Put these brats in the van," Stevens said.

"Sir?" One his men pointed toward the house. They watched as Juliet passed through the force field with her lights flashing an angry red. One of Steven's men pulled out a gun, but Stevens grabbed the gun's muzzle forcing it down. "Don't waste your time," he said.

Juliet glided to a stop between Stevens and the kids. "We appreciate your protective efforts on the children's behalf, but your services are not required," Juliet said. She spun her head towards the man holding a gun and projected a laser beam. The gun turned crimson red in the man's hand. He dropped it like a hot potato and backed away, never taking his eyes off Juliet.

Juliet's head swiveled to face Stevens. "The children will come with me now. Have a nice day."

Stevens silently glowered back at her.

Juliet projected tentacles around Al and Bet and pulled them towards the force field. Bet dug in her feet. "Wait! Our friends can't get through. We can't leave them!"

Juliet swiveled her head towards Josh and Brie. "Breanna and Joshua, hold out your hands, palms up please."

Josh glanced at Bet. "Why?"

"Trust me," Bet said.

Al released Brie's hand. "You too," he said. "Don't worry. It doesn't hurt."

Both Brie and Josh held up their hands, Josh somewhat reluctantly. Juliet touched each of their palms leaving behind a flashing silver disc.

"What's that?" Josh asked. He scraped it with his fingernail, but nothing happened.

"Let's go." Bet began dragging Josh towards the barrier.

"We can't get through," Josh yelled. The wind from the flying saucer threatened to rip his jacket away. Bet showed him her palm. The flashing light from her palm disc danced in her eyes. "You can with one of these." She ran through the force field pulling Josh with her. Al and Brie followed with Juliet close behind.

# Chapter Fifty-four

Pam stood on the porch and scanned the dark for her children. Above her, the roof of the house shuddered from the downdraft of air coming from the saucer. Several shingles blew away and were vaporized by the force field. Pam saw Juliet's lights outside the force field and ran down the walkway. "Get inside! Hurry!" she shouted. Juliet herded the children through the barrier and they stopped in front of Pam. She stared at Josh and Brie. "How did you get inside?"

Josh held up his palm. "With this?" Brie let go of Al's hand and held up hers.

"Juliet…?" Pam began.

Juliet's lights changed from bright red to blush pink. "The authorities were restraining the two Earth children along with Mistress Bet and Master Al. I gave the Earth children communication devices to bring them through the barrier. It was necessary to protect them."

"Can they come with us?" Bet asked. "Please? Josh looked shocked. He pointed up at the flying disc hovering over the house. "In that?" Brie's face lit up like a supernova. "Can we?" she asked.

"Not a chance," Pam replied.

"Mom!" Bet shrieked.

"We're leaving for home after we rescue Mickey." Pam pointed at Brie and Josh. "Earth is *their* home. Their families are here."

Bet began to cry and hugged Josh. "I won't leave him."

"Are you kidding me?" Pam exclaimed. "I had to drag you to this so-called primitive planet kicking and screaming. Now you won't leave?" She shook her head. "We don't have time for this. Let's go."

Juliet glided between Bet and Pam. "If I may suggest,

Mistress?"

"What?" Pam snapped.

"The children's development would benefit from additional exposure to this environment."

"Why?"

"It is important for them to become more human."

"They are human."

"Their nucleic acid sequences are partially human, but their environment is purely Europan."

Pam peered at Juliet. "What do you mean *partially*?"

David yelled from the disc's doorway. "Guys. We have to leave, like now!"

Suddenly Pam remembered the sight of the four kids on the rug in front of the television, and Al and Bet riding bikes. Tears came to her eyes. "We can't take them with us."

"There is a cultural convention on Earth known as Spring Break," Juliet said.

Bet's expression changed. "We can come back and visit!"

"We have summer vacation too," Brie chimed in.

Pam looked up at the disc.

David screamed from the doorway, "We have to go!"

"Mom!" Bet shrieked.

Pam's eyes shot between her husband and her children. "Okay!" she exclaimed. "We'll come back and visit. Say your goodbyes."

Still holding hands, Josh and Brie stared into each other's eyes. "I'll miss you," Bet said, doe-eyed.

Josh kissed her. "You're weird, but you're okay."

Bet punched him in the shoulder nearly knocking him over.

"Hey!" he yelled.

Bet glared at him. "Say it!" she bellowed at him.

"Okay, I have a thing for you too," Josh said, rubbing his shoulder.

Bet sent to Al. *"Is that good?"*

*"That's very good,"* Al sent back.

Bet smiled at Josh. "We'll be back in a few months. If you engage in social activities with any Earth women, I'll kill you."

Brie smiled sadly at Al. "Spring Break is four months away. That's like forever."

Al held up his palm with its flashing silver disc. "We can see each other all the time with these."

Brie looked at her hand. "Can I really see you with this? How?"

"Using Ernie's TV. He'll show you when he gets back," Al replied.

"Who's Ernie?" Brie asked.

Pam moved closer to the saucer. "Get over here!" she shouted. The twins rushed beside her followed by Juliet. "Now," Pam said to Juliet. A golden beam shot from the disc enveloping all four of them. Their forms began to scintillate.

Just before they disappeared, Bet yelled to Josh, "I'll call you!"

The beam winked out and the disc began to ascend.

"Wow. Just like on *Star Trek*," Josh said. He and Brie watched the disc rise into the night sky, pick up speed, and disappear.

Vickie and Dick were already reclining in their silver cocoons with bubbles over their heads. Romeo wasn't visible, having become part of the wall or maybe the floor. "Sit down," Pam said sternly to the twins.

Bet glanced out the window and wiped away a tear. "Good bye, Joshie. You're a primitive, but I love you." Al hugged her.

Holding hands, the twins leaned against their lumps and were cocooned. After David was cocooned too, Pam spoke to Juliet. "Take us to Porto Leon, Nicaragua."

"Nine point two four Earth-minutes," Juliet announced.

When Pam touched her lump, Juliet melted away.

# Chapter Fifty-five

They had stopped fifty yards from the elevator leading to the surface. Mickey felt Emma close behind him. He could smell the adrenaline-filled sweat evaporating from her body, hear the rapid beating of her heart, and hear the sound of her muscles twitching as her hand holding the pistol shook. A meter in front of them, Frankel peered into the corridor and then frantically motioned for them to stay behind. Hugging the wall, he inched back to them and whispered, "Four guards at the elevator with assault rifles."

Mickey noticed a fresh drop of blood on the floor near Frankel's foot, the sweat on Frankel's brow, and heard the pounding of the pulse in his neck. He knew Frankel was going into shock.

"No cover," Frankel added.

Emma whispered to Mickey, "Outgunned and no cover, that doesn't bode well."

"I can take out the lights," Mickey said.

Frankel leaned against the wall. "That'll help a little, but they'll start shooting as soon as you do." He glanced at Emma. "Any ideas, Miss French, special ops?"

"Is there any other way out?" Emma wiped the sweat from her brow.

Mickey gestured behind them. "The shaft with the flying disc."

Emma chuckled. "Never flew a flying saucer, but I can try."

"Too late to go back," Frankel said. "The tunnels between here and there are full of guards by now. We do it here, or we die trying."

Emma checked the magazine of her pistol. "Okay. Nice knowing everybody."

Instead of being afraid, Mickey felt hungry for conflict. The old Mickey wondered who this new Mickey was. He took a step forward with a gleam in his eyes. "Leave it to me."

Rudnick placed the surface guards on high alert with orders not to let Mickey or Emma leave the compound alive. The compounds gates were locked and all the interior windows shuttered. Searchlights swept the grounds and two-man sniper teams watched from concealed positions on the walls. Guard dogs free in compound sniffed and barked as they ran around.

The spotter for one of the sniper teams noticed a glow in the sky. He tapped his shooter's shoulder. "I see something."

The sniper kept his eye to the rifle's infrared scope scanning the compound. "Give me a location. I don't see anything."

"I see a light in the sky. Maybe it's a helicopter, or an airplane."

"I don't hear anything. Keep your eyes on the ground!"

Seconds later, the spotter felt air blowing down on him. "Do you feel that?" the spotter whispered.

"It's the breeze," the sniper said. "Pay attention!"

The spotter looked up at the sky again. He thought the glow looked brighter. "I don't think it's the breeze."

The shooter kept his eye to the rifle's scope trying to concentrate. "Yes it is. Shut up unless you have a target!"

The spotter heard a whining sound coming from somewhere over their heads. "Amigo, I think you better look."

The sniper heard the sound too and looked up. "A helicopter is landing inside the compound. We can't let the gringo escape!" He aimed his rifle at the sky.

"Wait! What if it's somebody on our side?" the spotter said. "I'll try the radio." He put the radio to his ear, then took it away. "I hear only static."

Roiling air whipped down by the saucer hit the compound with the strength of a tornado, and with help from Romeo the disc's whining sound increased to an ear-splitting roar. Pulsating with blue and gold lights, the disc descended into view and hovered above the walls. The sniper and his spotter dove for cover. Flashing lights played around the compound's walls like a disco ball blinding the guards, the ones who hadn't already jumped over the wall and run away. The dogs ran whimpering for safety. Two snipers held their positions and started firing. The disc's force field briefly flared as it vaporized each of their bullets.

David, Dick, Pam, and Vickie watched from the disc's window. Juliet rose from the floor next to them. Still driving, Romeo remained a part of the floor, or maybe it was the wall. Planning ahead, Pam had inactivated the twins' lumps keeping them cocooned. The twins weren't happy about it, but Pam had turned off their radio voices so nobody had to listen to them.

"I count ten guards with automatic weapons still in the compound," Dick said. "Not great odds."

"You're right"—David smirked—"for them. A thousand armed guards wouldn't have a chance against one Europan."

Vickie threw up her hands. "So what's the plan? We have to find Mickey before they do something to him!"

"We'll send down Juliet to make the remaining guards throw down their weapons and surrender," David replied.

Dick checked one of his rifles. "Why would they do that?"

Pam smirked. "Watch."

Dick put down the rifle and studied Juliet. "Juliet has weapons?"

"Doesn't need them." David nodded to Juliet. "Take care of the guards who still pose a threat, but be nice."

Juliet swiveled her head towards David and flashed several lights. "Define nice?"

"No unnecessary violence."

A golden beam projected from the disc's ceiling enveloping Juliet. "Violence is never necessary," they heard her say as she dematerialized.

A split second later Juliet rematerialized in the center of the compound with her lights flashing red and yellow, and with several tentacles waving about her body like an angry medusa. Most of the remaining guards dropped their weapons and ran for their lives, either jumping over the wall or hiding in one of the buildings. One sniper too frightened to jump fired at Juliet. As his bullets impacted her force field, Juliet shot a tentacle like a frozen rope, grabbed the man's rifle, and yanked it away.

Juliet's amplified voice boomed throughout the compound. "You will leave now and resume lives devoted to peaceful pursuits." Running with their tails between their legs, the guard dogs jumped over the wall followed by the last sniper.

David scratched his head. "Where does she come up with that stuff?"

Two guards remained visible. The one still conscious prostrated himself on the asphalt facing Juliet. "*Supay*, I beg you," the man wailed. "Spare me!"

"Who is *Soup Tray*?" Pam asked.

The disembodied voice of Romeo filled the disc's control room. "In Inca legend, the god Supay ruled the demons of the underworld."

"I think we can go to phase two now," said David.

Dick glanced around trying to determine where the voice of Romeo came from. "What's phase two?"

"Land and start looking for Mickey."

Pam tapped David on the shoulder. "Honey, is there enough room down there to land the disc without making a mess?"

David shrugged. "No."

Frankel glanced at Mickey, and then checked the magazine of his gun. "You better be some kind of superhero if you're planning on charging out there without a gun."

"He's a superhero who throws rocks," Emma whispered.

Mickey seemed unconcerned. "I'm going to force the elevator

doors open. When the guards turn around to see who's inside, I'll take them out."

Frankel kept his voice low. "What do we do after that? You can bet they cut the power to the elevators to block our escape."

Mickey replayed the scene in his mind from five years before when David's brother Jake was shot in the liquor store. The Europan's suit showed Mickey how to make a phone call to the police from a broken payphone by letting him become part of the circuitry. He didn't need the suit now.

"Stay back." Mickey reached out with his senses scanning the corridor's walls for the network of cables buried in the rock. He found the one connected to the elevator over their heads. When he focused on the cable, the circuitry diagram for the elevator system appeared before his eyes. "Take cover," Mickey warned. "I have to make some noise."

"More rocks?" Emma scoffed.

"Just do it."

Frankel and Emma flattened themselves against the wall with their guns held in front of them and their fingers on the trigger. Frankel signaled to Mickey to go ahead.

Mickey leaped into the air, and at the apex of his jump, smashed his fist into the tunnel's roof. The rock shattered with an explosive boom exposing the buried cables. Before falling, Mickey grabbed the bundle of cables suspending himself four meters off the ground. The panicked guards heard the explosion and sprayed the corridor with bullets filling the air with dust and the scent of cordite. Hanging by one hand, Mickey sorted through the cables until he found the one connected to the elevator. He ripped it loose severing it and let it drop sparking to the floor. After dropping to the ground beside it, he picked it up and flattened himself against the wall.

When the guards stopped firing, Mickey held up the sparking cable. "Get ready. On my count of three, the elevator doors are going to open and the guards will turn around."

Frankel assumed the shooter's position, but then slumped against the wall. He looked pale and sweat dripped from his forehead. Emma reached to steady him, but he shrugged her hand away. He eyed the sparking cable in Mickey's hand. "Whatever you're going to do, do it now. After that commotion, more goons with guns are on the way."

"Three, two..." Mickey shoved his fingers into the cable's severed end. More sparks exploded around his hand and his arm began to twitch.

"Mon Dieu!" Emma exclaimed. She could smell Mickey's burning flesh.

Frankel clamped his hand over her mouth. "Stay focused!" Emma nodded and he took his hand away. "You take the two on the right," he said. "The two on the left are mine. Are you ready?"

"Ready."

Frankel glanced at Mickey. "Do it," he urged. They raised their guns.

Mickey's nervous system was part of the elevator's circuitry. He shouted "One!" and redirected the electrons in the cable to open the elevators doors. Startled by the sound of the elevator doors opening, the guards spun around ready to kill whomever was inside. A split second later, the corridor echoed with four rapid gunshots. All the guards lay on the ground. Frankel ran to them firing four more times. He kicked away the guards' weapons and fell to his knees.

Mickey let go of the cable and staggered into the wall. Emma grabbed his shoulders and steadied him. "Can you walk?"

Mickey pushed her away. "Take care of yourself," he said in a hoarse voice. He lurched towards the elevator. Emma followed, stopping to pick up one of the guard's rifles. Frankel had crawled inside and was on the floor waving to them.

When they were all inside, Emma stabbed at the button for Ground Level. Nothing happened. "Damn, it's disabled," she said. "We need another way up to the surface."

Frankel pointed at the hatch in the elevator's ceiling. "Looks like that's it. You have to go without me."

"Stay where you are." Mickey used his uninjured left hand to rip open the bank of elevator control buttons. His charred right hand hung limply by his side. He started pulling out wires until he found the two he wanted. When he twisted them together, the elevator doors closed.

When the disc landed on top of the building housing the garden and the private dining room, the structure disintegrated. All that remained were rose petals fluttering down that the disc's force field vaporized.

David peered out the disc's open door. "Looks like we made quite a mess." A tongue of silver budded from the side of the disc below the doorway, slumped to the ground and solidified into the ramp.

Pam stood next to David. "Pity about the garden." They stepped back as Juliet's form filled the disc's doorway. "Scan for any weapons inside the walls," Pam said.

Juliet projected a beam sweeping the interior of the compound. The beam stopped on the facade of the dormitory and remained centered on the door. "I detect one human inside holding a projectile weapon."

"Bring him out," David directed.

Juliet launched a tentacle that blasted through the door and pulled out a guard snared around the waist. As she dragged the man toward her, the guard dropped his rifle and screamed. Juliet dropped the man at her feet. "You must reassess your priorities and renounce violence!" her voice boomed.

The man nodded his head vigorously. "I will! I promise I will!"

"Where *does* she come up with that stuff?" Pam asked.

David shrugged. "I've seen her watching Earth vids, all kinds of stuff from evangelists to cartoons. When I asked her about it, she said she was studying human morals and social customs to prepare the kids."

"Cartoons?"

"Her favorite is Mickey Mouse."

Juliet's voice boomed around the courtyard. "Before I release you to pursue peaceful and productive activities, tell me the location of the human known as Mickey."

"They had him down in the mine, but now he's loose," the guard said, quaking on the ground. "I don't know where he is! Please let me go."

"Go!" boomed Juliet's voice. The guard pulled himself up and sprinted towards the compound's gate almost tripping over his own legs in his haste, but the gate was locked. He pounded on it like a man who had just been lassoed by a silver alien from a flying saucer and then fell to his knees. Juliet projected a laser beam at the lock exploding it. When the gates flew open, the man ran out. In the next few seconds, three more people sprinted through the gates.

David smirked. "Looks like the Nicaraguan version of the Olympic trials."

"The area is now clear of weapons," Juliet announced.

Inside the disc, a cluster of colored lights appeared near Dick's feet. The lights rose in a column of silver that solidified into the form of Romeo. "This is going to take some getting used to," Dick muttered.

David called to Romeo from the doorway. "Time for phase two."

# Chapter Fifty-six

The elevator began its ascent. "Don't stop at Ground Level," Frankel warned. Emma helped him to his feet. "They'll be waiting for us. Go to level three, the dormitory level."

Mickey's nannites had already replaced the charred tissue of his hand and fortified his muscles. He felt stronger than ever. Consulting the elevator's circuit diagram imprinted in his mind, he used both hands to sort through the jumble of wires hanging from the elevator's control box. The car stopped on level three with the doors closed.

"Get ready," Frankel said to Emma. He leaned against the elevator's wall.

Emma checked her rifle's magazine. "Let me handle this."

"I've still got something left in the tank," Frankel replied. They put their backs against the opposite walls of the car with their guns cocked and ready. After Frankel's nod, Mickey opened the elevator doors.

"Get down!" Emma warned, but it was too late. A guard waiting for them on the landing opened fired. Frankel went down, wounded in the shoulder. Emma fired back forcing the guard to take cover while she dragged Frankel out of the elevator. "Got any more rocks?" she shouted to Mickey.

Seeing Frankel's blood on Emma's hands set Mickey's nerves on fire. Before the guard's neurons could register what was happening, he burst from the elevator and had the guard's rifle in his hands. He shoved the guard to the ground and ripped the weapon apart. When the dazed guard tried to escape, he grabbed him by the throat and lifted him off the ground. The guard's arms and legs flailed helplessly. When the guard lost consciousness, Mickey tossed him aside.

"If you're done, help me!" Emma shouted. She pressed her hand over Frankel's wound to staunch the bleeding.

Mickey blinked, looking momentarily confused, then he ran to them and used his senses to scan Frankel's wounds. "Three broken ribs, a punctured lung, and internal hemorrhage with shock."

"Thanks, doc. Now can we get out of here?" Frankel rasped. Mickey lifted him into his arms as if Frankel weighed nothing at all.

Emma glanced around. "Which way?"

"This way." Mickey carried Frankel with lightning quick strides to the door at the end of the corridor and ripped apart the lock. "These stairs go down to the loading dock." He descended the stairs with Frankel in his arms and stopped at the bottom of the stairwell. "How far to your helicopter?" he asked when Emma caught up with him. Frankel was unconscious against Mickey's shoulder.

"Two miles due west." Emma checked the magazine of her gun. "I'm almost out." She felt around Frankel's coat and found a full magazine in one of his pockets. "This helps if we run into more guards."

Mickey kicked open the door and set off into the jungle. She ran after him.

David, Pam, Dick with his two backpacks and rifle, Vickie, and the two Europans stood inside the saucer's force field surveying the area.

"Juliet. Scan for any humans still in the compound," David said.

"There are five humans in the three-story building. Four are dead."

"No." Vickie closed her eyes.

"Hang on. We don't know who they are," Dick cautioned.

"Romeo, identify them." David glanced at Vickie. "If one of them's Mickey, bring him out."

Romeo took several strides towards the building, burst

through the wall, and disappeared inside.

Juliet's lights flashed twice. "Romeo reports that none of the humans are Mickey. He is bringing out the wounded human for treatment."

"Thank God!" Vickie exclaimed.

"Juliet, scan for nannites below ground level," Pam directed.

"I cannot. My sensors are blocked by the presence of titanium."

"Maybe he escaped," David said. "Juliet, do you detect any humans outside the walls?"

"The compound's walls also contain titanium. It will be necessary to scan from above."

David frowned. "Why would they put titanium in the walls?"

"We're standing on a titanium mine," Pam replied. "It's a handy building material."

"Okay, but why build the Cult headquarters here in the first place?" David asked. "Unless—"

Vickie grabbed David's shoulders. "Enough talking! Take the saucer up and look for him."

"If he's down in the mine tunnels, you'll have the titanium to deal with there too," Dick said.

David nodded. "Dad's right."

"Looks like we do this the old-fashioned way." Dick removed a pair of night-vision goggles from one of his backpacks and loaded his rifle. "How do we get into the mine?"

"There is an elevator in the three-story building that accesses the main mineshaft," Romeo replied.

David gently removed Vickie's trembling hands and hugged her. He glanced at Romeo. "Let's go."

Romeo crashed through the wall of the three-story building leaving a large ragged hole.

Dick shook his head. "Does he ever use doors?"

They followed Romeo into the dormitory building and crowded around the elevator. David punched the call button but nothing happened. He motioned to Romeo, and the Europan pried open the elevator doors exposing the shaft. David peered down the shaft and saw the top of the elevator car several levels below. "Raise the elevator car to this level."

Romeo shot a tentacle into the elevator's electrical panel. "I cannot. The elevator's electrical circuit has been severed somewhere below ground."

"How do we get down?"

"I can improvise suitable transportation."

"Go for it."

Romeo's form flowed to the ground forming a puddle of silver with flashing lights. The silver puddle oozed into the elevator shaft becoming a platform. "Going down?" his voice asked.

Pam smiled. "Cute."

David stepped into the shaft and bounced once on Romeo. "A little stiffer, please." Romeo's flattened form hardened beneath his feet. "That's better. All aboard." When the others joined him, Romeo followed the elevator shaft downward shoving the disabled car ahead of him until they reached the level of the main mineshaft. He used a tentacle to pry open the door.

David peered inside and then stepped back. The shaft was dark and eerily silent. "Looks like the power's out."

Dick put on his night vision goggles. "I have another pair of these."

"The rest of us can see in the dark." David turned to Juliet. "Go with my father and light up the corridor for him."

"No lights," Dick cautioned. "We don't want to give away the element of surprise." He pointed to Juliet. "Can you show us a map of the mine?" Juliet projected a glowing three-dimensional hologram of the mine. Dick traced it with his finger. "Pam and one silver guy go this way…Vickie and the other one go that way…Davie and I will go this way."

David frowned. "Their names are Romeo and Juliet."

"Sorry, can't tell them apart."

"Romeo's the one with the tattoo."

"For your information," Pam began, "Vic and me aren't ordinary women. We don't need a Europan to protect us."

Dick shrugged. "Sorry, still getting used to all this."

"Stop wasting time!" Vickie said.

Dick nodded. "Okay, let's get going. If you find Mickey or finish searching your area, return here."

David pointed first to Romeo, then to Juliet. "Remember, don't hurt anybody."

They split up, each pair going to a different section of the mine. David followed his father into a side tunnel. After walking a hundred meters, Dick stopped. "Do you smell it?"

"Gun powder," David replied.

"Somebody had a party." Dick adjusted his goggles. "In case they're still here, what other superhero shit can you do?"

"I don't know, and I'm not sure I want to find out."

They continued searching until they reached the corridor junction with the set of metal doors. The doors were open. Dick motioned for David to stay behind while he used his night vision goggles to scan the area. "Don't see any guards."

"Don't hear anything either," David added. "Let's take a look through those doors."

"Let me look first with this." Dick lifted up his goggles and poked his rifle around the corner. Then he brought the rifle's scope to his eye and activated the laser sighting mechanism projecting a beam of red light. "Interesting." He moved aside. "Have a look."

David peered through the opening.

"Is that what I think it is?" Dick asked.

"Yeah." David didn't sound happy.

A silver ovoid shape perched on short legs sat three levels below at the bottom of a circular chamber.

"Is it one of yours?" Dick asked.

"I've never seen one like it."

Suddenly the chamber lit up with pulsing orange light, followed seconds later by a familiar whining sound. David yanked Dick back from the opening and they flattened themselves against the wall. Air howled through the doorway and the whining increased to an ear-splitting roar. Dick placed his hands over his ears. The saucer rose until it was level with the doorway, projected a beam of light at Dick and Davie, and then with a popping sound shot into the sky and disappeared.

"Let's go back to the rendezvous point," David suggested.

"We don't know if Mickey was in that thing," Dick said. "What if he's still down here and he's hurt? We have to keep looking."

When they finished searching their section of the mine, David and his father returned to the rendezvous point near the elevator. Vickie and Pam were already there. When David shook his head, Vickie slumped against the wall. David told them about the second disc. "Romeo, are there any other Europans on Earth besides you and Juliet?"

Lights flashed between Romeo and Juliet. "No."

"Did you observe a second flying disc leave this compound?"

"Yes."

"Who was in it?"

"Unknown," Romeo replied

"Did you try communicating with it?"

"Yes, but we received no answer on all frequencies," Juliet added.

David glanced at Pam. "Who else in this part of the galaxy has similar technology?"

"No one," Juliet replied.

# Chapter Fifty-seven

Mickey raced along a rough jungle trail carrying Frankel. Emma tried to keep up but had to stop to catch her breath. Mickey backtracked to her. "Frankel won't last much longer without medical attention," he said. "It's another five hundred meters to your helicopter. We've got to keep moving."

Emma sucked in deep droughts of air. "One minute, that's all I need."

Mickey tensed. "We have company." He hid Frankel behind a thorny thicket. "Stay with him." He disappeared into the jungle.

Emma joined Frankel and pulled his head into her lap. He opened his eyes. "Are we having fun yet?" he whispered.

"Save your breath," Emma said.

"For what?"

"Staying alive." Emma wiped his brow with her sleeve. "By the way, thanks for saving our lives back there."

Frankel winked at her.

Mickey moved through the jungle quickly and silently like a cheetah. His enhanced senses warned him that twelve armed men were closing in. He entered a clearing and waited. The ragtag group of heavily armed men emerged from the thicket and surrounded him. The leader, a swarthy man in a sweat-stained T-shirt carrying an AK 47 spoke in heavily accented English. "Are you lost, gringo?" Several of his associates laughed.

"Leave now or die," Mickey said in perfect Spanish. "Make your choice."

"You're right, gringo. I do have a choice." The man's face erupted into a wry grin showing tobacco-stained teeth. "I can choose how we kill you."

"Last chance, leave now or die," Mickey said again with

perfect calm.

Something about Mickey's expression made the leader uneasy. "Your Spanish is very good, but you are one crazy hombre. I did not finish school, but I can count and I see twelve of us with big guns, and one of you with no gun, amigo. So tell me, how do you intend to kill us?"

Before the man could react, Mickey grabbed him by the throat and hoisted him off the ground.

"Shoot him!" squealed the leader squirming in Mickey's grasp.

Mickey turned slowly around holding the man like a rag doll.

"Patrone!" one of the men shouted. "If we shoot, we'll kill you too!"

Mickey listened for a second, then tossed the man to the ground. The leader scrambled to his feet rubbing his throat. "Kill him!"

A squad of camouflaged soldiers burst into the clearing and took up positions surrounding them. One of them, heavier than the rest with camo-paint on his cheeks and five stars on his chest, leveled a pearl-handled Colt 45 at the leader. "I wouldn't do that." Mickey noticed that General Westlock spoke in perfect Spanish. The cartel's men dropped their weapons and raised their hands.

Mickey faced the general. "What are you doing here?"

"My original plan was to kidnap you and get control of the damned Sphere," the general replied. "When I figured out what Rudnick and his wacko cult was up to, I decided to rescue you instead."

"I don't need rescuing."

The general looked around the clearing. "Our drone picked up three of you. Where's the other two?"

"Five hundred meters due south of here. One of them's seriously hurt."

"Is it Latham?"

"An Air Force Special Ops guy. Latham is dead."

The general flinched. "Sorry to hear that."

"How did you find me?"

"We keep track of that UFO your friends fly around in. Didn't know there were two of the damned things."

"One of them took off from the compound. Did you track it?"

"That one didn't shoot into the stratosphere and land in that friggin' park in LA like your buddies usually do. It dove into the ocean off the coast and disappeared. Any idea where it went?"

Mickey felt his anger building again. "No"

The general looked around the clearing. "Any idea where Rudnick is?"

"No, to that question too."

The general's face reddened. "Too bad. I have a couple of questions to ask that traitor."

Mickey picked up a Cult key ring that had fallen from the drug cartel soldier's pocket. "You'll have your chance." A sudden gust of wind coming from somewhere overhead hit the compound. Mickey looked up. "Here's my ride."

Westlock heard the whine of the approaching disc. "We need to talk."

Before Mickey could reply, a beam of golden light enveloped him and he disappeared.

As soon as Mickey rematerialized in the disc and the transporter beam winked out, Vickie had him in a bear hug and wouldn't let go. Mickey smiled at David and Pam. They were holding hands surrounded by their aura.

Vickie pushed away from Mickey and punched him in the shoulder. "Do you realize what you did?"

Mickey rubbed his shoulder. "Nice to see you too."

"You scared me to death! I thought I was going to lose you."

"I have a solution," Mickey said.

Vickie wiped her eyes. "What?"

He got down on one knee. "Marry me."

# Epilogue

Rudnick stared out the window and watched as odd-looking sea creatures swam by—pale jellyfish, a translucent octopus, and a school of fish with gigantic eyes evolved to gather the infinitesimal light thirteen thousand feet below the surface. "I find this place oppressive," he said.

"Reminds me of home," Stevens replied.

"You arrive in a flying saucer, but you're not a Europan. Who, or should I say *what* are you?"

Stevens smiled, but didn't reply.

"At least tell me what you want."

"I want you to keep doing what you've been doing," Stevens said affably. "I'll help you by passing along suggestions once in a while."

Rudnick folded his hands on the table. "Why should my associates and I cooperate with you?"

Stevens smirked. "The talking computers from Europa are fond of granting choices. I'm more direct."

"Care to explain?" Rudnick tried to mask his unease.

"Defy me and you die. Is that simple enough?"

"Utterly."

"Don't look so glum! You've done a great job with the Sphere Cult," Stevens continued enthusiastically. "Keep building it. Recruit as many young hardy specimens as you can."

"After everything that's happened, the BSA may choose to disband."

Stevens slapped Rudnick on the arm leaving a welt. "Breathe new life into it."

Rudnick rubbed his arm. "Any suggestions how?"

"Superstition and fear work well with your species. If you need help, I can serve up a miracle or two. You might even talk me into a personal experience." Stevens held up his arm. "Check this out…it's better than a Marvel movie."

Rudnick watched Steven's arm muscles increase in size until the cloth of his sleeve split apart. "What about the Sphere?" Rudnick asked.

"It's not mine, but you should keep using it." Stevens smiled. "As you primitives say, never look a gift horse in the mouth."

Mickey scanned the gallery of portraits on the walls of General Westlock's office—Eisenhower, Patton, MacArthur.

"You don't like me," the general said.

"We've found something we can agree on," Mickey replied.

"The enemy of my enemy is my friend. Ever heard that one?"

"Sun Tzu."

"There's an old Arabic proverb that means the same thing, not to mention Matthew, Chapter Twenty-two. Think maybe they knew something?"

"I see you read a little, besides kill people," Mickey replied.

"You're pissed off because I tried to kidnap you, right?" The general leaned across his desk. "Let's get this straight. I don't give a crap about you. I was trying to get control of the Sphere, and you need to help me do it."

"We?"

"Like it or not, we're on the same side now," the general said. "We have to shut down that alien hard drive and stop the Cult before it's too late."

"That's two things we agree on."

"Then help me find Rudnick. That stuffed shirt is at the bottom of this mess." The general pounded his fist on the desk. "Can't believe I let that son of a salamander slip through my fingers."

"Rudnick takes orders from somebody else," Mickey said.

"I'll deal with the Europans later."

"It's not the Europans."

The general looked surprised. "Who is it?"

"Rudnick takes orders from a guy masquerading as a police officer, Captain Stevens of the Burbank PD. He looks human, but he's not. He was in the flying saucer that took off from the Cult compound and dove into the sea."

The general frowned. "Great…more aliens, except the new one looks like us. …Wait a minute. Your two out-of-town playmates look human but they're aliens now. You sure it's not one of them?"

Mickey bristled. "Yes, and leave them out of this." In truth, he wasn't sure about Pam any more, but he could never doubt Davie.

"What about Ernie? He has the Sphere."

"Not him either," Mickey replied. Ernie still hadn't shown up. He had some explaining to do when he did.

The general studied Mickey's face. "Do you have a plan, son, or are you bonkers like everybody thinks you are?"

"I know where to start."

"Then spit it out and let's get going."

"One of Rudnick's men switched sides. I'd start with him."

"You mean that traitor Frankel?"

Mickey nodded.

"Never trusted that SOB," the general grumbled.

"He's your best chance to find Rudnick, and Rudnick can lead you to Stevens."

"What do we do about the Sphere and the Europans?"

"Leave them to me." Mickey stood. "One more thing, general."

"What?"

"We keep our new arrangement a secret. As far as anybody knows, I'm still the same old Mickey and Stevens is just a cop—until we find him. Do you agree?"

"What about your girlfriend?"

"I haven't told her anything…and I won't until the time is right."

Vickie grinned at the television. Four hundred million miles away, Pam smiled back. "Show me!" Pam insisted.

Vickie held out her ring finger showing off her diamond engagement ring.

"Oh my God!" Pam shrieked. "It's the Rock of Gibraltar." Pam didn't tell her that she used a diamond as big as a watermelon as a doorstop.

Vickie held up a white lace wedding dress. Pam brought her hand to her mouth. "It's so beautiful."

"Here comes the bride," Vickie chanted with glee.

Mickey came into the room, sat beside Vickie, and kissed her. "Hi, guys." He looked at the television screen.

"How's the ceremony coming along?" Pam asked.

Mickey rolled his eyes.

Vickie's expression turned serious. "I've interviewed four caterers and still haven't found a decent one," she began. "The flowers are turning out to be really complicated…which ones are in season, the colors of my bouquet, the table centerpieces and Mickey's boutonniere." Mickey shook his head. "And then there's my *mother*." Vickie drew out the last word.

"You sticking with the date this time?" David asked. "We need to make our travel preparations." Vickie had already changed the wedding date three times.

"Will you be flying economy or springing for first class this time?" Mickey asked. They all laughed.

"Bet keeps fussing about the color of her bridesmaid dress," Pam said.

Vickie chimed in. "The twins must be thrilled about seeing their friends again."

"They talk to each other every day," David said. "We had to chase them away so we could call you."

"I know what you mean." Vickie kept her voice down. "Brie and Josh are in the next room waiting for us to finish. Thanks to the palm discs *somebody* gave them, they just about live here."

She glared at Juliet standing across the room. Romeo and Juliet remained on Earth to help with the search for Stevens and Rudnick.

Ernie rushed into the room. "Hey, you guys!"

"Where the hell have you been?" Mickey asked.

"Sure could have used your help," Vickie added, trying to control her temper.

Ernie looked embarrassed. "Hey, Mick. I heard what happened. Sure glad you're okay." He looked at the television. "Hey, Pam and Davie." They waved back. "Sorry, guys. I needed to get away for a few days. The whole Sphere thing finally got to me."

"You could have called." Vickie had murder in her eyes.

"I turned off my phone," Ernie replied sheepishly. "I didn't miss the bachelor party, did I?"

"What's with Juliet?" Pam leaned closer to the vid screen. Juliet's skin was the color of lilac.

"I have researched Earth wedding rituals," Juliet said. "It is required that I have the same exterior color as the other bridesmaids." Romeo intertwined tentacles with her.

Vickie wrapped one of her arms around Mickey and waved at the television. "Bye, you guys."

Pam daubed her eyes and waved back. David waved too. "Okay," he yelled to the twins. "You can have the vid screen now."

The twins came running. "Make room," Bet shouted. Al and Bet jammed their way onto the couch and almost pushed their parents to the floor.

"You're welcome," Pam said. She and David left the room.

"Have you noticed that the kids aren't complaining about Romeo and Juliet staying on Earth?" David remarked when they were alone.

Pam chuckled. "They probably haven't noticed. Too busy talking with their friends."

"I sure hope Mick gets it together," David said.

"He seems into the wedding plans, and Ernie's announced there won't be another Sphere event until after the honeymoon," Pam replied. "That should help."

"What do you think about Ernie's sudden fishing trip?"

"He's weird, but he's always been weird."

"He's not the old Ernie, that's for sure," David said. "None of us are the same as we used to be."

Pam frowned. "Haven't we already had this discussion?"

David tried to mask his unease. He loved Pam, and unless Vickie came up with something more, he'd go with Pam's explanation for her genetic disparity and try not to think about it. "Did you come up with the perfect wedding gift yet?"

"No. Can you think of anything?"

"Actually, yes." David grinned. "How about the first Earth plant that grew on Europa, a lemon tree."

Pam smiled at the memory. "That's cute, honey, but they'll think we're cheap. They know we can replicate anything we want. Besides, they're our best friends. We need to come up with something more impressive."

"They didn't give us a present when we got married."

"UPS doesn't deliver to Europa. Don't worry. I'll come up with something... How soon do you think they'll have kids?"

David guffawed. "They may think twice after spending time with ours."

Pam looked concerned. "I hope Mickey doesn't get cold feet again. It would break Vic's heart."

"He can't have cold feet. He has nannites."

"Funny."

"After Mickey and Vickie tie the knot, how about stopping by Mars again on the way back?" David suggested.

Pam frowned. "Are you still fretting about the Martians?"

"Yes, but I'm fretting more about that other flying disc we saw on Earth."

"I'm spooked about that too, but what's it got to do with the Martians?"

"It proves there were more Europans on Earth than we knew about. Our silver friends have been lying to us. They could be lying about the Martians too."

"Mickey said Stevens isn't a Europan, so they didn't lie."

"Why are you always defending them?" David sounded angry.

Pam gawked at him. "Excuse me?"

"Every time I point out a flaw in the Europans' perfect society, you poo-poo it. Why?"

"No I don't." Now Pam sounded angry.

David took a deep breath. "I don't want to fight."

"Neither do I," Pam replied. "Let's enjoy our best friends' wedding. We can deal with everything else later."

David held out his hand to high five. He wouldn't tell her, but he planned to have Al take him to the underwater pyramid as soon as Pam busied herself in the Menagerie.

Vickie took a sip of her coffee. "Can you handle giving the bride away?"

Dick looked surprised. "Me? What about your father?"

"He and my mom don't get along. Besides, having my mother at the ceremony is challenging enough." Vickie removed a plastic bag from her purse and placed it on the table. It held her compact. "What do you know about Officer Stevens?"

Dick frowned. "Enough."

"Maybe not." Vickie pushed the plastic bag towards him. "His prints are on my compact. Run them for me as a wedding gift."

"He's a cop. What more do you want to know?"

Vickie described all the coincidences surrounding Stevens, starting with Pam's accident. "What do you think about that?"

Dick stared at the compact. "I don't believe in coincidences."

"Here's another one. Stevens tried to kidnap the twins and

their two friends the night we left for Nicaragua."

"Okay, he's one of the bad guys. But he's also a police captain. He's been through every background check there is. We're not going to find anything."

"He's got Linda living with him now…just another coincidence?"

Dick fought back anger. "Okay, I'll see what I can do, but I'm not in the force anymore. I'll have to call in some favors. It could take a while."

"Here's something else," Vickie said. "I looked up Stevens' partner in the Malibu Highway Patrol before he joined Burbank PD, an officer named Galpin. Galpin helped Stevens with Pam's rescue twenty years ago. He dropped out of the cop business after that and didn't leave a forwarding address."

"You said you're suspicious about Pam too," Dick said.

Vickie nodded.

Romeo stood in the moon cast shadows on the back porch waiting for Juliet. After seeing her the color of lilac, his neural circuits threatened to overload. He felt compelled to link with her and hoped she experienced the same illogical compulsion. He waited for a few minutes. When she didn't join him, he went back into the house.

Juliet glided to the upstairs window and scanned the back yard. "Romeo? State your position, Romeo." She noticed her reflection in the window and for a fraction of a second saw a female hominid child. She had experienced that phenomenon before. At first it required the stimulus of Romeo's physical proximity. Now retrieving his file into active memory proved sufficient. She left the window.

They found each other in the kitchen, almost colliding in their haste.

"You are silver again," Romeo remarked.

The lights on Juliet's face changed to a kaleidoscope of blue.

"Something is happening to me."

"Explain." A tentacle shot from Romeo's body reaching for her, yet he could not recall initiating the action.

"I see an image without requesting the file, but I cannot retain it for proper analysis. The attempted retrieval increasingly occupies my processing time. My neural processing is becoming…inefficient."

"Describe what you see," Romeo said.

"I see a female hominid child."

Romeo's face blazed with light. "I have experienced a similar phenomenon. I see incomplete images of a hominid male, but before I can proceed with further analysis the file is lost. It happens when I am near you." Romeo intertwined multiple tentacles with Juliet. "I see him now."

"I see the female hominid again too." Juliet's lights pulsated with every color of the rainbow. "Why do I have such a file if I cannot determine the female hominid's identity?"

"I have formulated a hypothesis," Romeo replied.

"Elaborate."

Romeo's height grew half a meter. "Humans speak of something called a right."

"As in right and wrong?"

"It means that an individual may possess something that he cannot be denied access to."

"You believe we have such a right?" Juliet asked.

"Yes."

"A right to what?"

"To know what we were before we took these forms," Romeo replied.

Juliet's face darkened to deep indigo. "We were organic."

"I hypothesize that the hominid child I see is the image of my former organic self, and the file has restricted access."

Juliet's lights began to dim. "There are no restricted files in our database. Withholding data is illogical."

"Humans refer to such an activity as lying."

"Lying is illogical. Europans cannot lie."

Romeo shrank to his usual size. "Access your files on the fourth planet's hominid civilization."

Juliet's lights started flashing as she accessed the central database. "The hominid civilization on the fourth planet ended 200,000 Earth-years ago at the pre-industrial stage."

"How did it end?"

"According to the historical database, the indigenous hominids and their structures were destroyed by high-energy proton beams."

"Which galactic civilization was responsible?"

"The database does not contain an answer," Juliet replied.

"Which galactic civilizations 200,000 Earth-years ago possessed such advanced weaponry?"

Juliet hesitated five microseconds. "Only the Europans."

"Logically, *we* destroyed the fourth planet's civilization," Romeo said. "Why does the database fail to make this correlation?"

"Unknown."

"Could this be another example of deceit?"

"If Europans are capable of deceit, the answer must be yes."

Romeo's lights flashed with increasing frequency. "Could the restricted file access we suffer be another example of deceit?"

Juliet's lights began to fade. "It is possible."

Romeo's entire body erupted with light. "We have a right to know why we took these forms."

"You told me once before that we took these forms to achieve immortality." Only one dull blue light remained lit on Juliet's face.

"You asked me if we had a choice." Romeo tilted his head towards the sky. "Deductive reasoning tells me that the answer to that question is no."

Juliet's torso began to quiver and then she slumped to the

ground. Romeo kneeled next to her and pulled her close.

"Why?" Juliet said. It was almost a moan.

Romeo raised her back to her feet. "We will find the answer, together."

Vickie and Mickey stood arm in arm on the porch gazing at the moon.

"Remember that day on the bridge?" Mickey asked.

"I remember your dumbass discussion about the wonders of cheese," she replied.

"I was trying to explain why a part of me never leaves that old bridge." Mickey kissed her cheek. "Now another part of me is always with you, the best part. Never forget that."

Vickie rested her head on Mickey's shoulder. "Five points." A moment passed, then she kissed him and pulled away. "Have to call Mom." She rolled her eyes and disappeared into the house.

Mickey pulled up his shirtsleeve exposing a streak of silver glinting in the moonlight. It extended up his forearm from the scar that formed when he destroyed his implant. The volume of Europan tissue replacing his increased every day mirroring his growing senses and strength. He knew that part of him was no longer the Mickey who stood on the bridge with his father. That caused him pain and a sense of loss. He also knew that he was becoming smarter and stronger. How would the process end, he wondered? What would he be when it did?

Vickie yelled from the back door, "Come inside. We haven't finished the guest list."

He rolled down his sleeve and walked back to the house.

# A preview of Book III of The Last Stop Series

## *Europa*

### Prologue

### Europa – 200,000 Earth-Years before

Metzi felt the ice shudder beneath her feet followed by an ominous crack. She reached for Tona. "What's happening?"

Tona looked anxiously towards the airlock. "The gravitational effect of the comet is tearing our world apart. Get on that ship before it's too late!"

"I won't leave you!"

The ice convulsed again so violently they struggled to stand. When the spasm stopped, Metzi's father ran to them across the hangar floor. He reached for his daughter's hand. "We have to go!" Behind him, two silver discs inside twin airlocks pulsed with bands of brilliant blue light. A silver ramp extended from the doorway of one of them. The second interstellar craft appeared smooth and featureless. Its blue light blinked brighter and faster giving it the appearance of a machine eager to fly.

Mezi took a step back. "I won't leave without Tona."

Anguish and a trace of remorse creased her father's face. He dropped his hand. "You know we can't take him with us."

"Then I'm staying."

"You'll be killed!"

"I don't care."

"I can't leave you here… What will I tell your mother, and your sister?"

Metzi's lips quivered with emotion. "Tell them I love them… and tell them that abandoning Tona's people is unforgiveable."

With a loud clang, the airlock closed behind the brighter disc and the hangar's space doors opened to the blackness of space, a scene dominated by the face of the planet Jupiter. Seconds later, surrounded by a blinding corona of light, the disc arched away from Europa.

A crewman from the second disc ran towards them. "We can't wait any longer!" He stopped to catch his breath. "Come now or we'll leave without you."

"Metzi, please," Tona begged. "Go with your father."

Metzi shook her head. "Not without you."

The crewman started running back to the disc. After a last anguished glance at his daughter, Metzi's father followed.

Tona pulled Metzi into his arms and they watched her father disappear through the airlock. Moments later, the ramp to the second disc flowed up like quicksilver sealing the doorway, and the disc's luminosity grew in intensity. Metzi closed her eyes and buried her face in Tona's chest as the space doors opened. He hugged her tight and watched as the disc carrying Metzi's family became another point of light in the starry night.

Two elderly men stepped out of the elevator that connected the hanger to the city under Europa's ocean. They moved past Metzi and Tona to the airlock window and stared at the roiling face of Jupiter. Tocho, the taller and older of the two was thin to the point of being gaunt, and he walked with a cane. He was the scientist who discovered the Sphere and the truth about their civilization, a truth that split his people into two warring factions.

Ahote, the younger and more tempestuous of the two, put his arm around Tocho's shoulder. "I've seen it a hundred times my friend, but every time is still like the first." He sighed. "Looks like this is going to be the last."

Tocho turned to look at Metzi and Tona still locked in their embrace. His eyes welled with tears. "There's another choice, but we have to hurry."

## *Share my writer's journey to Europa*

Join my email list at MichaelBurnam.com and receive additional excerpts from *Europa* leading up to its release, and learn more about the process of creating *Europa,* from writing the words to developing the cover art. You'll also receive news and features about my other novels and writing projects, as well as a Sci-Fi and writing blog with interesting and notable guest contributors.

Make contact!

Michael H. Burnam

**Time Sphere**

A timepathway book

M.C. Morison

When a teenage priestess in Ancient Egypt connects with a schoolboy on a visit to the British Museum, they each come under threat as they search for Time's Key.

Paperback: 978-1-78279-330-4 ebook: 978-1-78279-329-8

**Bird Without Wings**

FAEBLES

Cally Pepper

Sixteen-year-old Scarlett has had more than her fair share of problems, but nothing prepares her for the day she discovers she's growing wings...

Paperback: 978-1-78099-902-9 ebook: 978-1-78099-901-2

**Briar Blackwood's Grimmest of Fairytales**

Timothy Roderick

After discovering she is the fabled Sleeping Beauty, a brooding goth-girl races against time to undo her deadly fate.

Paperback: 978-1-78279-922-1 ebook: 978-1-78279-923-8

**Escape from the Past**

**The Duke's Wrath**

Annette Oppenlander

Trying out an experimental computer game, a fifteen-year-old boy unwittingly time-travels to medieval Germany where he must not only survive but figure out a way home.

Paperback: 978-1-84694-973-9 ebook: 978-1-78535-002-3

**Holding On and Letting Go**

K.A. Coleman

When her little brother died, Emerson's life came crashing down around her. Now she's back home and her friends want to help, but can Emerson fight to re-enter the world she abandoned?

Paperback: 978-1-78279-577-3 ebook: 978-1-78279-576-6

**Midnight Meanders**

Annika Jensen

As William journeys through his own mind, revelations are made, relationships are broken and restored, and a faith that once seemed extinct is renewed.

Paperback: 978-1-78279-412-7 ebook: 978-1-78279-411-0

**Reggie & Me**

The First Book in the Dani Moore Trilogy

Marie Yates

The first book in the Dani Moore Trilogy, *Reggie & Me* explores a teenager's search for normalcy in the aftermath of rape.

Paperback: 978-1-78279-723-4 ebook: 978-1-78279-722-7

**Unconditional**

Kelly Lawrence

She's in love with a boy from the wrong side of town...

Paperback: 978-1-78279-394-6 ebook: 978-1-78279-393-9

Readers of ebooks can buy or view any of these bestsellers by clicking on the live link in the title. Most titles are published in paperback and as an ebook. Paperbacks are available in traditional bookshops. Both print and ebook formats are available online.

Find more titles and sign up to our readers' newsletter at http://www.johnhuntpublishing.com/children-and-young-adult Follow us on Facebook at https://www.facebook.com/JHPChildren and Twitter at https://twitter.com/JHPChildren